# Bessie Bell and the Goblin King
## Tales of Aylfenhame, Book 3

Charlotte E. English

Copyright © 2016 Charlotte E. English

Cover art © 2016 Elsa Kroese

Illustrations copyright 2016 by the PicSees

All rights reserved.

ISBN: 9492824011
ISBN-13: 978-9492824011

# CHAPTER ONE

*Good evenin' to ye, an' well met! Welcome to the Tilby toll-bridge. Steady, now. Yer horses are havin' a hard time seein' through the fog, an' when it's dark t' boot, well! Ye'll want to go good an' slowly through the town. Not that ye'll meet any other folk on the road. Yer carriage is likely to be the only one sailin' the streets o' Tilby at this hour.*

*I'm Mister Balligumph, yer friendly toll collector. But don't let that worry ye! Mayhap we've met before — I can't altogether tell in the dark o' night, yer face is a mite too hidden-like. But either way, the toll's not steep. I'll not be needin' any coin from ye — what would a troll do wi' English money? It's a little bit of information I'm after. A bit about ye will suffice. What brings ye to our fine Tilby-town in the depths o' November, an' on such a damp an' foggy night? Thas all I need, an' ye can pass. An' if ye're minded to tell me somethin' else — somethin' by way of a secret, like — then I might tell ye a tale by way o' thanks.*

*There's been some mighty strange goin's on in these parts this autumn. Oh, I know thas not entirely out o' character fer Tilby. Ye might've heard one or two oddly stories about us before — mayhap from me. I talk to a lot o' folk. But this one's the strangest yet, an' a touch on the dark side.*

*Ye'd like to hear more? Tis a recent tale, all happenin' only a few short weeks back. I had best warm up yer carriage a trifle before I begin — 'tis cold t' be sittin' long wi' no heat. There, thas better.*

*And so, to my tale. It began, in point o' fact, on a night much like this — dark an' chilly an' deep in fog. Rumours had been flyin' about fer a week or two aforehand, 'bout a menace on the roads. Travellers bore tales o' shadows an' strange noises an' flamin' eyes in the night. 'Twas wishy-washy mutterin's to be sure, but most folk agreed: wanderin' about at the dead o' night may be a poor idea. But fer Bessie Bell, it weren't rightly a matter o' choice...*

In the humble opinion of Bessie Bell, housemaid, the residents of Hapworth Manor bore a remarkable talent for making a vast quantity of mess in a short space of time. Crouched as she was over the drawing-room carpet, she had plentiful leisure to reflect upon their slovenly habits as she sweated over the sweeping-up. Just how was it possible for four people to leave a pristine room in such an abominable state every single evening? She took pride in her work, and she knew that the drawing-room had been spotless only that morning. Now it was a deplorable mess, and it was *her* unhappy task to render it respectable once more. And there was a fresh, new stain for her to endeavour to remove, for some obliging guest had spilled Mrs. Adair's expensive tea all over her floor, and Bessie had been instructed to ensure that naught remained of the mishap by morning.

The Adair family were reckoned as good employers, and not wholly unjustly. They were generous enough with the wages they paid to their servants; they did not stint on such necessities as nourishing food and warm clothes for the winter, as some families did; and the room Bessie slept in each night was shared with only one other servant. These were not inconsiderable benefits.

But in other respects, they left a great deal to be desired. Mrs Adair was exacting in her requirements, almost ferociously so. Bessie rose at four every morning, in order to ensure that the fires were lit for the family before they were pleased to rise. From that hour until ten or eleven o' clock in the evening, her day was filled with back-breaking labour, and it was not unusual for her to be bidden to clean a room twice over, if Mrs Adair was dissatisfied with her work.

'I will help you with that, Bess-Bess,' said a small, mild voice from near Bessie's elbow.

Bess smiled gratefully at the speaker. Derritharn was a brownie, and though she was only as tall as Bess's knee, she was a hard worker, an efficient cleaner, and the only being in the world Bess could call friend.

'Thank you, Derri,' said Bess. 'We are gettin' tired, no doubt, but with a *little* more effort, I am thinkin' we'll be done. And then we can go to bed.' She sighed, and added, 'If *milady* will permit it.'

Derritharn's little becurled head drooped with weariness, and she wiped her tiny hands upon the ragged grey dress she wore, nodding her agreement. 'And about time as well! 'Twas a long day and no mistake.'

Like many towns and villages in England, the Lincolnshire town of Tilby possessed, alongside its human residents, a population of the fae. These varied creatures had chosen, for whatever reason, to leave their natural home of Aylfenhame and settle in human households. Hapworth Manor was home to several brownies who assisted Bessie and the other housemaids with keeping the house clean. Mrs Adair, rather unwisely, treated them more as slaves than servants; too satisfied was she with the unpaid labour she received from these gentle beings, and she worked them every bit as hard as she did Bessie. As such, brownies rarely remained long in the Adairs' service. Neither did housemaids.

Heartened by the thought of her bed, Bess attacked her work with renewed energy. Her bed was narrow and hard and not nearly so well-smothered with warm blankets as she would like, but at least it was *hers*. And in it she could lie down, stretch herself out, and welcome the sweet oblivion from her daily toil that she so badly required — even if her slumber tended to be all too brief.

She and Derritharn finished cleaning the carpet, using wadded cloths to protect their hands, and moved on to tidying the rest of the chamber. This work was soon complete, and Bess recognised the end of her working day with relief. But just as she was collecting up the rags and brushes she had been using in her labour, she heard the door creak as it opened.

'That,' said a male voice, 'makes far too much noise. You will see that the hinges are oiled before you retire to your bed.'

Bess controlled her instinctive scowl with an effort. Mr. Edward Adair, the son of the house, had a repellent habit of waylaying her as she went about her duties. His manner was autocratic, and he invariably found additional work for her to do.

Not only that, but he watched her with lascivious eyes every moment she remained in his presence. With his immaculate dark hair and sculpted features he was considered uncommonly handsome, and the other housemaids giggled over his long, appreciative looks. But Bess deplored his character too much to appreciate the undeniable beauty of his face, and the way he stared could not gratify her. She read more than appreciation in his eyes: she read… *intent*.

Alas, she could not contrive to avoid him altogether. Nor could she point out that the hour was far advanced, and she ought to be asleep. What Mr. Adair required must be done, and Bess could only bob a reluctant curtsey and murmur something assenting.

But he stood in the doorway, blocking her egress. She was obliged to pause and wait, her eyes respectfully lowered, in hope of being permitted to leave. Usually he would look his fill upon her face and figure, and then leave her be.

Tonight, though, he stepped farther into the room and shut the door behind him. 'A little later,' he decided. 'First, I have another duty for you.'

To Bess's disgust, he approached until he stood only a few inches away from her. He stared down at her, his beautiful blue eyes cold and hard. 'Bessie, isn't it?' he said. Abruptly, he reached out and tore off the frilled white cap she was obliged to wear. 'Take your hair down,' he ordered.

Bess's eyes narrowed, and a flicker of anger flared in her heart. She took a step back, shaking her head. 'Sir, I have work to do. Mrs. Sanders is expectin' me below stairs—' She hoped that invoking the name of the housekeeper might give him pause, but the gambit failed.

'Never mind,' he interrupted, and advanced upon her once more. 'I'll do it.' He began yanking the pins out of her hair and dragging long tendrils of it out of the formerly neat arrangement, hurting her but blatantly uncaring. He ran her black, wavy locks through his fingers, and then tugged sharply. Surprise left her unable to suppress her involuntary cry of pain, and he smiled. 'Forget Mrs. Sanders.'

'Sir—'

'Not another word,' he said, his smile gone. 'As my servant, you are obliged to attend to any duty I should require of you. Do you understand?'

Bessie understood. She felt a flicker of fear – and a surge of fierce anger. *This*, on top of all of the day's trials! She lifted her chin. 'I was hired to clean the house,' she said firmly. 'Sir.'

'Your duties are as I define them.' He advanced and took hold of her in a hard, cruel grip, one hand tangled painfully in her hair. He kissed her shrinking mouth with violent force, and began pushing her backwards towards the wall behind her.

Bess knew that his behaviour was not uncommon. Some housemaids accepted such *duties* as an inevitable part of their lives, and submitted; some even enjoyed the attention, provided the young master was handsome enough. But Bess could never submit. She fought his bruising grip, panting with the effort to free herself before he could succeed in pinning her. But he was much stronger than she, and her struggles only hurt her and angered him.

'Stop that,' he growled, tightening his grip on her hair until she cried out with the pain of it. He began dragging at her clothes, and Bess heard the tearing sound of fabric ripping through.

Then abruptly he gave a yelp of pain, and released Bess to stare down in bewilderment at Derritharn. The brownie looked smaller than ever, contrasted against his considerable height. But she wielded a tiny metal bucket with both hands, her expression ferocious. She swung it back and smashed it against Edward Adair's shins twice more, as hard as she could, and shouted, 'You leave Bess-Bess alone! You're frightening her!'

Mr. Adair kicked Derritharn, and the brownie fell to the ground with a cry of pain. She lay in a miserable little heap and did not move.

Bess glared at the arrogant boy, making no effort to disguise her hatred of him. 'That,' she said slowly, 'was *not* the best decision you've ever made.' She caught up the bucket Derritharn had dropped, paused a moment to take aim, and swung it at Adair's head. It connected with a satisfying *thunk,* and he yelped with pain.

Bess raised her weapon for a second blow. ''Tis a tiny tool, but solid, no?' She made a show of hefting the miniature bucket, and swung it back and forth. 'Hurts just a touch when it connects with your foolish noggin, don't it now? Shall I have another go?'

To her satisfaction, Adair fell back, his face a mask of wrath. 'You will regret your actions today, *maid.*'

'Eh.' Bess kept her grip on the bucket, in case he should decide to try again. 'I doubt it.'

Then again, perhaps she might. For she heard the door handle turn, and then the hinges creaked once more as somebody opened it. Bess had no time to hide the bucket she still wielded, and could only phrase the swiftest of silent prayers that it was but Mrs. Sanders come to check on the maids' progress.

Alas, it was not.

'What is the matter in here?' said Mrs. Adair, with regal displeasure. 'I thought I heard—' She broke off in surprise, and stared at the vision before her. Bessie could well imagine the scene as her employer saw it. Her upper housemaid with her black hair loose in a wild cloud around her face and her arm raised, clutching a tiny bucket with obvious intent to cause harm. Her precious son in full retreat before this vision of fury, his forehead already purpling with a fresh bruise. And a tiny household brownie (whose name she would never remember), lying in a crumpled heap not far away.

Bess was foolish enough to hope that the obvious explanation would occur to Mrs. Adair, and that she might be lenient.

*Fool,* she thought in disgust as Mrs. Adair's face darkened with an anger directed at Bessie.

'Bell?' she said. 'Perhaps you would care to explain why it is that you have assaulted my son.'

'Because he assaulted *me.*' Bessie would not shrink before that disapproving gaze, and she would *not* abase herself with apologies. She was not in the wrong.

'She lies, mother.' Edward Adair, curse him, did not even trouble himself to invent a plausible tale to defend his indefensible conduct. He knew that he need only accuse her of falsehood, and his mother would support him.

Which she did. 'You will leave this house at once,' she said to Bessie. 'You will not, of course, receive a character.'

Shocked to her core, Bessie could only gape in dismay. Turned off in the middle of the night, and without the reference that would allow her to seek another respectable post? She ought not to be surprised, but she *was* — and a little afraid. The hour approached midnight, the weather was inclement, and with no family living, she had nowhere to go.

But she could match Mrs. Adair for majesty. 'Nothing could persuade me to remain in this house another instant,' she said with all the dignity she could muster, though her heart pounded as she spoke. She set down the bucket, dismissed her erstwhile employers from her notice, and went to Derritharn's side. The brownie had picked herself up, though she bore an unsteady appearance.

'Well, now,' said Bess as she steadied her friend. 'You took a tumble, but I think yer not much hurt. Is that the case?'

Derritharn nodded, her small mouth pursed with disapproval. 'I'll not stay another instant either, Bess-Bess. And no brownie will ever set foot in Hapworth Manor again — I'll see to that.'

Bessie felt a small glow of satisfaction at this statement. She doubted that the loss of her brownies would instil any particular sense of their own wrongdoing in Mrs. Adair or her son, but it was something.

'Come, then,' she said. 'Off we go.' She picked up Derritharn and left the drawing-room without a backwards glance, not deigning to acknowledge either of the tormentors she left behind.

'Your hands are shaking,' said Derritharn as Bess climbed the long staircases up to her attic chamber.

'Aye, but only a mite. They'll pull themselves together in a minute, or two.'

Derri disappeared while Bess packed her few belongings, and the very little money she had saved. Bess's heart sank, for she felt it unlikely that she would ever meet the brownie again, and she was fond of her.

But as Bess made her way back down the stairs, Derri rejoined her, a tiny bag slung over her shoulder. 'The others are leaving tonight,' she said. 'They will spread the word.'

'And you?' Bess eyed the luggage Derritharn carried, and tried not to hope too much.

'I am coming with you. Though I hope you will carry me some of the way, for my legs are rather short.'

Bess beamed her relief, and a little of her tension eased. At least she would not be *quite* alone. 'You're the best friend I ever had, and I'm right delighted to have you along.' She stooped at once and scooped up Derritharn, tucking her inside the woollen cloak she wore. 'Though I warn you, I have not the smallest notion of where we are goin'.'

'That's all right,' said Derri comfortably. 'Wherever we go, I am sure it will be better than here.'

Bess could not but agree. She quit Hapworth Manor without speaking to another soul, and trudged away from the house and into the foggy night, her heart a mixture of sensations. In spite of her dismay and indignation at the night's events, and her fear at the challenge now before her, she could not stifle a sense of relief at leaving the Adair family far behind.

## CHAPTER TWO

*Oh, when I think o' that family an' their right dastardly treatment o' Bess, I could break sommat! She ain't the first, neither. Tis plain wrong, an' someday I'll find a way to give 'em what they deserve. Thas a promise.*
*But Bess, now. Couldn't have happened to a lass wi' more pluck. Some misses, eh, ye turn 'em out o' they homes in the dead o' night an' they'd collapse into a fit o' hysterics. An' who could blame 'em, considerin'? But Bessie Bell is made o' sterner stuff. Off she went into the night, wi' nowhere to go an' no plan... an' thas when the interestin' things started to happen. I'll say on.*

The night was not so cold as Bess had feared, which cheered her a little. But it was also foggier than she had imagined, and she had not been able to procure a light for herself. She could see barely a yard in front of her face, and was obliged to move slowly indeed in order to avoid tumbling into a ditch. The sensation was strange: she could see little but swathes of white fog, and even sounds were muffled. She felt adrift in a cocoon of mist.

As such, she judged it wisest to keep to the road. She could not expect to find her way safely through woodland under such conditions, nor would it avail her much if she could. Her plan, such as it was, went no further than finding some wayside inn to sleep at for the night, even if it were in a stable. She had money enough for one or two nights spent thus, or so she hoped.

But she had misjudged how far out of the way was Hapworth Manor. She walked mile after mile, always following the largest road (as far as she could judge). Nothing occurred to raise her hopes; no lights shone in the distance, no promising sounds reached her ears.

She could not even tell how long she had been walking. Time seemed to slow as she trudged on, and the sameness of the foggy world she journeyed through led her to feel, after some time, that she was making no progress at all.

The chill began to seep into her bones, and her hair grew wet and heavy under the clinging mist. Her body ached with weariness, and her thoughts were thick and sluggish with exhaustion. 'Derri,' she said at last. 'I have to admit that I am not leadin' us in any useful direction. And I have no notion what to do about it.'

Derritharn stirred in her swaddling cloak nest. ''Tis a difficulty,' she acknowledged. 'I will stop sleeping, and start thinking instead.'

But Bess's straining eyes alighted, at last, on something new: a faint light, shining in the distance. 'Stay a moment!' she said. 'Feast yer eyes on *that*.'

Derri peeked out of the cloak, and squeaked her approval. 'Perhaps it is an inn!'

'That's my thinkin' too,' agreed Bess. But she was forced to revise her ideas, for it soon became apparent that the lights were moving. 'Nay! Tis a traveller. Mayhap a coach. One of them bigguns, wi' the lanterns atop.' Her heart lifted at the thought, for if it was a mail coach or some such, she could entreat the driver to take her up with it.

*If* she could contrive to halt it. The contraption approached rapidly, and soon she could hear the sounds of hoofbeats. It was driving faster than it ought, she thought, given the conditions. She had no light with her, nothing to announce her presence. Indeed, she was in danger of being run down if she tried to stop the coach, for the driver could not possibly see her until he was almost on top of her.

Ah well. If she did not make the attempt, she was like to perish of damp and chill and hunger before she found any shelter. She positioned herself in the road, near enough to the edge to jump out of the way if she had to, and waited.

'Bess-Bess...?' said Derritharn as the hoofbeats grew louder.

'Oh,' said Bessie. 'Aye, you'd better get down. I wouldn't like for the both of us to be flattened.'

There was no time for more. Horses loomed abruptly out of the mist: a matched pair, black as night. Bess tensed, her heart pounding wildly as the equipage barrelled down upon her.

The horses snorted and neighed in surprise at finding an obstacle in their path, and one of them shied. Bess heard a male voice cursing. She waited until the last possible instant before leaping aside, heart palpitating with terror — and hope, that her foolish gambit had been enough.

For a moment it looked as though the carriage would *not* stop, and Bess's spirits sank. It bowled on, sweeping past her in a flurry of wind and the scent of sweating horse, and was swallowed up by the mist once more.

But the sound of hoofbeats slowed, and then stopped abruptly. It was not the gradual fading of the horses disappearing into the fog, and Bess's hopes rose again. She clutched a shaking Derritharn to herself and stepped back into the road, hurrying after the coach.

When she grew nearer to the vehicle, she was able to see at once that it was not a mail-coach after all, nor anything nearly so large — or so promising. It was a gentleman's carriage, the kind that seated but one or two, and the driver was the sole occupant. Oddly, there was no sign of the lanterns she had seen in the distance.

Its owner sat up high, gentling his startled horses with soothing words. His head turned slightly as Bess approached, and she knew he was aware of her presence, but he neither spoke to her nor looked at her until his horses had ceased their restive behaviour and stood, quiet and calm, once more.

Then he stared down at Bess.

In the darkness, she could discern little about him. He wore a dark coat or cloak and a wide-brimmed rain hat, which contrived to conceal his figure and much of his face. She could neither see nor imagine the expression of his eyes, and must attempt to judge his reaction to her presence by the quality of his silence alone. Which was no easy feat.

Bess tried not to feel afraid, and failed. Weariness defeated her, and the remembrance of Edward Adair's ungentle attentions of only a few hours before. She was in no fit state of mind to be encountering *another* lone gentleman tonight, by herself, and with no hope whatsoever of help, should matters go awry. But she could not retreat either, for he was her only hope of assistance.

'You are out late,' he said at last. 'And alone?'

'Yes, sir.' His tone had not been altogether unwelcoming, but nor had it been kind. 'I am in a spot of trouble, and must beg yer aid.'

She felt it to be a hopeless request as she spoke, for she knew herself to be far from the type of female he would have any inclination to assist. But he did not bark a negative and instantly drive on, as she had expected, and a flicker of hope flared in her heart.

He looked away, in the direction of his horses and the empty road ahead. Bess felt that his manner expressed some sort of frustration. 'You may have it, provided that assisting you does not interfere with my endeavour.'

'I need shelter,' she replied. 'An inn or sommat will serve me well, if you know of one in the neighbourhood. Failin' that, a barn or a stable or *anythin'*.'

'We are miles from any inn, and where there is no inn, there is no stable either.'

'A farm?' said Bess, with failing hopes.

He sighed irritably. 'I haven't the smallest notion. It has not occurred to me to consider the question of local farms.'

'Fair enough. Them as drives carriages got no cause to worry about such things.'

'Those, my dear girl,' said the gentleman blandly, but with a hint of annoyance. 'Those *who drive* carriages, and it is *have* in this context, not *got*. Quite apart from which, this is not a carriage but a curricle.'

'That's the way,' agreed Bess. 'Find fault wi' my speech, and you set yourself nice and high over the likes of me.' She smiled as she spoke, but her words were born of frustration. It was of no use to *her* for him to quibble, either about local geography *or* about her grammar.

The gentleman looked at her through narrowed eyes. 'Some would call it unwise, to give sauce to your betters. Especially when that better is a stranger, and you are alone, and it is late at night.'

Bessie patted the nose of the nearest of his horses. 'No sauce, sir,' she said blithely. 'I'm admirin' yer strategy. Tis a sound one, and I'm thinkin' you've had some practice.'

He sighed deeply, and the reins twitched in his hands. She thought for an alarming instant that he was going to drive away and leave her after all, but he did not. 'Where did you come from, infernal wench?'

'Hapworth Manor.' Bess did not care to elaborate, but it did not appear that she needed to. He looked sharply at her as she spoke the name of the Adair family home, and his silence spoke volumes.

At last he said, 'I should not feel interested in such a deplorable minx as I fear you will prove to be, but it seems I cannot help it.'

Bess grinned. 'You know pluck when you see it, sir.'

'That I do. Up you come, then. There is but just room enough, I imagine, though you will have to hold that bag of yours upon your lap.'

Bess clambered up at once, taking care neither to drop nor to reveal Derritharn, and settled herself upon the seat next to the gentleman. 'Thank you for your help, sir. I was at me wits' end.'

'As well you might be. It is no night to be abroad.' He set his horses in motion and the carriage — *curricle* — moved off at a smart pace. The wind was cold, and Bess sat huddled around Derri for warmth.

'There is a blanket on the floor,' he said briefly. 'You may use it if you wish.'

Bess required no second invitation. She felt around upon the floor near her feet, and her frozen fingers soon discovered a heap of something thick and soft. She drew it over her legs and tucked her hands beneath it, grateful for the warmth it soon imparted.

Her reluctant companion was silent for some time, and she received the impression that he was concentrating too intently to have any attention to spare for her. He would have to, of course, in order to successfully drive his curricle through the darkness and the fog. Which raised the question in Bess's mind: what manner of fool took any kind of carriage out on such a night? And alone, at that?

'I suppose it's an urgent endeavour,' she said at last. The words emerged a little oddly, for her lips had frozen stiff in the chill wind.

He glanced at her sharply, as though he had forgotten her existence. 'It is pressing. I ought, perhaps, to have warned you of its nature before I took you up. But leaving you behind alone would have been far more unwise, I believe.'

Bess absorbed that. 'It is some manner of dangerous undertakin', I collect.'

'If it is successful. If it is not, we will merely be chilled to the bone and mightily bored.' He glanced her way once more, and added, 'Or rather, I will be. It is my hope that I will be rid of my passenger before too long.'

'I ain't the troublesome sort,' Bessie offered.

'You are already causing trouble. Or *complications*, which is much the same thing.'

'Aye, well. 'Tis all much more troublesome to *me*, as it happens.'

'No doubt. Incidentally, "I am not troublesome" would be correct.'

'Yessir.'

He stopped speaking abruptly, and she once again felt that his attention had travelled far from her. She began to say something else, but he hushed her with a few words, and she fell silent.

He reined in his curricle, and they sat in strained silence for some moments. He was listening hard, but she had no notion what he was listening *for*.

'If you should happen to see eyes in the dark,' he said after a time, and in a languid, conversational tone, 'I beg you will mention the fact.'

'Eyes in the dark,' repeated Bessie. 'Right enough.'

He said nothing more.

'I suppose it'd be too much to ask why you are expectin' to see such a thing?'

'I have not time for your questions. Be silent, or I shall be forced to abandon you.'

Bess was left to speculate as to the meaning, and probable owner, of the eyes in question. It did not sound especially promising, but then there was nothing in the phrase by itself that ought rightly to inspire the shiver of dread that ran over her skin at the idea. He might merely be looking for a cat, or some other such creature. She would blame her unsettled feelings upon the depth of the night, the thickness of the fog, the chill in the air, and her own lingering tension from the events of earlier in the evening.

This approach functioned perfectly to restore her calm – at least, until she saw the eyes.

They had been clattering up and down lowish hills for some time, by which she judged them to be adrift somewhere in the midst of the Lincolnshire Wolds. Having slowly ascended a hill somewhat taller than the rest, they reached the peak and began to descend; and as they bowled into the valley at its base at a ground-eating trot (a petrifying pace, considering that the fog still concealed virtually everything around them), Bess saw a flicker of bright, sharp light like blue flame, floating in the mist some way off to her left. She stared hard into the fog, and realised with a thrill of horror that the twin motes of light resembled eyes.

'Mister?' she said.

'Green,' he replied.

'What?'

'Mr. Green.'

'I ain't askin' for yer name, though it's right nice to know. I'm happenin' to mention the fact that them eyes you was lookin' for are right over yonder.' She pointed.

He stared in the direction she indicated, and let out a low hiss. The sound shocked Bessie, for it was wholly at odds with the cultured speech and refined manner of a gentleman that he had hitherto displayed. 'Hold on tightly,' he said, and in spite of his apparent displeasure the languid tone had not left his voice. 'We are going to pick up the pace a little.'

He flicked the reins, and his horses dashed into a canter – and then, to her disbelief, a gallop. They careened wildly through the fog at a terrifying speed – and then, to crown Bess's horror, the curricle veered off the road and plunged into the woods. Their pace did not in the slightest degree slacken. Rank upon rank of shadowy black tree-branches loomed out of the blank whiteness and reached bare, twiggy fingers for Bess; she hunched in her seat, dipping her head low, and their grip missed. Branch after branch went sailing overhead and away, while the trunks of the trees and black, shadowy bushes loomed and faded on either side of the curricle. Derri shifted in Bess's grip, squeaking with terror, but Bess could only clutch her tiny friend and pray.

All the while, those flickering eyes of cold flame danced ahead of them, always out of reach.

'How is it that you can see where you're goin'!' shrieked Bess.

'In fact, I cannot!' said Mr. Green. 'We are not guided by my eyes.'

This made no sense to Bessie. Was it better or worse if some unknowable power guided the curricle through the maze of the woodland? *How* was it possible? It began to be apparent to Bess – if the cold-burning eyes were not enough of a clue – that she had been taken up by no ordinary gentleman.

The eyes grew suddenly larger, and Bess stared in horror into the depths of blue, frozen fire burning with a malevolent glare. This she bore with fortitude, though her heart beat quicker than she had ever known in her life.

She was rather *more* startled when Mr. Green – hitherto civilised in his behaviour, if a trifle odd – suddenly let out a vast cry; a terrible, dark sound loaded with incomprehensible words. Then he dropped the reins and leapt from the curricle with another horrific shout. The curricle continued on without slackening its pace in the smallest degree, proving that Mr. Green really had not been guiding its progress at all.

Bess clutched the seat and hung on grimly, resisting the temptation to throw herself from the wildly racing vehicle before it could contrive to plough into something, and kill her outright.

It was not, she thought, the most relaxing night of her life.

Just as a scream bubbled its way up into her throat and threatened to tear loose, the curricle's frantic pace finally slowed, and the vehicle came to a stop. This development did not please Bess as much as she would have preferred, for she had fetched up at the feet of the most frightening creature she had ever beheld in her life.

It was a horse, or something along those lines. Far larger than any horse had any right to be, it towered over the curricle – and therefore over her, in spite of her normally advantageous position atop the seat. Its hide was dense, roiling storm-cloud, or so it appeared to her (possibly fanciful) eye. Dark grey laced through with night-black and frozen-white, the horse blended into the fog as though it wore the inclement weather like a cloak.

Its eyes were those she had seen in the distance: enormous, winter-blue and crackling with impossible flame.

Bess's breath stopped.

'Tatterfoal,' she breathed.

'That he is,' said Mr. Green, who stood at the beast's head. 'Have you ever seen a mightier steed?'

Bess could find no words with which to respond. Her fool of a preserver (if he could be called such) appeared to be trying to *befriend* the beast. Bess decided on the spot that he was cracked in the head.

*Tatterfoal?* All the county knew of the nightmare creature. Some tales named him a horse, others a donkey, but all agreed that he was a fell beast indeed, wicked as winter and twice as cold. He had walked the hills of the Wolds many long years ago, terrifying unwary travellers and leading them astray. He took over a person's reason, so the tales said; hopelessly bewitched, they wandered blithely into the winter-struck woods and were never seen again.

These were tales of a long-lost menace; none had heard tell of Tatterfoal's presence for generations. But mothers still used its legend to keep their children in order, and to discourage them from venturing too far from the fireside. It worked, because Tatterfoal was *terrifying*.

And Mr. Green was *chatting* with it.

'There, foolish beast,' he said conversationally. 'I have not the faintest notion what you are doing partying abroad in England without your master's leave. It had better be a good explanation, for he will be more than a little displeased with you otherwise. Hmm? You did *not* have his leave, my dear pony, for he would remember granting it. Would he not, now? That is the gravest falsehood, and you had better not tell any more of *those*.'

Bess listened to half of this speech in a state of powerful terror, expecting any moment to see the fell beast snap her foolish driver's head off and then come after her. But before many words had passed his lips, it became apparent that no such calamity was imminent. She could find no explanation for Tatterfoal's apparent docility; nor for the fact that Mr. Green had, by all appearances, deliberately set out into the fog with the intention of encountering precisely this monster.

It was enough, for the present, to feel that her own life was not in imminent danger. Bess sat in rapt contemplation of the scene as Mr. Green continued to talk nonsense to the nightmarish horse.

But in the midst of this one-sided conversation, Tatterfoal abruptly reared, kicked up its heels and galloped away. Roiling wisps of storm-grey cloud shot through with lightning trailed after it, and dissipated without trace into the fog. Mr. Green stared after the vanished horse in open-mouthed dismay, and then fell to calling and cursing with growing rage. He spoke words Bessie could not understand; they burst forth in a torrent of anger, dark and snarling, and she could not suppress a shiver at the menace they seemed to carry.

But Tatterfoal did not return.

Mr. Green fell silent at last, returned to his abandoned vehicle and climbed back into the driver's seat. He gathered up the reins, but this time he made no pretence of employing them to set his horses in motion. He merely waved his hand and muttered, 'Off we go, then,' and the horses turned themselves and began plodding back in, presumably, the direction of the road they had left behind some time ago.

Bess waited in expectation of receiving some manner of explanation, but none was forthcoming. At last she said, 'Tis not that I mean to pry, you understand. But that were… Tatterfoal.'

'That it were.' Mr. Green's lips twisted in annoyance. '*Was*. That it was.'

'And it seems to me that he were kind enough *not* to swallow you whole.'

'He would not dare.'

'By that I am to understand that you are more terrifyin' than Tatterfoal.'

Mr. Green glanced sideways at her. 'You are positively overflowing with questions.'

'Ain't that natural enough? Considerin' what just happened in front of my eyes.'

'I thought you might be frightened.'

'Oh, I was,' Bessie agreed comfortably. 'Until I saw His Scariness actin' like a placid pony on a jaunt through the park. And then I was curious instead.'

'I am afraid your curiosity is destined to remain unsatisfied.'

Bess might have pressed him further, but that it occurred to her that the fog was dissipating. Nay, *had* dissipated; barely a wisp of it was left, for all that it had been as dense as a winter blanket only a few minutes before.

'Now, that's mighty strange,' she said, twisting in her seat to look about herself. She could not see much more of the wood than before, as the sun had not yet risen. But she could see the wide trunks of aged trees rising all around her, bark black in the darkness.

'Tatterfoal brings the fog,' said Mr. Green. 'Have you not heard that before?'

'Nay, that's no part of any legend I ever heard.'

Mr. Green grunted.

'Come to think of it, Tatterfoal ain't been seen in a hundred years. So they say.'

'Oh, not nearly so long as that.'

Bessie sighed, and fell silent. Clearly, her probing would avail her nothing; Mr. Green would be neither tricked nor persuaded into explaining himself.

'Bess-Bess,' came a faint whisper from within her cloak. Bessie peeked inside. 'Be wary of *him*,' said Derritharn.

Bess did not need to be told. Despite his kindness in taking her up with him, the rest of his behaviour clearly proclaimed that he was no ordinary English gentleman. She did wonder what else Derritharn had detected that prompted her to issue a special warning, but she could not question the brownie on that point without their being overheard.

'You should know,' said Mr. Green in a bland tone, 'that I have very sharp ears.'

Oh. 'Come on out, then, Derri,' she said. 'May as well, if your hidey-hole's discovered.'

Derritharn poked out her nose, and shivered violently. 'I'll not, if it is all the same to you. That there is a cold wind.'

Mr. Green snapped his fingers, and a moment later a ball of faint light materialised in the air over Bess's head. The light grew rapidly in strength, until she could see her surroundings clearly.

'Course,' said Bess, gazing at the mesmerising silvery glow. 'There be will-o-the-wykes followin' in yer wake as well. I might have expected as much.'

'They are fond of me,' said Mr. Green. He sat looking intently at Bess, and she returned his scrutiny while she had the opportunity, for she was mightily curious about the strange fellow whose assistance she had been forced to beg.

His figure remained a mystery inside the great black driving-coat he wore, and the rain hat still covered some part of his face. But she could see that he was unusually pale of complexion, with a firm mouth sardonically tilted at the edge. She caught a flash of bright eyes as he briefly met her gaze.

'It is not every day one encounters a plague of a curiosity-ridden housemaid wandering the roads at all hours, and alone,' he said. 'When she turns out to be bearing a denizen of Aylfenhame secreted inside her shabby wool cloak, then I would say it is a unique event indeed.'

*Aylfenhame.* The word repeated inside Bess's mind, growing larger with every echo. Aylfenhame was the fae realm, separate from England but sometimes accessible – at least, to the fortunate few. Or unfortunate. The tales of the realm of the Ayliri, as its human-like denizens were known, were myriad and varied. Some spoke of wonders and riches and magics marvellous beyond belief; others of black-hearted curses and nightmares, like Tatterfoal. Some few of its creatures chose to live in England, like Derritharn and her kin. Most, however, remained aloof from Bess's world, and never came there.

'Are *you* a denizen of Aylfenhame?' she said, unabashedly brazen.

He chuckled. 'Do I not look human enough, to your eye?'

'I cannot tell,' said Bess at once. 'Not under all that cloth coverin' you up from head to toe.'

'Well, it is far too cold to strip for your amusement this evening.'

Bess blinked. 'I—'

His sardonic smile widened. 'Yes?'

'Hm.' She eyed him with displeasure. 'You like to divert me questions by tryin' to shock me.'

'Ah. And you are not easy to shock. That I have had ample opportunity to observe.'

Thinking of the hideous vision of Tatterfoal and her decision *not* to run away screaming, Bess nodded affirmatively. 'Though not for lack of tryin' on your part.'

'Mm. Do stop plaguing me with questions, however. I must decide what is to be done with you.'

The curricle found the road and lumbered back onto it. There it paused, stretched across the road, apparently waiting.

'Dunnot trouble yourself,' said Bess. 'Me and Derri will decide what to do wi' ourselves. Just take us to an inn, or some such place.'

'I could do that,' he agreed. 'But I do not think I shall.'

Derritharn shivered, and clutched at Bess's cloak. 'Alas and woe, for 'tis too late to be wary!'

Mr. Green rolled his eyes heavenward. 'Silence, creature. I am not going to harm your human.'

'Settin' me down someplace safe would go a long way towards reassurin' us both,' said Bess.

'Which is precisely my intention, but an inn will not do. No—do not speak, if you will be so kind. You are not in full possession of the facts. Being observed in *my* company will have done your safety little good, tonight.'

'Well, then, I wish you had left us in the road!' said Bess, with some asperity.

Mr. Green made no response to this sally. He muttered something Bess did not understand and the curricle stirred into motion once more, righting itself upon the road by way of a right-hand turn. The horses began to trot and then to canter, bowling smartly along under the now-visible moon.

'I did not precisely understand the extent of the peril, at the time,' Mr. Green said at last. 'Even if I had, only a blackguard would leave a young woman alone upon the road past the midnight hour. And whatever else I may be, Bess-Bess, I am *not* a blackguard.'

'You,' said Bess with dignity, 'may call me Miss Bell.'

He laughed delightedly at that, then tore off his hat and tossed it away with a flick of his wrist. 'What an intriguing young beast you are.'

His hair proved to be red and wild, and worn longer than was typically fashionable for a gentleman. Bess watched it whipping in the wind, and considered. What could be the motive behind this stranger's actions? The things she had seen tonight would have had her scoffing in disbelief, only a few hours before.

But strangely, she did not feel in any danger from him, in spite of Derritharn's obvious unease. In fact, she could find nothing that might account for her brownie friend's distrust. Edward Adair's mere presence had always made Bess uneasy, from the first moment she had encountered him; something of his nature had shown itself in his manner and his behaviour right away. But in spite of *this* gentleman's comfort with such nightmares as Tatterfoal, Bess did not feel the same concerns about Mr. Green. He had spoken brusquely to her, but in essentials he had been naught but kindness.

Always supposing that he *did* intend to convey her to safety. Perhaps he intended to take her somewhere out-of-the-way, where she would be beyond the reach of help. Bess frowned as she attempted to picture this scene. Somehow, she could not believe it of Mr. Green — not least because he seemed wholly uninterested in her person. He scarcely seemed aware that she was female.

Perhaps she was being a fool to trust him. She would listen to Derri, and be ready to run at the first sign of trouble. Accordingly, she sat tensely beside him throughout the rest of the strange journey, clutching Derri in one arm while the other rested atop the mean bundle of possessions she had managed to bring away with her.

But flight did not prove necessary. Their journey ended some twenty minutes later, when the curricle drew up outside of a mansion house. It was not nearly so large as Hapworth Manor, but it was substantial enough: the residence of wealthy people. The moon shone silvery upon its pale stone walls, and many windows glittered faintly in the darkness.

'This is Somerdale,' said Mr. Green as his horses came to a stop. 'It is the home of some friends of mine. They will treat you well, and keep you safe. I am also certain they will assist you in finding a new place.'

He meant a new place in service, of course, and it was natural that he should assume she would want to take up another position as a maid. But as he uttered the words, Bess knew without doubt that she never wished to work in service again. *Never.* The beginnings of a new plan had taken hold in her mind, and she had every intention of pursuing it.

That, however, was none of Mr. Green's business. She permitted herself to be assisted down from the curricle, still prepared to flee if it should prove necessary. As Mr. Green marched up to the front door and rapped loudly upon it, Bess held a whispered consultation with Derritharn.

'What think you, Derri? Now's our chance to run, if we want to get away.'

Derri shook her head. 'Nay, he spoke truly. This place is safe.'

'Oh? And how do you know that?'

'Because it is *Somerdale*.'

'That makes no sense to me.'

'Did you not hear of the Aylfendeanes?'

'The wha… oh! You mean Miss Ellerby?'

'That I do. *They* live here.'

'Well then, that makes sense after all.' And it did. The neighbourhood of Tilby had been lively with interest over the story of Miss Isabel Ellerby, several weeks before. The young lady had fled a perfectly respectable – indeed, advantageous – marriage in favour of wedding herself to an Aylir. Out of *Aylfenhame*. Bess had never set eyes upon any of the people in the tale, of course, and she had half imagined it to be the purest nonsense; as unlikely a story as that of Tatterfoal. But they were said to have settled near Tilby itself, defying the disapproval of the more censorious of the town's gossips.

And if Derri believed it…

Bess clutched her cloak more tightly around herself, overtaken by a sudden and surprising hope. Oh, goodness! If she had been able to choose one place in the whole of Tilby to flee to after her ordeal, this would be her choice. Could the story really be true?

Mr. Green had succeeded in eliciting a response, and the front door opened. A middle-aged woman – probably the housekeeper – stood framed there, dressed in a nightgown and with a shawl around her shoulders.

'You must wake your mistress, with my apologies,' said Mr. Green. 'There is an urgent matter requiring her attention.'

Did he mean her? Bess was unsure how she felt about being characterised as an *urgent matter*. It sounded most unpleasant. But the housekeeper made no objection, which suggested that she knew Mr. Green. She disappeared inside the house, and Mr. Green beckoned Bess herself forward.

Bessie caught up her bundle of clothing and approached. Within moments she was standing in the hall of Somerdale, abruptly aware of how uncomfortably cold she was. She felt an undesirable degree of discomfort besides, for the grand owners of Somerdale could not wish to be roused from their beds over a mere maid such as herself.

But she was no more blessed with options now than she had been to begin with, so she waited. Within a few minutes she heard footsteps upon the stairs, and the light of a candle approached to join that of the single flame burning in the hallway.

'Grunewald!' said a woman's voice. 'Whatever is the matter? I hope nothing is amiss with Sophy—oh!'

The woman stopped before Bess, and looked her over. Bess had quieted some of her discomfort by composing a little speech in her mind with which she hoped to pacify her would-be hostess, but every word of it fled when she saw who was to be burdened with her problems.

The woman was taller than Bess herself, and might be taken for human. But even in the wavering light of the candle, Bess could see that her abundant brown hair was threaded through with tendrils of pure gold; not the "gold" of bright blonde but real, shimmering gold. Her eyes were faintly slanted, and an odd, pale green colour Bess had never before beheld. Her face was uncommonly beautiful, and a hundred things about it proclaimed that she was not human at all.

Bess gasped, unable to help herself. The tale was *true!* Not only had Miss Isabel Ellerby married one of the Ayliri, but she was Aylir herself.

Miss Ellerby – or rather, Mrs. Aylfendeane – was kind enough to ignore Bess's reaction. 'Dear me, I see that something highly untoward has happened,' she said with a kind smile. 'Are you very cold indeed? I think that you must be. Mrs. Glover, would you be so kind as to prepare the lavender room for our guest? With as many hot bricks as can be spared, please. Oh, and do have a bath drawn!'

Bess heard these instructions with disbelief, and growing alarm. Perhaps, in the poor light, Mrs. Aylfendeane had failed to observe the nature of Bess's garments. 'Oh no, not for the likes of me!' she said. 'Not that I wouldn't be grateful for somewhere to sleep—' and Bess swayed on her feet as she said this, aware anew of the extent of her exhaustion '—but any out of the way chamber'd do for me, ma'am. In the attic, mayhap.'

But Mrs. Aylfendeane merely patted her shoulder. 'Nonsense. You are chilled to the bone, and require proper care if you are not to be ill. Stay a moment, Mrs. Glover.' She turned to Mr. Green, who stood in silence inside the huge front door. 'Will you be staying, Grunewald? I hope so, for the hour is far advanced.'

'I ought not, but perhaps I must,' he said. Bess thought he spoke of reluctance without feeling it; his manner was more suggestive of wariness.

'Those instructions again for Mr. Green, Mrs. Glover,' said the Aylir lady. 'The jade room.'

Mrs. Glover went away, and Bess set down her bundle of clothes. She felt awkward – more than awkward – dropping such a mean parcel upon the polished hardwood floor of this grand hall, but she was simply too tired to carry it any longer. The bundle was collected shortly afterwards by a footman, who bore it away up the stairs. Bessie was ushered after him by Mrs. Aylfendeane herself, and with the greatest kindness. The room she was shown too was far too grand, of course, but Bess barely noticed – except to register that a tiny brownie-sized cot had been set up for Derritharn, with its own hot brick.

It stood to reason that the Aylfendeanes would be prepared to host fae guests, of course, but Bess was so touched by this extra gesture that she felt tears start to her eyes. So much solicitude struck her on the raw, after the disastrous day she had suffered through. Mrs. Aylfendeane would hear nothing of her thanks, however. She merely instructed Bess to appear at any time she chose in the morning, and that breakfast would await her. Then she withdrew.

Bess waited only long enough to ensure that Derri was comfortably settled before she collapsed into bed. It occurred to her, distantly, that it was the softest, warmest, most delicious bed in which she had ever taken her repose. She had little opportunity to relish these facts, because within seconds she was asleep.

## CHAPTER THREE

Grunewald left Somerdale before dawn on the following morning, having enjoyed but a few hours of slumber. He barely felt the effects of his lost sleep, for he was enjoying a mixture of intrigue and alarm which kept his brain lively and his steps energetic. The theft of Tatterfoal could be no good news, but in the face of this emergency, he felt more alive than he had in years. Mr. Green of Hyde Place, and the dissipated life that he led under the disguise, seemed far away indeed.

Grunewald bent his lively mind to the problem with alacrity. Anyone who knew of Tatterfoal must know of the horse's advantages. The fog which attended upon his every step cloaked the actions of both horse and rider from prying eyes; Tatterfoal's terrifying appearance, combined with the legends of ill-luck and horror which had grown up around him, kept interfering parties at bay; and he was, besides all this, the fastest mount ever known – when he chose to run. The question of *how* somebody had contrived to make off with the horse may prove difficult to answer, but Grunewald had no difficulty imagining *why* somebody would go to the lengths and risks of stealing the creature; he was the perfect accomplice for dark deeds.

And uncatchable. Grunewald harboured no hopes whatsoever of being able to run down whoever had stolen the horse; not if they caught wind of his pursuit, and urged Tatterfoal into flight. His only hope was to position himself cleverly, choosing somewhere the creature was likely to pass through, and by this means contrive to catch sight of whoever had taken possession of his prize mount. The fog was an obstacle, to be sure, but he had retainers aplenty at his command.

He did not judge that Tatterfoal would emerge until after sunset, which gave him some hours in which to make his arrangements. He embarked at once for that area of the countryside in which he had encountered the horse the night before, and set about summoning assistance. Placing himself in, as near as he could judge, the very spot in which he had previously intercepted Tatterfoal, he dismounted from the sadly ordinary mare he had borrowed from the Aylfendeanes' stables and uttered a string of words rarely heard in England before.

The sun had yet to fully rise, and he stood cloaked in shadow but barely touched by the sluggish, grey light of dawn. His breath steamed in the cold air, and he felt the creeping chill of October seeping through the layers of his coat. He felt a flicker of impatience, then, when minutes passed with no response, and no sound save the faint creaking of the trees in the rising winds.

Then a tiny ball of cold, greenish-pale light winked into being near his face and bobbed a greeting.

'About time,' Grunewald growled.

Three others soon joined the first, and then half a dozen more. Grunewald waited until each of the dark, looming trees around him had sprouted lights like bunches of grapes, and the clearing was aglow with wisp-light. Then, still speaking the ancient Darkling tongue, he issued his instructions. When he had finished, the wisps flickered their compliance and streamed away. Soon, Grunewald was left in near darkness once more.

The wisps would spread out across Tilton Wood, dampen their lights to almost nothing, and wait for a glimpse of Tatterfoal. That such subterfuge was necessary was not in question; Grunewald's pursuit of the goblin horse the night before had ended in disappointment. He had caught up with Tatterfoal, to be sure, but lost him again; and whoever had taken possession of him had abandoned the horse and disappeared. If he wished to catch sight of the rider as well, he would need all the assistance his wisps could give him, and their light alone could reliably penetrate the thick, drifting fog which clung to Tatterfoal's heels.

The sun rose, though its light was feeble and hidden behind a thick blanket of grey cloud. Grunewald spent the daylight hours recruiting further assistance from the shy leafling fae that populated Tilton Wood, and an occasional hob or hob-goblin tucked into underground burrows beneath the trees. By the end of the day, he was hungry, cold and tired, but he had achieved his goal: the woods and hills surrounding Tilby were alive with watchers, and he had taken care to position some few near to Hapworth Manor.

He had but one task left, that being to hope that Tatterfoal would return this evening.

In this, he was not disappointed. Drenching fog seeped up from the ground almost as soon as the sun disappeared, and the chill night grew colder still. Grunewald did not move from his appointed position. He did not think it coincidence that he had encountered Tatterfoal in the depths of Tilton Wood, and there he intended to stay.

Time drifted past. His hair grew wet and dripping beneath the chill fingers of the fog, and his coat and boots soaked through. After some hours of vigil, he felt frozen to his core and began to shiver.

This hardship he ignored. He stood, immoveable and still, in a cocoon of thick white fog, unable to see more than two feet around him. With nothing to fix his attention upon and naught to do, his mind drifted, turning over myriad notions as to the meaning of Tatterfoal's theft.

That it had something to do with the Adairs, he could not help but wonder, for Hapworth Manor was situated but a mile from his present position. He had entered the environs of Tilby by chance, the year before, in company with another: an Aylir of Aylfenhame named Aubranael, disguised at the time as a human gentleman. The ensuing caper had amused him, but he had been particularly intrigued by the town of Tilby. Its enveloping woods, called Tilton by the residents, struck him as beyond the ordinary; some quality to its trees and carpeting mosses and its filtering green lights, some note to its verdant aromas, seemed to him unusually primeval — even fae. The town was blessed with an unusually thriving population of fae creatures, though he did not imagine that the townsfolk were aware of it beyond the brownies which took up residence with them.

And then there was the bridge-keeper, Balligumph. Grunewald had travelled widely throughout England, and he knew well how unusual the toll-keeper was. A troll, come out of Aylfenhame to keep the Tilby bridge? It was but a modest crossing at that, too small to warrant any kind of toll. And the price asked for passage was strange, too: not coin, but information.

Oh, Tilby was certainly unusual. Intrigued, Grunewald had remained even after Aubranael had left, and sought to discover more. His enquiries had led him all the way to the Chronicler's Library in the royal city of Mirramay, in Aylfenhame; and there he had learned... a few things.

The town of Tilby was situated directly across the divide from the ancient Aylfenhame town of Grenlowe. He now suspected that it had long borne close connections with the fae lands, and that the fae had left more than one lingering mark upon the place.

He suspected still more that some of those connections had taken root among the populace of the town – its *human* populace. This suspicion had been confirmed recently, when a sweet young woman known as Miss Ellerby had discovered Ayliri heritage and the powers to match, and had accordingly become a witch.

That there were more families hereabouts with fae blood, Grunewald no longer doubted; but that they were all as innocently placed, and as inherently harmless, as Isabel Aylfendeane and her fledgling powers, he could not feel confident of. The Library of Mirramay had revealed disturbing hints of powerful Ayliri bloodlines mingled with equally powerful English families, and Grunewald's misgivings had grown. Even the Chronicler's records could offer little by way of fixed information, and Grunewald had taken it upon himself to try to discover more.

And now, the business of Tatterfoal. The two things may not be connected at all; but on the other hand, they might. Grunewald kept his mind open to possibilities, and waited.

His thoughts drifted to the hapless maid he had rescued on the previous night. She was wasted on the Adairs, and on service; that he had quickly seen. She had borne her abrupt dismissal with composure, and gamely set out into an inclement night with no fears beyond the reasonable. Moreover, she had been brought face-to-face with Tatterfoal and had proved remarkably impervious to the horse's terrors. He regretted bearing her along on that venture, but there had not been sufficient time to deposit her somewhere without losing his quarry.

She interested him, and more than a little. Her lack of deference did not offend him; rather, it was refreshing – though if she had spoken to her former masters in the same fashion, he considered it no surprise at all that she had been turned off. Her spirit impressed him, and her wit amused him. It was a matter of some faint regret that he would, in all likelihood, see little of her henceforth – if he ever saw her again.

A faint sound reached his ears through the muffling fog: the breaking of a stick, and the dull *thud* of a hoofbeat. All thoughts of the black-haired maid fled from his mind; with a strong effort of will he resisted the urge to turn in search of the sound, and continued to wait.

Another *thud*, and another. Hoofbeats indeed. Grunewald stopped breathing as the sounds came closer. A faint, dark shadow moved in the fog up ahead.

Grunewald whispered a word, and a light flared in the darkness: a wisp had erupted into life. More followed, and within moments the woods were drenched in a stark, piercing wisp-light which blazed through the fog, and revealed the dark form of Tatterfoal.

*And his rider*. Grunewald felt a moment's fierce satisfaction, for his subterfuge had worked: his quarry, unaware of any surveillance, had not yet fled. The rider looked sharply around, blinking in the sudden light, and with a wordless cry he applied his heels to Tatterfoal's flanks and disappeared into the night and the fog.

The encounter lasted no more than three seconds, but it had been enough: Grunewald had seen. What he had glimpsed shocked him to the core, for the rider's visage had been as familiar to Grunewald as... well, as his own.

Rage filled him. Abandoning his hiding-place, he darted for his mare, swung himself up upon her back and rode in furious pursuit of Tatterfoal, screaming wordless fury. But though he rode long into the night, he never caught up with his wayward goblin mount, or the rider who had stolen the beast's loyalty.

\* \* \*

Bess woke to find the hour far advanced. The sun was up and shining full upon Somerdale, which caused her to feel wonder and regret in equal measure. She could not remember the last time she had risen from her bed in daylight; it was a rare thing, even in the heart of summer. In the midst of October, it was unheard of and unthinkable.

Which meant she was shamefully late in presenting herself to her kind hostess.

Worse – or, perhaps, better yet – someone had been into Bessie's room while she slept. A fire burned in the hearth, and a large jug of fresh water had been set next to the pretty porcelain wash basin which stood upon the dresser. Recognising the work of a housemaid, Bess could only stare. Only a single day ago, it had been *her* unhappy task to rise in the dark and the cold of the morning and light fires which other people would enjoy. How was it that she had, in so short a space of time, become one of the few to benefit from such labours?

*Best not get accustomed,* she cautioned herself, for it could not last. Besides, even in the midst of her pleasure at washing her face in clean, warm water, she felt a touch of guilt, for she could sympathise all too clearly with the probable feelings of the maid who had laid out these delights for her.

Derritharn was still asleep, and Bess left her to slumber. She was touched anew to note that Derri had also been provided for in the night. A tiny wash basin and jug were laid out for her, too, together with a clean (albeit still ragged) dress, and a hearty-looking breakfast. This would be the work of Somerdale's household brownies. Bess was heartened to see that they were as ready to welcome Derri as the Aylfendeanes were to welcome Bess herself. Having completed her ablutions, brought some semblance of order to her tangled black hair and changed her dress, Bess was able to go down to breakfast, comfortable in the knowledge that her friend was well taken care of.

Still, it went sorely against the grain with Bess to leave such a fine guest room and descend the main staircase to an even grander hall. She had to resist the temptation to search for a hidden, plainer staircase somewhere which would take her straight to the kitchens. She owned only two dresses, and even the finest of them was but faded red cotton. It had been old when she had received it, a cast-off begrudgingly bestowed by her former mistress. Now it was shabby and frayed, and Bessie felt like an imposter sweeping down the main stairs in such a garment.

But she was here by invitation, and a far kinder and more genuine invitation than she had ever before received. She dismissed such feelings, lifted her chin, and endeavoured to appear comfortable and unconcerned.

This lasted only until she arrived at the bottom of the staircase and realised that she had no notion of where next to go. She hesitated, unwilling to venture through any of the closed doors or down the corridors without some idea of where to present herself. If she were to intrude somewhere she was unwelcome, she would swiftly lose Mrs. Aylfendeane's goodwill, and then what would become of her?

As she was considering this problem, a door opened and the housekeeper she had glimpsed before – Mrs. Glover – appeared.

'There you are,' said Mrs. Glover without ceremony. 'There is breakfast for you in the kitchens.' She turned away at once, leaving Bess to follow as she could. Bess was more than content to do so; feeling, secretly, relieved that she would not be expected to take her breakfast anywhere as grand as her bedchamber had been.

But Mrs. Aylfendeane's voice prevented her escape. 'Ah, Bess!' she said. 'It is Bess, I believe? I am glad you have found your way down.'

Bess turned back. Her hostess stood in the middle of the hall, looking even more beautiful and marvellous than she had in the darkness of last night. Her sumptuous hair was coiled atop her head in a fashionable style, and arranged into ringlets in front. Her gown was of some kind of silk, Bess judged, though it was finer and stranger than any she had seen before, for it shimmered in three shades of green simultaneously, and rippled like water even when Mrs. Aylfendeane was standing still. A butterfly with violet wings sat at her waist.

'Ma'am.' Bess made a curtsey, which, to her horror, was returned.

'Mrs. Glover? Bess will take breakfast with us in the parlour, if you please.'

'Begging your pardon, ma'am. I thought that the young person would be more comfortable in the kitchen.'

'Miss Bell has endured a very difficult day and conducted herself remarkably well. Nonetheless, I believe she requires a little cosseting to fully restore her.' Mrs. Aylfendeane smiled at Bess. 'Besides which, Miss Bell, I am eager to speak with you about your adventure.'

Bess could hardly refuse. She followed her hostess into a pretty parlour which, she was relieved to discover, was not *too* grand, and accepted a chair at the table. A gentleman also sat there; Mr.

Aylfendeane, presumably. He was as well-dressed as his wife, in a cerulean waistcoat and snow-white shirt of similarly remarkable fabrics. He was also uncommonly handsome, with pale brown skin, long hair as black as Bess's own tied into a tail, and eyes of an unsettling burnished bronze colour. Bess received from him a smile every bit as kind as his wife's as she took her place at table.

There was no sign of Mr. Green.

Bess realised, belatedly, that the food was set out upon a sideboard behind her, and she was expected to serve herself. Too late; for as this darted through her brain, she found a plate set before her by Mrs. Aylfendeane herself. Mr. Aylfendeane filled up a cup of chocolate for her and set it by the plate.

For the first time in her life, Bess had no idea what to do or say. She was too far out of her depth. She ought rightly to be serving *them*, in the proper way of things! Or not even that, for serving at table was too high a duty for a mere housemaid.

She also failed to hide her feelings as completely as she was used to do, for Mr. Aylfendeane observed her distress. 'T'ain't quite a usual household, this,' he said, and not at all in the refined accents Bess had expected. 'Ye'll get the hang of it in a minute.' He winked at her, and applied himself to his own chocolate.

'Oh dear, that is true,' said Mrs. Aylfendeane as she sat down. 'I had not considered! It must seem very odd to you, and perhaps we have made you uncomfortable. But I hope you will overlook our blunder – or *mine*, indeed, for my husband has anticipated your feelings.'

Bessie blinked. The lady of Somerdale was apologising to *her*? 'I can truthfully say, ma'am, that I have never been treated so kindly in the whole course of my life.' Good heavens, the food alone was so far out of the ordinary way that Bess hardly knew how to eat it. There were fresh bread rolls with butter and preserves, three different cakes, and tea, together with the pot of chocolate. She had never enjoyed such a variety of food before, nor in such quantity; the pile upon her plate might ordinarily be expected to serve her for two breakfasts.

Nor was she accustomed to eating the moment she rose; ordinarily she would have completed some two or three hours of work first.

Mrs. Aylfendeane seemed nonplussed by Bess's statement, and her face darkened with some thought Bess could not identify. 'You came from Hapworth Manor, I understand?' she said.

'Aye, ma'am.' Bess said no more, for the extent of her hunger had at last penetrated through her haze of confusion, and she attacked her breakfast with energy.

'Mr. Green imparted some details of your story to me before he left the house,' said Mrs. Aylfendeane, partaking of her own breakfast in a far more ladylike fashion than Bess was proceeding to do. 'But I should like to hear it from your own lips, if you will indulge me.'

She would have to wait until Bess had finished eating, for having begun, she could not bear to stop. She felt as though a year had passed since her last meal, and nothing would do but that she clean every scrap of food from her plate, and every drop of tea and chocolate from the cups and pots set before her as well. Mr. Aylfendeane watched these proceedings with obvious amusement, but Bess could not feel abashed.

Once her meal was complete, Bess began to talk. She sensed that Mrs. Aylfendeane's question came from real interest, and from her expression when she spoke of Hapworth Manor, Bess risked a guess that the Adair family were not among the Aylfendeanes' favourite people in the neighbourhood. Even so, she softened some of the details of the event which had led to her expulsion from the Manor, and dispatched that part of the story as rapidly as she could. She hurried on to the moment when she had met Mr. Green – *if* that was his real name, for she distantly recalled his being addressed as something else at Somerdale.

When she had finished, both of her hosts sat for a moment in silent thought. Then Mrs. Aylfendeane said: 'You hit Edward Adair with a bucket?'

Bess blinked. 'Aye, ma'am.'

'You hit him in the *head* with a bucket?'

Bess braced herself for disapproval – until she realised that the lady was trying to resist an apparently strong urge to laugh. Mrs. Aylfendeane soon gave up on the futile endeavour and laughed heartily indeed, clapping her hands in satisfaction. 'I can scarcely think of a person more deserving! I applaud you. Grunewald said you were out of the common way, and he is perfectly right.'

'Grunewald? Ain't he called Mr. Green?'

'He is, when he chooses to be. But you have already had full opportunity to observe that he is not altogether an ordinary gentleman.'

'I reckon he is cracked in the head.'

'Oh? Why do you say so?'

'Anyone who goes up to a nightmare and pats it on the nose is missin' somethin' in the way of sanity.'

Mr. Aylfendeane grinned at that with obvious appreciation. 'I hope ye told 'im as much yerself.'

'No sir! I ain't nearly mad enough. If he can manage Tatterfoal like he was a bitty-lamb, he could eat the likes of *me* for lunch.'

'Oh, nonsense,' said Mrs. Aylfendeane. 'Grunewald would not hurt you. He has proved as much! He does not like to spread it about that he is *not* plain Mr. Green, but he has taken no objection to *your* being fully aware of it. He has not threatened you, has he?'

Bess snorted. 'He don't need to! He were kind to me when I needed it, and I am grateful to him to be sure. But I maintain he's as mad as they come.'

Mrs. Aylfendeane nodded, and sipped her tea with enviable calm. 'It is a strange business, to be sure. Did you ever hear of Tatterfoal before, my love?' This last was addressed to her husband, whose brows rose at the question.

'Mm. That I 'ave, though not a great deal. In the past, it was said t' be the favoured mount o' the Goblin King, an' never abroad but wi' his blessin'. As t' whether that's still true, ye'd have t' ask—'

'How interesting,' said Mrs. Aylfendeane, with a quick glance at Bess. 'I hardly think the Goblin King would terrorise our poor county with fog and nightmares, however.'

'Aye, well. As t' that, His Majesty's famously hard t' understand.'

Bess thought back to last evening. What had Mr. Green said? *I have not the faintest notion what you are doing partying abroad in England without your master's leave.* Tatterfoal's master was the Goblin King? A *king of Aylfenhame?* But if that was true, how came Mr. Green to know anything about it?

'Grunewald works for the King of the Goblins?' Bess blurted.

Mrs. Aylfendeane looked sharply at her. 'Did he say so to you?'

'No. But he called Tatterfoal a *pony*, if you please, and said that he didn't have leave to be partyin' in these parts. How would he know that, if he weren't workin' for Tatterfoal's master? *And*, 'twould explain why he was willin' to go right up to the beast.'

Mr. and Mrs. Aylfendeane exchanged a look. 'That is possible,' said the lady. 'But Bess, I believe we must consider the question of how we may assist you. Your returning to Hapworth Manor is out of the question, naturally, but I collect that you did not receive a character?'

Bess's mood darkened at once. 'Aye. Right enough.'

'How perfectly revolting,' she said in tones of strong disgust. 'But there I may be of assistance. I shall be happy to write you such testimonials as you require, and we will perhaps be able to find you a new position with some one or other of our friends.'

This was kindness, and everything Bess would have hoped for on the previous evening. But a deal had changed since. Her heart sank low at the prospect of returning to her housemaid's labour; so much so that she could not welcome Mrs. Aylfendeane's offer, no matter how kindly meant. She had never wished to go into service; it had merely been the only option available to her. Motherless since birth, her father had died eight years before, and considering her youth, inexperience and lack of either money or connections she had been obliged to keep herself thereafter by any means possible.

Now that she was a stout young woman of four-and-twenty, she *ought* to be able to do better for herself. But how? She was no more skilled now than she had been at sixteen, except at such delights as cleaning fireplaces, stuffing mattresses, mending bed linen and beating carpets. She could not expect to be taken as an apprentice at any higher profession; not at her age, and with no money to offer to a prospective master.

Her options, in short, were limited indeed. After eight years of toil, she was no nearer to improving her situation.

'You need not answer at once,' said Mrs. Aylfendeane. 'There is time to consider.'

Was there? She could hardly expect this obliging couple to continue to house her while she debated her choices — especially knowing that, in the end, her choices numbered but one.

'I must accept your offer,' said Bess. 'And I thank you for it.'

Mrs. Aylfendeane looked concerned, and a frown appeared upon her perfect brow. 'I do rather wish that—' she began, but she did not complete the sentence. She stopped speaking, lips parted upon whatever the next word would have been. 'I think I hear...' she said, and then turned to her husband. 'Do you hear that?'

'Aye, love,' he said grimly. 'I hear it well enough.'

Bess heard nothing out of the way at all, and she was confused. But within a few moments, something odd reached her ears: strains of music, distant but coming closer.

It was strange music at that, utterly removed from the popular ditties and ballads Bess had heard before. The melody was a fluid ripple of notes played at a rapid, almost frantic, pace, and the piercing notes of a pipe rose above it all.

The Aylfendeanes rose from their chairs and went into the hall, forgetting Bess entirely. She trailed after them, puzzled, as the music grew louder. Soon it began to seem as though the melody emanated from directly outside the house; moments later there came a loud rapping upon the great front door of Somerdale House.

A butler had appeared from somewhere, and now went forward to open the door. But Mr. Aylfendeane waved him back, and went to admit the visitors himself. He threw open both doors, and Bess received a clear view of a marvellous and surprising sight.

In the preceding months, a band of Ayliri musicians and their attendant dancers had been wandering across England, attending assemblies and balls all over the country. They were known as The Piper's Rade, and their appearance — though looked upon with suspicion, at first — had come to be welcomed, even celebrated. But when the summer came to an end, the Rade's progress had apparently ended as well.

Until now? For the array of colour spread before Bess's wondering gaze could be nothing else. A company of Ayliri had drawn up in front of the house; Bess counted at least eight of them, all mounted atop long-legged horses whose coats shone in strange and beautiful colours. Their riders were still more magnificent: each wore an approximation of the fashions of English gentry, but cut from silks and velvets of impossibly rich colours. Their clothes shimmered in the weak morning sun, decked in ribbons and lace and glittering with magic.

Even this astonishing magnificence could not cast their wearers' beauty into the shade, for the Ayliri were more handsome than Bess would have imagined possible. Their skin ranged in hue from icy-pale to as dark as chocolate; their features were sculpted perfection, almost eerily beautiful; their eyes and hair were of the shades and hues of flowers and precious jewels.

Their leader was the Piper. He held a curiously curled pipe to his lips and played a whirling melody upon it, and this he did not cease until the doors of Somerdale were opened to him. Then he dismounted, revealing himself to be remarkably tall. His hair, worn long and loose, was indigo in hue, and his eyes were an intense violet.

He also appeared to be in a flaming temper. He strode up to the door and demanded, without preamble, 'Has Grunewald been here?'

'Aye,' said Mr. Aylfendeane, surprised. 'Last night.'

The piper scowled. 'Oh, he was up to a deal of mischief last night! Tell me at once. Are you in some way involved in this matter?'

'We are unsure to what matter you refer, Lyrriant,' said Mrs. Aylfendeane in a calm way. 'Do, please, elaborate.'

Lyrriant's eyes narrowed. 'Do not seek to dissemble. I can only be referring to the abrupt reappearance of Tatterfoal in these parts.'

'Then of course, it is naught to do with us.'

Lyrriant stepped closer to her, his manner far from conciliatory. This angered Mr. Aylfendeane, who took his wife's hand and drew her closer to himself. 'Do not seek t' frighten my wife, Lyrriant. Tell us at once what's the matter wi' ye.'

'*Grunewald* is the matter,' snarled Lyrriant. 'For him to go riding about the countryside upon such a mount as *that*! You, above all others, must realise the dangers of such reckless behaviour.'

'I do not believe he was riding Tatterfoal at all,' said Mrs. Aylfendeane. 'Indeed, he is as much puzzled by the horse's appearance as any of us.'

Lyrriant's scowl deepened. 'Naught but the purest falsehood. He was observed.'

'Oh? By who?'

'Oh, by many! Too many to imagine that they are all mistaken. If Grunewald has told you that it was not *he* atop Tatterfoal's cursed back, then he has lied to you.'

Mr. and Mrs. Aylfendeane exchanged a troubled look. And then, inevitably, both of them looked at Bess.

'But we have a witness,' said Mrs. Aylfendeane.

Lyrriant's violet gaze turned upon Bess, and with no very friendly expression. His lip curled. 'This is your witness?'

Bessie stepped forward. 'I was wi' the one you're callin' Grunewald last night, sir. And I can vouch for what he has told the Aylfendeanes. He were chasin' Tatterfoal and tryin' to catch him. He was not ridin' the beast.'

Her words set up a murmur of comment from the piper's attendants, which he hushed with a wave of one long-fingered hand. He looked hard at Bess. 'Explain.'

Bess was obliged to recount her story all over again, which she did as succinctly as possible — not least because a cold autumn wind was blowing into the house, and she had not the garments to withstand the chill in any comfort. It did not appear to her that Lyrriant believed her tale, which caused her some pique. But he did not altogether discount it, either.

'You appear to be sincere,' he said when she had done. 'But if your story is the truth, then there would have to be two Grunewalds wandering about in Lincolnshire.'

'Wi' the arts o' Glamour, that's not impossible,' said Mr. Aylfendeane.

Lyrriant nodded. 'But if someone has stolen his semblance, answer me this: Which of the two is the real Grunewald, and which the lie?'

'The real Grunewald is the one who visited *us* last evening,' said Mrs. Aylfendeane. 'I would swear to it.'

'I hope that you are correct,' said Lyrriant. 'But if you are, we must face the possibility that this semblance is capable of fooling even His Majesty's most loyal servants. And that is no pleasing prospect.'

'Are ye sure ye didn't wake up Mister Tatterfoal yer own selves?' said Mr. Aylfendeane. 'Wi' yer ridin' and pipin' about, ye've been wakin' up a deal o' long-lost folk.'

'Tatterfoal is beyond our power to influence. He answers to none but His Majesty.' Lyrriant strode to his horse — jade-coloured, its pearly mane whipping in the wind — and jumped back onto the creature's back. 'If he returns, notify me,' he said. Without awaiting a response, he lifted his pipe to his lips and began, once more, to play. His mount darted forward, and Lyrriant rode away from Somerdale at a rolling canter. The rest of the Rade fell in behind him, and the whole party thundered away.

Bess and the Aylfendeanes watched their departure until every last scrap of colour and light had faded from sight, and the Piper's music could no longer be heard. Then, at last, the butler was permitted to close the doors of Somerdale upon the chill wind.

'I wish Lyrriant did not have to be *quite* so dictatorial,' said Mrs.

Aylfendeane with a sigh. 'I confess, I do not see why it should matter to him that Tatterfoal roams the countryside.'

'It used t' be said tha' the appearance o' Tatterfoal presaged some kind o' disaster,' said Mr. Aylfendeane. 'I am inclined t' doubt that it means any such thing, but mayhap Lyrriant disagrees.'

Mrs. Aylfendeane looked worried by this suggestion, and her husband immediately fell to reassuring her. But Bess said nothing. Her mind was busy, turning over everything that Lyrriant had said. One part of his speech was of particular interest to her: *Tatterfoal answers to none but His Majesty.*

'Are ye full certain, love, tha' last night's visitor was Grunewald?' said Mr. Aylfendeane. This question recalled Bess's attention, for she had been wondering the same thing.

His wife gave the matter some thought, her brow furrowed. 'I am sure of it. Consider. If there is an imposter wandering about Lincolnshire in Grunewald's form, and this person is responsible for the appearance of Tatterfoal, then we must assume that his intentions are at least questionable, if not outright malevolent. But the person *we* met last evening took the trouble of bringing poor Bess here, out of naught but kindness. Would an imposter have done it?'

It did not appear to occur to Mrs. Aylfendeane that she had said anything to cause any alarm. But an alternative interpretation of last night's events evidently entered her husband's mind, and his gaze settled upon Bess with a hint of suspicion.

Bess could easily guess the direction of his thoughts. 'I am everythin' I claim to be, I swear it!' she protested. 'I never met Mr. Green, or whatever he calls hisself, before yesterday, and he took me up in his curricle pretty unwillingly.'

'Let us not forget Derritharn, love,' added Mrs. Aylfendeane. 'I am persuaded that she would never consent to take up with anyone who could not be trusted.'

'There I must disagree wi' ye,' said her husband. 'Brownies are simple folk, true enough, and rarely get themselves mixed up in such matters. But it 'appens. An' Derritharn is no more known t' us than Bess.'

'I will ask Alleny,' said Mrs. Aylfendeane.

As though summoned by the mere mention of her name, a brownie darted into the hall moments later and presented herself at her mistress's feet. Her hair was corn-coloured, and she wore a tattered sage-green dress. 'Aye, Mrs. Isabel?' said she.

'I would like you to vouch for Derritharn, if you can. And for Derritharn's companion.' Mrs. Aylfendeane gestured at Bess.

Alleny looked Bess over carefully. 'I know naught of the human, but Derri, now! Her granny is cousin to my gramper, and her brother Balso is wed wi' my niece Valline.'

'Ah! So she is well-known to you. And has she indeed been resident at Hapworth Manor, until recently?'

'Oh yes! Though we *told* her them was a bad lot.' Alleny put her hands upon her hips and tutted. 'She would not listen!'

'Derri has known me all of this past year,' offered Bess. 'She would know if I was not meself.'

'Thank you, Alleny,' said Mrs. Aylfendeane, and the brownie dashed away again. Bess did not think her words had entirely satisfied both of her hosts, which injured her a little. But with the likes of Tatterfoal abroad, she could not blame them for being wary.

Any lingering suspicion Mr. Aylfendeane may have felt about Bess did not manifest in any alteration in his treatment of her. They kept Bessie with them for most of the day, and the lady of the house questioned her closely about her life, her skills and her interests — most likely with a view to finding Bess a suitable new position thereafter. But it pleased Bess nonetheless, for no one had ever taken such an interest in her before. She and her husband were also forthcoming about themselves, and answered Bess's questions with the greatest good nature, though she took care to ask nothing too personal or probing. She did not wish to give them cause, however inadvertently, to suspect her of harbouring some ulterior motive for her show of interest.

Derritharn came down in the afternoon and joined Bess and their hosts in the parlour. Bess noticed that Mr. Aylfendeane found myriad subtle ways to test Derri's knowledge of Bess, and her loyalty, without seeming to examine her. This did not unduly trouble Bess, for she knew that Derri could say nothing out of place, and she gave her host full credit for subtlety and sensitivity in his questioning. If Bessie was part of some plan to introduce a threat at Somerdale, then of course he must discover it, in order to protect his family. But by the end of the afternoon, she felt that these fears had been assuaged.

She herself remained unsettled. By the end of a day spent in near idleness, the question of how best to dispose of herself was as pressing as ever, but still unanswered. The matter was driven from Bess's mind when, come four o' clock, dense fog began to drift over the fields and soon engulfed Somerdale. The weak and fading October sunlight vanished altogether, and within a few minutes all was darkness outside the house.

Mrs. Aylfendeane rose and went to the parlour window. 'I can see nothing!' she reported. 'It is worse than last evening, I am sure of it.'

'Tatterfoal,' said Bess.

Mr. Aylfendeane looked at her. 'The fog?'

'Aye. Mr. Green said Tatterfoal brings it.'

'He is out there somewhere, then,' said Mrs. Aylfendeane. 'I wonder what it is that he wants in these parts?'

Half an hour passed in a state of some tension. Bessie could not settle, for she was too well able to picture Tatterfoal in all his nightmarish glory marauding through the Wolds — and not, in all likelihood, very far away. Was Mr. Green out in the fog once again, chasing down his errant steed? Would he be any more successful at bringing him back under mastery, this time?

Soon afterwards there came a violent pounding upon the door, which caused Bess to startle almost out of her wits, for the sound was amplified beyond all reason; it seemed to shake the very house itself. The Aylfendeanes shot out of their chairs and, as one, left the room. Bess went after, and arrived in the hall just in time to see Mr. Green come striding through the front door. He ignored the butler who, half-indignant and half-atremble, attempted to ask him his business.

Bess received her first clear view of the man who had assisted her. He was taller than she had thought, and though he still wore the great black driving-coat of last evening, she received the impression that his was a spare, trim frame. His skin was excessively pale, almost stark white; his shock of red hair stood out all the more prominently in contrast.

His eyes were bright, vivid leaf-green, and at the present moment they were livid with fury.

'Isabel!' he bellowed. 'The effrontery! The thrice-damned *nerve!* That traitorous, lily-livered, fatuous-minded *pony* is not merely wandering about taking his ease among your beautiful Lincolnshire hills. He is here by instruction! Nay, by cordial *invitation!* And whose the instructions, you might ask, sent the ridiculous creature flitting about the English countryside like an oversized butterfly?' He paused with awful deliberation as he took a deep breath. '*MINE!*' he roared.

'My own blessed invitation, if you please! For who should I have glimpsed tearing about upon the poppinjay's back but my own self!'

'We 'ave discovered the same, this mornin', by way o' Lyrriant,' said Mr. Aylfendeane.

'Oh, you have! How very obliging of him! I suppose he has told the rest of the neighbourhood as well! Dear folk of Lincolnshire, if you wish to know by whose order your roads and hills are being terrorised by a vision of hell itself, you need look no further than Mr. Green, of Hyde Place!' Grunewald was working himself into a visible fit of apoplexy, for with every word his pale complexion grew a shade redder, and his eyes flamed with rage.

Mrs. Aylfendeane went towards him with her hands outstretched. 'I do not imagine him to have done any such thing, Grunewald. I assured him, of course, that Tatterfoal's appearance was none of *your* doing, and that we had heard as much from your own self only last night.'

Mr. Aylfendeane pointed to Bess. 'You do recognise tha' young lady, I suppose?'

Mr. Green's livid gaze fell upon Bess, who merely raised an eyebrow in response. 'Yes, of course I recognise the baggage,' he snapped. 'What has that to say to anything?' Enlightenment dawned, and if anything, his rage grew fiercer. 'Oh, I *see!*' he said with awful sarcasm. 'There was some question, was there, that your visitor of last night was the *other* Grunewald, and the baggage some manner of accomplice! Permit me to reassure you! That deuced tangle of problems fell into my lap by the most *damnable* piece of ill-luck and it was of the greatest inconvenience!'

Bess bridled at that. 'Gentleman, are you so? I have met pigs wi' better manners.'

Grunewald pointed one long, thin finger at Bess. 'You watch your mouth, my girl! I am in no humour to brook any of your sauce this evening!'

'Then you'd best address me with a bit more courtesy! For I had no desire whatsoever to be hauled off on your hare-brained venture, and that you know full well! You think I *enjoyed* it, I suppose! That I congratulated meself on runnin' into *you* just at the right moment to be swept up into the maddest ride of my life and imaginin's both, when I was already cold and tired and more frightened than I have ever been in all my years! You were welcome to leave me in the road where you found me wi' my blessin', and so I said to your face once before!'

Grunewald looked as though he would cheerfully throttle her, which only angered Bess the more. Impossible man! If he thought he could so easily disrespect *her* because she was naught but a maid, he was full mistaken!

'Grunewald, do please calm yourself,' said Mrs. Aylfendeane. 'Bess, please! It is clear that there is something gravely amiss and we must discover what it is together. This howling at each other is of no conceivable use.'

Grunewald's fierce gaze fixed upon Isabel, and Bess feared that he would next begin to shout at her. But he took a big, big breath and let it out, and his rage seemed to dissipate along with it. 'I apologise,' he said shortly. 'You are perfectly right.' He bowed, first to the

Aylfendeanes and then — to Bess's astonishment — to her as well. 'Yes, baggage, I also apologise to you. Of course, it was not your fault that you strayed into my path, and it was not much to your benefit either.'

'Well,' said Bess, disconcerted. 'To be fair, you did bring me here. I only wish we could've dispensed wi' the mad part aforehand.'

A twinkle of amusement appeared in Grunewald's eyes. 'Yes, well. It does not appear to have produced anywhere near so lasting an effect as I had hoped, for here is the wretched creature returned!' He looked at the Aylfendeanes, and his expression grew sober indeed. 'Isabel. Tal. It is not merely my *semblance* that has been stolen, do you understand? For semblance alone would not fool Tatterfoal. No, whoever has helped himself to my image is able to mimic me to my core, and *that* not only angers but terrifies me. There is no end to the trouble such a person could cause — not only to me, but to others. To England. To Aylfenhame.'

Silence met these words. Bessie was more appalled by Grunewald's seriousness, and his acknowledgement of fear, than she had ever been by his rage. She did not yet know the full secret of Grunewald's identity, whatever her suspicions might be; but that he was a strange and powerful being, *that* she had no doubt of. Anything capable of terrifying *him* was fearsome indeed.

'Is there some way we can be of assistance?' said Mrs. Aylfendeane. 'You did not come here merely to deliver yourself of a tirade, I imagine.'

'I have some hopes that you can. I must discover who is behind this masquerade, but the Glamour is too perfect; even I cannot expect to penetrate it without significant assistance.' Grunewald stared intently at Somerdale's lady. 'You are a witch.'

'I am,' said Mrs. Aylfendeane guardedly. 'But of no great talent, I am afraid.'

'Thou art bein' overly modest, again,' said a voice Bess had never yet heard. To her amazement, the most peculiar creature emerged from some shadowed corner where it had lain entirely undetected. The beast resembled a cat, though its ears were those of a bear and its face was somewhat bat-like. Its fur, thick and luxurious, was striped in brown and gold, and the tip of its long tail was crowned with a crimson tuft. 'Thou'rt new t' the witchin' arts, but nonetheless thou'rt passing skilled at Craftin'.'

Grunewald stooped to stroke the creature's ears, which ministrations it did not at all seem to mind, for it wrapped its tail around his knees and purred. 'Tafferty, I rely upon you to support me!' said Grunewald. 'You and Isabel are my best hope of a speedy resolution.'

'Aye, I understand,' said Tafferty. 'Thou hast fairy ointment in thy thoughts, I collect?'

'I do.'

Isabel gasped, and Tafferty's tail twitched. 'Thou'rt askin' a great deal, admittedly.'

'I know it,' said Grunewald. 'But will you try?' This last was directed to Mrs. Aylfendeane, with a look of such soulful entreaty that Bess did not think *she* could have resisted it.

'I will try,' said Mrs. Aylfendeane doubtfully. 'With Tafferty's help, perhaps I might... oh, but I do not know what it is to be out of! I have no materials for such creations at Somerdale.'

Grunewald collected a packet of soft cloth from a pocket in his driving coat, and handed it over. 'Wild thyme, four-leaf clovers and snowfoot boletes,' he said. 'And but two strands of butterbyne moss.'

'Thou'rt already astray wi' thy mushrooms,' said Tafferty. 'Tis velvet queen parasols we require, with the boletes.'

Grunewald frowned. 'In truth? Perhaps my information is unsound. Nonetheless, will you make the attempt?'

Isabel took the packet with a nod. 'I could not refuse, though I beg you will not allow your hopes to rise too high. Tafferty is right: I am but new to the arts.'

Grunewald smiled upon her with a glow of gratitude, and perhaps more. It entered Bess's thoughts that he harboured a degree of special fondness for Mrs. Aylfendeane. 'Thank you, Isabel.'

The Aylfendeanes went away with the talkative, striped creature, leaving Bessie alone with Grunewald. He appeared to have forgotten Bess's existence, for he stared after Isabel with a meditative expression, and did not move.

'You cannot simply catch ahold of this person and remove them from the neighbourhood?' Bess enquired.

'Not a chance,' Grunewald said absently. 'His choice of Tatterfoal as steed is no accident, for there is no swifter creature in your world or mine. I would need Tatterfoal to catch him. Nay, *better* than Tatterfoal.'

Bessie accepted that without further comment, and her thoughts took a swift turn. 'I am wonderin',' she said conversationally. 'How does a person get to be a witch?'

Grunewald blinked at her, and it took a moment before his eyes focused upon her face. 'What? Oh. Have a fancy to take up witching, have you?'

'It seems to me a deal more interestin' than sweepin' floors.'

'No doubt. Unfortunately, it is not an art one may simply decide to practice. It comes with blood heritage from Aylfenhame, and even then, but few are able to attempt it.'

Bess sighed. 'Tiresome. Does it sometimes seem to you that all the best things are kept for those wi' the right bloodline? Tis a mite dull for those of us wi' the poor luck to be born from naught but mud.'

'Perfectly true, but alongside your understandable cynicism you must consider two points. Firstly, that one may just as easily inherit burdens and disasters with one's bloodline as advantages, and the two sets of birth-gifts often occur together. Secondly, that a lack of inherited advantages need not curtail *your* choices. Only a fool or a weakling abandons themselves to disappointment merely because they were not dealt a perfect hand of cards at birth.'

Bess was briefly silenced. She could not reasonably argue with any of his points, for she felt the sense of them keenly enough. But it did not alter the fact that her *choices*, as he termed them, were but few. 'What would you do, in my shoes?' she said.

He took her question literally, and glanced at her feet. 'Cast-off shoes from a careless mistress, rather an older gift than is reasonable. Worn to the point of being not only uncomfortable but, I should imagine, painful.'

Bess's feet had blossomed with a few new blisters after last night's wanderings, and she nodded.

'I would stop walking around in someone else's shoes,' he concluded.

'Shoes ain't exactly in the habit of growin' on trees around here.'

'Then you must go somewhere else.'

Bess snorted, and abandoned the conversation. It was evident that Mr. Green's thoughts were on his own problems rather than hers, which was reasonable enough; she could hardly expect him to care what became of her. Why, he still called her *baggage*. Nonetheless, she felt a moment's resentment that he, dripping in wealth as he was, could so flippantly cast out such advice. Where else was she to go — some place where shoes grew on trees? What nonsense.

Derritharn appeared at Bess's feet. 'There is a shoe-tree in Avarindle,' she offered, quite as though she had heard Bess's sour reflections.

Bess frowned. 'A what?'

'A shoe tree. A wood-gnome fell on hard times and had no shoes for his children. So he buried a worn old shoe in the ground and wished and shed a few tears, for his children were crying with the pain of their cold and sore feet. Tis said that a passing witch heard and cast an enchantment, and the next day a tree grew upon the spot. And it sprouted shoes, of all shapes and sizes.'

'Derri, you are makin' that up,' said Bess suspiciously. 'Such wonders don't happen, not even in Aylfenhame.'

Derritharn smiled up at Bess. 'It is as true as that I stand here.'

'I'll be needin' a bit more'n a magic shoe-tree to make a life for meself.'

'Oh, yes,' said Derri. 'But it would be a fine start.'

Bessie had no further comments to make, being outfaced by the sheer absurdity of Derritharn's arguments. She left Grunewald to his agitated pacing and Derri to improve her friendships with the brownies of Somerdale, and wandered into the garden. The time of year was not conducive to any impressive display of verdure, but she welcomed the solitude, and revelled in the unaccustomed freedom to wander in the garden in the middle of the morning. At this hour, only a day previously, she would likely have been busily engaged in airing the beds of Hapworth Manor, with a long day's duties still ahead of her.

Her resolve strengthened. She must not, at all costs, permit dreary necessity to force her back into service. She felt in her heart that she was made for more; that she wasted herself and all her resources of wit and liveliness, her youthful strength and her passionate nature on the menial life of a housemaid.

But where in England could she go in search of better? Who would ever be moved to give her the opportunity to better herself?

Nowhere. That she knew. But another idea had seeded in her mind, and Bess spent some little time engaged in the consideration of this new possibility. Aylfenhame. Thither Miss Ellerby had gone, and returned a witch — and an Aylir. Nor was hers the only such story, for a year or more ago the reverend's daughter had likewise ventured Aylfenwards. Bess had heard the tales with lively interest, but never had she thought that she would seek to follow the example of those fine ladies. Nor that she would be granted any opportunity to do so.

Now the interest was hers, and opportunity also, if she could only find a way to take it. Bess wandered and thought for some time, until her fingers were numb with cold. When she returned into the house, she bore with her the beginnings of a plan.

# CHAPTER FOUR

*Strange happenin's, are they not? When word o' Tatterfoal's return reached my ears, I was none too happy. That ye can bet on. Tatterfoal! And in my neighbourhood! Poor news indeed. An' puzzlin'. I knew right off tha' sommat odd were goin' on. I know Grunewald. Odd fellow, an' no mistake, but not one to set such a beast wanderin' the roads at will.*

*So I weren't surprised to learn that he had a fetch. Ye know the term? An apparition o' some kind, tha' looks just like another. In this case, most likely some kind o' Glamour bein' employed to change th' appearance o' someone wi' questionable intentions. Who it could be, though? I 'ad no notion. Considerin' th' events o' the summer, however, I thought it poor news indeed. What wi' Mrs. Aylfendeane's adventure not long since, an' the darklin' bein's she had come into contact with, I 'ad to wonder if it were related.*

*Well, it were a while afore I learned anythin' along those lines. Many another strange event was to come first, an' poor Bessie Bell were right in the middle of 'em all.*

*Well. I say poor lass, but between you an' me, I think it were all a deal more to 'er likin' than she might 'ave wished t' admit.*

Bessie was invited to dinner.

Not merely dismissed to take her dinner in the kitchen with the servants, as she had expected, but invited to dine with the Aylfendeanes and Grunewald. Not only that, but Mrs. Aylfendeane sent her own maid to Bessie for the arranging of her hair, and lent to her a fine, wine-red gown to wear for the occasion.

At first discomfited by this unlooked-for and puzzling solicitude,

Bess soon came to enjoy it – particularly when she donned the rustling silk down, and admired the new vision of herself in the mirror. The maid – Sally, Bess soon learned, a girl only a year or two younger than herself – was skilled indeed, and Bess barely recognised her own black curls, organised as they were into an elegant style, with ringlets at the fore. Sally did not appear to resent her instructions, in spite of Bess's obviously being on a social level with herself. Her confidence in the Aylfendeanes' judgement seemed absolute.

Bess descended the stairs feeling like another person entirely. Her skirts felt heavy and luxurious around her legs; the neckline of the gown, while modest enough, displayed her natural assets in a fashion she was wholly unused to; and with her hair nicely done, she felt quite a lady.

When she saw the look of surprised appreciation in Grunewald's eyes as she walked into the drawing-room, her satisfaction was complete. She observed Mrs. Aylfendeane casting an intrigued glance at Grunewald at the same moment, and began to wonder whether the lady's motive in treating Bess so had aught to do with him.

The mood over dinner, however, was subdued. Bess gathered at once that Mrs. Aylfendeane's attempts to create fairy ointment had not been successful. The lady seemed to feel her failure keenly, for her spirits were low, and her manner apologetic.

'It is of no moment,' Grunewald assured her. 'I wish you will not torment yourself about it. I knew it to be but a small chance, and there are others I can ask.'

Mrs. Aylfendeane raised her eyes to his face in surprise. 'Can that be true? I had understood it to be a rarity indeed.'

'Oh, yes. A decided rarity. But there is another witch of my acquaintance who may be able to produce it. Hidenory, you will perhaps remember her?' He paused in the act of bringing a portion of stewed pork to his mouth, and frowned. 'I need merely persuade her compliance, which, I grant you, is no inconsiderable task. Besides that, I may go in search of another capable witch. There are others in Aylfenhame, one assumes. And then there are the Markets.'

'Hidenory!' said Mrs. Aylfendeane. 'I know that Sophy would be interested to know of her whereabouts!'

'Ye'll not have much luck at th' Markets, I fear,' said Mr. Aylfendeane. 'I 'ave found them t' be lackin', these days. Not what they used t' be.'

Grunewald scowled. 'Alas, I must agree with you. Baubles and trinkets and little else! But I must make the attempt. I have some hopes of Grenlowe, but if that should fail… I will call a Goblin Market.'

Mr. Aylfendeane's response to that was but a shocked silence, and he stared at his dinner guest with eyes rather wide. 'Nay, surely it 'asn't come t' that,' he finally ventured.

Grunewald's eyes sparkled with some amusement. 'Come, come! What tales have been told abroad? The Goblin Market is not so bad as all that.'

Mr. Aylfendeane grinned. 'Oh, do ye say so? 'Tis said that if ye 'appen t' be in the market fer the darkest o' wares, the Goblin Market is the place t' be. Curses an' poisons an' tricksy enchantments, all that manner o' thing. Is tha' not so?'

Grunewald served himself from a dish of pudding before him. 'Oh, that is largely the truth,' he admitted.

'Oh, Grunewald!' said Mrs. Aylfendeane. 'Surely you cannot consent to make such questionable goods available in Aylfenhame, all in search of a mere ointment?'

Grunewald eyed her with an unreadable expression. 'I should lament the necessity, my dear Isabel, though the consequences are likely to be considerably less severe than I see you imagine. But perhaps you do not fully understand the problem I am facing. It is no minor undertaking, to impersonate such a being as myself.' Here his gaze strayed to Bess's face, and he did not elaborate on what he meant by that statement. 'It has not been done merely for the imposter's entertainment. I do not yet understand the purpose behind it, but that it may prove to be a grave threat to more than this neighbourhood's peace I have little doubt.'

Isabel sighed deeply. 'Yes, yes. I quite see that the matter is urgent.'

Bess felt sorely out of her depth. 'What is meant by the Goblin Market?' she ventured to ask.

'It is the largest market in Aylfenhame,' said Grunewald. 'And that is because any kind of goods may be sold there, with no restrictions, as there are in other markets. It takes place but rarely, for it is called at need.'

He had omitted some important details. 'Called by who?' Bess asked shrewdly. 'Are you able to call such a thing?'

Grunewald scowled. 'My compliments to your cook, Mrs. Aylfendeane,' he said, instead of answering Bess. 'Rarely have I tasted such a fine sago pudding.'

Mr. Aylfendeane laughed softly, and his wife looked conscious. 'Thank you, Grunewald,' said Mrs. Aylfendeane smoothly. 'I will ensure your compliments are conveyed.'

'I will learn the truth some day or other,' said Bess. 'There can be no use tryin' to keep it from me.'

Grunewald's eyes narrowed as he looked at her. 'I fear you may be perfectly correct, baggage, but I should like to postpone that day as long as possible.'

Bess smiled at him. 'No secret is safe around me, sir.'

'I imagine not. On which topic,' said Grunewald unexpectedly, and he turned his attention fully upon Bessie. 'Perhaps you will answer a question for me.'

'Course I will,' said Bess in some confusion.

'The Adairs. How long were you employed in that household?'

'One year only,' said Bess with a grimace, for it had felt longer than a single year.

'That is full long enough. Tell me: Did you ever chance to observe anything unusual? Particularly as regards the behaviour of the family.'

'Why would you ask that?' she said, wary and surprised.

'Odd visitors,' Grunewald pressed. 'A member of the family behaving in uncharacteristic ways. Particularly recently.'

Bess thought. 'Old Mr. Adair has been sufferin' poor health these past weeks,' she offered. 'He keeps to his rooms more'n he comes out, and when he shows hisself he's lookin' peaky.'

This modest offering did not seem such as to interest Grunewald, but he appeared thoughtful. 'Thank you, Miss Bell,' he said formally. 'If you should happen to remember any other such snippets of information, I beg you will inform me.'

'Why should you be interested in the Adairs?' asked Mrs. Aylfendeane.

Grunewald shook his head. 'I am not certain that I am, yet. But something in this neighbourhood is of interest to whoever has taken possession of Tatterfoal, and I am inclined to feel that it may be no coincidence that Bess here was in the same vicinity with the creature.'

The idea that the appearance of Tatterfoal might have anything to do with her former employers startled Bess considerably, and for a time she had naught to say. Her mind set to work, turning over every encounter with any of the Adair family she had experienced in the final weeks of her employment. But little occurred to her to mention, beyond the poor health of the elder Mr. Adair. It was hardly surprising; the great families considered it their duty to keep their private business from the knowledge of their servants, and sometimes they were even successful.

'I suppose the Market will be held in Aylfenhame?' Bessie said some time later, when a lull in the conversation offered her an opportunity.

'Invariably,' said Grunewald.

Bess nodded. 'And when are you callin' it?'

Grunewald's leaf-green gaze settled upon her, and narrowed. 'Why should you ask?'

Bess finished the last of her excellent fruit jellies, and set down her spoon. 'Because,' she said, and met Grunewald's gaze squarely, 'I would like to go.'

'Absolutely not.'

'How ungenerous.'

'That it may be, but my answer stands.'

Bessie glared at him. 'I will go as your servant if I must! I can be useful.'

'If I require that kind of service, I have loyal retainers aplenty to take along.'

'Then take me along for my sake.'

Grunewald's brows lifted. 'My dear girl, I am leaving you behind for your sake. You can have no notion what you are asking.'

'Then explain it to me.'

Grunewald sat back with a sigh and cast his gaze heavenwards, as though asking the Powers how he had come to be saddled with her. 'The Goblin Market is no safe place for a lady. Or, indeed, for anybody. In fact, nowhere in Gadrahst is safe. The Goblin Realm is dark, strange and sometimes unfriendly to outsiders. I will not be able to guarantee your safety.'

'Happily, I ain't askin' you to.'

'Or indeed your survival.'

That gave Bess pause, though she shrugged it off. 'There ain't a great deal waitin' for me in England. I'll take a risk.'

Grunewald's brows lowered. 'I have important and dangerous

business to see to. I will have neither time nor leisure to attend to you as well.' When Bess began to speak, he held up a hand to interrupt her. 'No more, please. If you wish to travel into Aylfenhame, I refer you to our obliging hosts for assistance. They will manage the matter much more comfortably than I.'

Bess was silenced. She felt at once that this would not quite do, but she could not imagine why that should be so. There could be little doubt that Mrs. Aylfendeane and her husband would assist Bess; they had made their kind intentions more than clear. But where would she be sent? How would she manage? What would become of her?

Grunewald, at least, was familiar to her. This, she knew, was but flimsy reasoning, but she had no better. 'I would rather go wi' you,' she said.

Grunewald blinked. 'Why?'

Bess shrugged her shoulders, enjoying the way her silk gown rustled as she did so. 'I dunnot know.'

Grunewald appeared to have no response to make. His face was expressive of surprise, and other emotions Bess could not name, and he did not speak. The silence stretched, until Mrs. Aylfendeane spoke.

'Allow me to assure you, Bess, that Grunewald is perfectly correct. If you do not wish to re-enter service, I can understand your feelings most readily, and we will be happy to assist you in travelling to Aylfenhame. I have a friend there who will be glad to receive you.'

Bess thanked her hostess sincerely, though her words did not change her feelings with regards to Grunewald. That puzzled her, for why should she care for his company? He was abrupt and rude, even if he was also kind. Even if he also treated her as a person, albeit a troublesome one – not merely as a servant.

The topic was allowed to pass, and a less contentious subject embarked upon. Bess did not raise it again.

The fog did not come that night, which puzzled the Aylfendeanes and Grunewald more than it reassured them. Had Tatterfoal and his rider achieved whatever purpose had called them into Lincolnshire, or had something occurred to draw them away? If the latter, where might they now be occupying themselves, and with what dark intentions? The household retired to bed early, uniformly concerned, and Bess, too, was content to seek her bed.

She knew that Grunewald was likely to depart early upon the morning. Her habits were such as to ensure that she would wake well before dawn, which could only be to her advantage. Prior to retiring, she ensured that her minimal belongings were packed and that the slightly better of her two gowns was laid out for the morning. With these preparations made, she drifted into sleep with her mind full of hopes – and fears, which she ignored.

When Grunewald appeared in the hall of Somerdale shortly after dawn the next morning, Bess was waiting for him. Her cloak was tied around her shoulders, her shabby winter bonnet was in place, and her small bundle of possessions waited by her feet.

She was alone. Derritharn had settled well at Somerdale, and Bess was loath to disrupt her comfort, especially with a view to carting her into such uncertain territory as Grunewald had described. She would miss Derri, but the brownie would be safe, comfortable and happy. Bess considered that to be more important.

Grunewald stopped abruptly when he saw Bess and the hopeful face she turned upon him. His brows snapped downwards, and he actually growled. 'It is to be an ambush, is it? A pretty plan indeed! If you appear before me ready to depart and with that infernal beseeching look, you imagine I shall change my mind!'

'Oh, certainly!' said Bess with a smile. 'For tis merely my own safety at stake, and since it is mine, I can do as I choose wi' that.'

'The responsibility falls upon me, however, as your guide. You will have to be protected, baggage, and who else shall there be to do so?'

Bess's smile grew. 'Why, me own self.'

'Foolish girl. You know naught of what you speak.'

'Right enough, no doubt.'

Grunewald made an exasperated noise and turned his back on her. He strode to the door without a backward glance, and it became obvious to Bess that he intended to simply walk away.

She collected up her bundle, and went after him.

'I will find a way to help you,' she said to his retreating back. 'What of the Adairs? There's none as knows them the way I do.'

'If I require more information about them, I will be sure to enquire.' Grunewald did not stop, or even slow his pace.

'Then I'll find a way to pay for passage.'

'Even supposing you did, it would change nothing.'

His curricle waited, and he had almost reached it. 'I really wish you might gi' me a chance,' Bess called up to him.

Grunewald stopped, and turned back to her. 'Why?' he asked in great puzzlement. 'I do not see why you should not be satisfied with accepting Mrs. Aylfendeane's offer.'

'Why, if I do that the adventure will be over entirely. I may never learn why Tatterfoal has been wanderin' again, nor who is the one wearin' your face. I'll have no chance to be part of that story, and no way of helpin' to rid these parts of the nasty creature.'

'It will be dangerous,' Grunewald repeated. 'Which part of that is failing to impress you?'

Bess grinned. 'Eh, as to that. Cleanin' carpets turned out to be more'n a little dangerous, too.'

A glimmer of amusement appeared in his vivid eyes. 'I cannot argue with that logic, baggage, but nonetheless I must decline. I'll not have leisure to see to you.' He turned from her and got up into the driving seat of his curricle.

'You'll not change your mind?'

Grunewald flashed her a wide smile, his eyes twinkling from beneath the brim of his hat. 'My dear baggage. I never change my mind.' The reins were in his hands; he nodded once at Bess, and urged his matched pair of black horses into motion.

Bess watched as the curricle bowled through the gates of Somerdale, and vanished. Well, then; she would have to find some other means of entering Aylfenhame, and of seeing the place called Gadrahst. Why it should matter to her, she did not fully understand, but that did not disturb her very much. Gadrahst, and the Goblin Market! His talk of danger she did not much regard; she had been in the presence of Tatterfoal, and contrived to keep her wits about her. She had been set adrift in the midst of the night, alone and with no conceivable means of seeking help, and she had not descended into hysterics. Why should she not face the Goblin Market with impunity?

But the opportunity to so test her strength and her resolve was denied her. Her only means of going into Aylfenhame at all lay with the Aylfendeanes. She thought it hardly likely that they would send her anywhere Grunewald had declined to take her; Mrs. Aylfendeane, a gentle soul herself, would be far too concerned for her safety. But once in Aylfenhame, perhaps she could contrive to find the place known as Gadrahst herself.

Decided, Bess turned her steps back towards the house. But before she could enter the grand doors, a curious sound and a glimpse of something strange attracted her attention. She thought she had heard a hiss; not that of a cat or other such beast, but an odd sound indeed. And her eye had detected a flash of red colour, somewhere to her right.

Bess looked, but could see nothing untoward. The sound was repeated more loudly, and there – another flicker of red.

Bess turned away from the doors of Somerdale and trod in the direction of these peculiar signals. She walked the length of the house and around the corner, entering a pretty shrubbery.

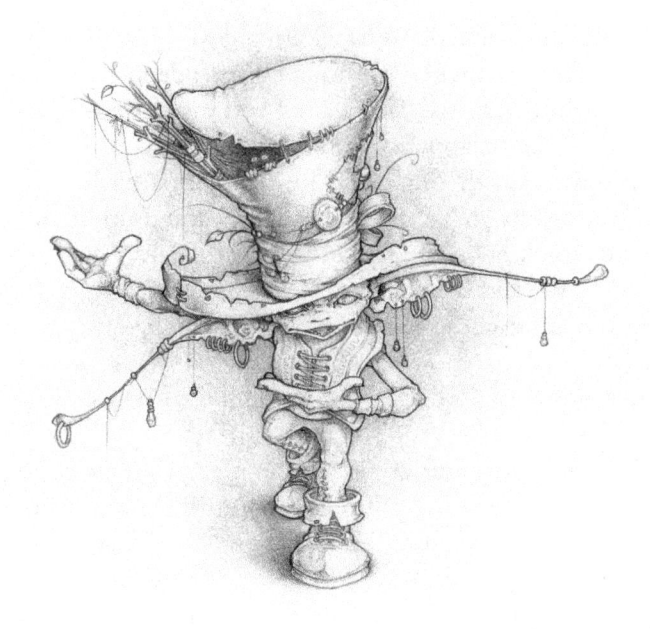

Standing betwixt two flourishing bushes was a curious creature, unquestionably fae. It – or he, Bess thought, judging from the jerkin and oversized hat he wore – was perhaps three feet tall, his skin the colour of oak. His head seemed fractionally too large for his body, an effect magnified by the preposterous hat. His ears were long and tapered at the tips, and he wore a fine collection of brass hoops and trinkets punched through the flesh of each one. The red colour Bess had seen came from the jerkin, which was velvet and rather fine. He beamed at Bess as she approached, showing an array of pearly teeth, and his moss-coloured eyes twinkled a welcome.

'Hello, Baggage,' he said, and swept a florid bow. How his enormous hat did not tumble off to fall at his feet, Bess could not imagine.

'Baggage!' she repeated. 'How came you by that name?'

The creature tapped one of his long, decorated ears. 'I was listening. You are on terms with the Gaustin, it appears.'

'I don't know any Gaustin. You mean Grunewald, I suppose.' Bess eyed the little man with some suspicion. 'What do you want wi' me?'

The smile widened. 'Why, I am one of the Gaustin's retainers!' And he swept another bow, though not so deep as the first.

'My congratulations,' Bess said. 'And my question?'

'Alas, my Gent appears to have abandoned us both. He ought to have taken me with him. And he ought not have been deaf to the pleas of a beauteous young lady.' He beamed up at Bess. This time, his smile struck her as crafty, and she grew wary.

'And?' she said. She folded her arms, and stared at the behatted creature in an uncompromising fashion. 'Oblige me by comin' to the point.'

'He is gone to Gadrahst, and there you wish also to go. Indeed?'

'Aye.'

'Well then, nothing could be simpler! I am going there myself, almost this moment. Why should we not travel together?'

Bess looked him over. 'What manner of bein' are you, and why are you fixin' to help me?'

'I am a Goblin of the Yarva tribe.' He fingered his hat, and tipped it slightly to Bess. 'Name of Idriggal. And you appear to be a young lady as has the Gaustin's ear.'

'In point of fact, I am fairly sure he took both of his ears along wi' him.'

'He listens to you.'

Bess raised an eyebrow. 'Considerin' I am standin' here talkin' to you instead of ridin' along wi' Grunewald, I'd have to say that he don't listen too well.'

'You are but a little acquainted with my Gent,' said Idriggal. 'He is of an uncompromising nature. If he had decided wholly against your company – or, indeed, against you – he would not have discussed the matter at all. But he did. And what's more…' Idriggal paused, and his eyes grew round. 'He thought about doing as you asked. I saw it.'

Bess was unimpressed by this vision of Grunewald's unusual tractability in her case. 'I don't see as that amounts to much.'

'Oh, it does,' said Idriggal softly. 'He has taken an interest in you. He was concerned for your safety.' He tipped his hat once more to Bess, a gesture of clear respect. 'If you were to ask him something else, I dare say he'd listen to that, too.'

'I see. So you want to take me wi' you to Gadrahst, and some time or other I'm to ask your Gent for somethin' you want.'

Idriggal bowed.

'You ain't worried that his Gentship'd be fearful angry wi' you for disobeyin' his orders?'

Idriggal snickered. 'He never ordered me not to take you into Gadrahst.'

'Order or not, he obviously wanted nothin' of the sort to happen! And what if I was to come a-cropper somewhere in them parts?'

'You will be under my protection.'

Bess eyed his diminutive frame with some scepticism. 'Oh?'

Idriggal smiled, and this time the expression struck her as outright menacing. 'You are used to brownies and other such gentle folk. Believe me, stature is all that I share with the likes of them.'

Bess's brows rose, but she would not argue the point with him. If he was ready to guarantee her safety, knowing the probable extent of Grunewald's wrath if she came into trouble, then he must have full reason for his confidence.

She thought over his proposal, keeping her eyes upon him as she did so. He merely smiled with calm serenity, and awaited her decision.

Bess felt there was more to his offer than was apparent, but she was not disinclined to take it up. It served her immediate purpose, and secured her a guide and protector in the process. It enabled her to achieve her goal without further troubling the Aylfendeanes, and it permitted her to make her own decision as to how, why and where to travel into the realm of Aylfenhame.

As to his bargain, it was little indeed he asked of her. She had merely to talk to Grunewald about some topic of his choosing; she could hardly be expected to control his decision.

'Very well,' she said, and picked up the bundle she had set down at her feet. 'Shall we go?'

Idriggal beamed at her. 'You are a lady of decision! Are you full ready to depart?'

Bess ought rightly to take formal leave of her hosts, she knew. But she had already left them a letter of thanks, written in Derri's pretty script, in the expectation of being carried away from Somerdale by Grunewald in the dark pre-dawn. The hour was still early; she could not expect that the Aylfendeanes would rise for some time yet, and she did not wish to wait. 'I am ready.'

'Then, it's away with us!' He held out a small, gnarled hand, which Bess took. 'I give you fair warning. We are going by the goblin ways, and they are not… pleasant, to your kind.'

'Eh. Try emptyin' chamber-pots of a mornin', and you'll know unpleasant.'

Idriggal snickered. 'Here's off!' he cried.

That was all the warning Bess received. His grip on her fingers tightened; she was wrenched sideways with powerful force, and the world dissolved into blackness.

# CHAPTER FIVE

When Grunewald departed Somerdale for Aylfenhame, it was with an incongruous vision of Bess in mind. Not as he had last seen her, bundled in layers of her shabby clothing and wearing, he suspected, every item of use that she owned. She appeared in his thoughts as she had presented herself last evening, wearing one of Mrs. Aylfendeane's gowns. The red silk had much become her; red suited her colouring, and her rich dark hair.

But her appearance did not interest him so much as her manner. Ordinarily, the mere alteration of attire ought not to so transform a person; as an experienced masquerader, he knew that very well indeed. But Bess had needed only that, he thought, to appear in a wholly different light. She had not the deference, the ignorance, or the sense of inferiority which often came with the position of a servant. Hers was a strong mind, and lively, and she well knew her own worth. Some elements of her behaviour had jarred with the vision: her table manners left something to be desired, and her speech gave her true station away. But she needed nothing by way of manner, posture, poise, conversation and ideas. That Isabel had discerned the same things, he had no doubt; for why else would she contrive to present Bessie at dinner, and in a fine gown?

He had little idea why the recollection of last night's dinner should live in his mind into the following morning, but he welcomed it as a distraction from the driving problem of his *fetch*.

Alas, it could be but brief, for the moment his thoughts once again wandered thither, the problem took full possession of his mind.

The knowledge that somebody of unknown identity had taken possession of *his* semblance, so successfully as to fool everyone in the neighbourhood of Tilby, and even Tatterfoal! The appearance he wore – the pale skin, the thin frame and red hair – were naught but Glamour in truth, and there existed no especial reason why another artist in illusion might not adopt the same characteristics. But to do so with such skill! Sufficient even to impress Grunewald himself! Who was it that wielded such powers, and why had they chosen to adopt his visage?

He could lose no time in discovering the identity of the imposter. From Somerdale, he travelled at once to Hyde Place, the manor house he had taken possession of in the previous year, and left his horse and equipage in the hands of a groom. He went directly to his study, a room he had not seen in some weeks, so occupied had he been elsewhere, and crossed to a large, verdant tapestry which hung in between two of the long windows upon the outer wall. He touched the fine silk fabric, and whispered a single word.

The tapestry shimmered. Ordinarily, it depicted a flourishing, ancient forest carpeted in moss and ferns. Now those rich green colours swirled together into a confused morass of forestal hues, and then solidified into a door hovering in between two mighty, tall oaks.

Grunewald reached out, took hold of the coiling bronze door handle, and twisted. The handle turned, and the door opened. On the other side, Grunewald saw not the rear gardens of Hyde Place over which the windows looked, but another room; one far away, over the border between Aylfenhame and England. He stepped through, his boots thudding dully upon the bare wooden planks of the floor, and shut the door behind him.

The room was built entirely from wood of a dusty, silvery grey colour, and was but sparsely furnished. Grunewald did not consider it worth his while to render it comfortable, since he spent but little time in his chambers in the town of Grenlowe; the twin tapestries merely served as a convenient doorway from Hyde Place in England into the Ayliri lands of Aylfenhame. He left the little wooden fae house at once, barely cognisant of the film of dust which lay across every surface.

It was market day in Grenlowe, which he had counted upon in his hurry to leave England that morning. The town was populous, and famed throughout Aylfenhame for its weekly market. It was said abroad that what one failed to find at the Grenlowe market was scarcely worth having; a sentiment with which Grunewald could not wholly agree. But his best chance of finding the goods he sought without the hassle and bustle of a Goblin Market lay in Grenlowe.

But he did not go immediately into the throng of coloured stalls. He directed his steps instead towards a particular shop with which he had become very familiar in the past year. Its name was Silverling, and its proprietors were friends upon whose support he could always rely.

He found Sophy seated alone in her favourite rocking chair, situated directly before the long shop window. A large pile of shimmering cloth lay in her lap, and her hands sought, with deft movements, to embroider some pattern into the surface. Her flyaway blonde hair escaped in lively curls from beneath the edges of her wispy lace cap. She greeted him with a delighted smile, and at once set aside her work.

'Why, Grunewald!' she said, rising to meet him. 'What an unexpected pleasure! Is something amiss in Tilby?'

He had long been in the habit of paying unannounced visits; indeed, he rarely found either opportunity or occasion for announcing his intentions beforehand. As such, this question surprised him. But she did not lack for perceptiveness; his manner, perhaps, or his expression had alerted her to the idea of trouble. 'Not entirely,' he said, with a return of her friendly courtesies. 'Do not be alarmed, for all is well with Isabel! But I must speak with you at once, and Aubranael.'

Sophy ushered him upstairs without a word of complaint or delay. They found Aubranael occupied at a small desk in an upper room. The tall, dark-skinned Aylir had married Sophy more than a year ago, and Grunewald had scarcely ever seen a more contented couple. Aubranael's perception did not lag behind his wife's; he, too, greeted Grunewald in the friendliest manner, but his dark eyes were sharp and alert as he looked at his friend. 'Green! What's afoot?'

Grunewald accepted the chair that Sophy directed him to, and sank gratefully into its soft, well-stuffed depths. He recounted the full tale of Tatterfoal and his *fetch*, sparing no detail – save that he saw no occasion for mentioning Bessie. His friends listened with quiet attention, and exchanged worried looks once he had finished.

'We have heard nothing of this,' said Aubranael. 'Word of your imposter has not yet travelled into Aylfenhame, I think.'

'Indeed,' said Grunewald grimly. 'That is part of my motive in coming, for I wished to warn you to be wary. If you should receive further visits from me, do take care to ensure that it *is* me. Until I can understand my imposter's reason for adopting my image, I cannot guess at his intentions, and I would not wish to imagine that he may successfully impose upon my friends.'

'We will take care,' Sophy promised.

Grunewald nodded. 'Besides that, I wished to entreat your assistance. There is *one* means by which such an illusion might be penetrated, and that is fairy ointment. With it, I will be able to see through any Glamour, no matter how skilful its composition. But I need not tell you how rare *that* has become.'

'No, indeed,' Sophy agreed. 'Do you attend the market?'

'That was my thought.'

She rose at once. 'Then we shall assist you in the search.' Aubranael was on his feet in an instant, and echoing his wife's offer.

Grunewald had known that he could count on them, but still a sense of gratitude swept through him. He had not, until recently, been blessed with the support of good, kind-hearted people, and he had forgotten how it felt. Indeed, he had despaired that he would ever know such felicity again. He shook both Sophy's and Aubranael's hands with fervent thanks, and attended them downstairs. Sophy recruited the rest of her household to his cause with a few brisk words, and soon a party of five set out into the streets of Grenlowe: Grunewald himself, Sophy and Aubranael, their friend and lodger Mary, and an unusually well-dressed brownie known as Thundigle.

The search occupied the rest of the day. By the time the sun began to set and the market closed, Grunewald felt sure that they had, between them, inspected every single stall at least twice. But no trace of fairy ointment had been discovered, nor any of the rarer ingredients he required for its manufacture. He was left with the disappointing feeling of having wasted not only his own time, but that of his friends as well.

His mood descended into a mixture of gloom, frustration and anger by the time he left Grenlowe. He would have to call the Goblin Market after all; no small undertaking, and fraught with some risk. No control whatsoever could be exerted over the wares offered in the Goblin Lands when the market took over the streets, and it attracted the attention of people even Grunewald would prefer to avoid.

But a market there must be.

As he left the darkening town of Grenlowe behind and sought passage into Gadrahst, his thoughts were sour. But at least he had taken the opportunity to warn Sophy and Aubranael, a measure which would protect *them* from harm and also, he hoped, limit the means by which his imposter might take advantage of Grunewald's visage.

And if there was to be a Market after all, he was gladder than ever that he had left Bessie safe behind at Somerdale, and out of the way either of harm or temptation.

\* \* \*

Bess rapidly discovered that *not pleasant* had been an understatement of near catastrophic proportions. She did not rightly know what it might feel like to be turned inside out, but the passage into Gadrahst gave her some inkling as to the probable sensations associated with such an experience. She suffered an excruciating minute, or perhaps ten, during which she felt that every part of her anatomy had been wrenched away, and afterwards hastily re-assembled in quite the wrong fashion. She could see nothing, but her ears were filled with a horrific jabber of voices pleasantly leavened with the sounds of high-pitched screams.

She collapsed, eventually, onto something that felt solid, but her head swam as though she were being spun about at speed. It took her some time to appreciate that the aroma assaulting her nostrils was the smell of her own discomfort, given tangible form by way of the contents of her stomach. Indeed, some of the screaming had probably been her own efforts also.

She lay still until her dizziness lessened, and then ventured to open her eyes.

The first thing she saw was Idriggal, standing not two feet from her. He looked wholly untouched by the passage; in fact he was dusting off his bright red waistcoat with an air of mild dissatisfaction.

'Tis not easy to clean mud out of velvet,' he informed her, when he noticed her scrutiny. 'I am only relieved that you contrived to keep your digestive antics to yourself.' He glanced askance, and added, 'Or nearly enough.'

'I can think of few worse happenin's than the ruin of your clothes, indeed,' agreed Bess. She raised herself shakily into a seated posture, and waited as her head swam anew. 'When you said *unpleasant*, 'twas no exaggeration.'

'Oh, not in the least. But may I say that you are bearing it well?' He grinned at her, flashing teeth.

'A deal of shriekin' and makin' a mess of meself weighs nothing wi' you, I suppose?'

'Very little,' he assured her. 'I have seen far worse.'

'Well, that's reassurin'.' Bess ventured to gain her feet, and shook out her dress. 'I'll need just a moment to remember how me legs work. Supposin' them still to be attached at all.'

Idriggal looked her over closely. 'You look unchanged.'

'That's somethin'.' Bess stretched, and shook herself. Her hair had tumbled down during the passage, and she felt the weight of it against her back. Not a respectable way to appear, at least in England. But she was far afield now.

'And so, we are in Gadrahst?' she enquired. Stable for the present, she found leisure to look about herself.

They had come out in some manner of village, or perhaps a town; Bess could not immediately determine its proportions. She stood on a patch of purplish grass behind a row of houses of eccentric style. In general, the buildings were much smaller than the houses of England; they were sized, she supposed, for goblins of Idriggal's stature. They were built with wooden frames, though she could see little of the timbers underneath the daub or plaster that covered them. They ranged in hue from muddy green to vivid purple, encompassing a range of earthy colours and some bright shades. Many small windows were fitted into the walls, and the doors were rounded in shape.

But not every building was diminutive. Interspersed amongst these at haphazard intervals were much taller structures, the size Bess would expect to see in a house. They sat oddly among their smaller brethren, creating an uneven appearance which Bess found charmingly eccentric. The area was quiet; she saw no one at all, save for her companion, and heard little.

Idriggal took a tiny, clear glass pipe from a pocket and put it to his lips. He made no effort to light it, or to activate it by any other means. Nonetheless, the pipe instantly changed colour to a fine raspberry hue, and began to spit bubbles of a similar shade from its bowl. Bess watched in some delight as a stream of them floated upwards into the cloudy sky. 'That we are,' he said around the pipe's delicate stem. 'Or in some small part of it. Gadrahst is on the large side, you understand. 'Tis known as the Goblin Lands elsewhere. We have come out in the town of Gorrotop, which happens to be where I live.' He took the pipe from his mouth and used it to point to one of the nearby houses. Bess had no trouble determining which he meant, for one stood out from the rest: it was diminutive in stature, like Idriggal himself, and painted the same bright red as his jerkin. 'Sadly,' he said with a wide smile, 'I cannot invite you in. But there's a wayhouse for folk of your size, not far away. I'll be installing you there.'

His pipe altered its hue, and began to produce watery-blue bubbles. Bess watched in some fascination. 'Thank you,' she said.

He bowed his head. 'I might just ask. What is it you are planning to do in our fair realm?'

Bess blinked. 'I don't rightly know,' she admitted. 'Gettin' here was the difficult part. Though, wi' that said, I would very much like to go to this Goblin Market I heard tell of.'

'It has yet to be called, but if that happens I undertake to escort you.'

'It will, I am fairly certain,' Bess assured him. 'Grunewald much desired it.'

'Aye, well. If the *Gaustin* wishes it, it'll come about.'

Bess tilted her head. 'What do you mean by that? The *Gaustin?*'

Idriggal raised one dark brow. 'Can you not guess?'

'If I could, would I be askin'?'

Idriggal puffed upon his peculiar pipe, his gaze thoughtful as he looked at her. 'Interesting. What do you know of Grunewald, if I may ask?'

'I met him as "Mr. Green", only two days gone. He were bowlin' about the lanes in his fancy wheeler wi' two black horses. Dancin' about in the middle of the night and in the worst fog I ever saw. I thought him naught but an ordinary fine gent, albeit wi' odd habits, but *then* he talked to Tatterfoal like the beast was an errant pony, and sent him packin'.' She shook her head. 'He ain't no typical gent, that I can see. But what he might rightly be, I dunnot know. Save that he is of Aylfenhame. It don't take much to see *that.*'

Idriggal nodded slowly. 'I've risked his displeasure enough, by bringing you into Gadrahst. I'll not risk it further by telling what he has chosen to conceal.'

Bess nodded. 'You're showin' sense there, Mr. Idriggal. I'd not like to cross Mr. Green neither.' She was uncertain what to make of Grunewald, in point of fact. He had shown her kindness and expressed concern for her safety, which was more than anybody had ever done for Bess before, in the whole course of her life. For that, she was grateful. He had wit and liveliness, which she appreciated. But he could also be dismissive and autocratic, and there was that in his eyes at times which hinted at worse capabilities hidden behind his urbane manner.

'You may call me Drig,' said her goblin friend. 'Seeing as we are to be such excellent friends.'

'Then you may call me Bess. I prefer it to "baggage", all told.'

Drig grinned. 'I can see that you might. Well, so. Are you right and proper again, and stable on those long pins?' He made a show of looking all the way up at Bess, rather exaggerating her height, for she was not so tall by the standards of England.

'That I am,' said Bess firmly. She took a few experimental steps, and when she did not promptly fall upon her face, she added, 'For certain. Lead on, Drig.'

Drig turned and sauntered away. He kept one hand upon the stem of his peculiar pipe — which was now producing sunny yellow bubbles — and tucked the other into a pocket of his jacket. Bess followed along as he wandered between two houses and entered a wide street laid down in dark cobblestones. She saw other goblins going about their business, none of them in any greater hurry than Drig seemed to be. They were predominantly of similar stature, though she saw an occasional rather taller goblin. They wore clothes in a surprising variety; the concept of particular, accepted fashions for attire did not seem to apply in Gorrotop.

Drig guided Bess down some few similar streets, and stopped at last outside of an unusually tall, narrow building in the midst of a long row. It towered three storeys higher than its nearest neighbours, though in width it could be barely more than fifteen feet. Its front was set with myriad windows, none of them matching in size, shape or colour, and it had multiple doors: one at ground level, through which Drig clearly proposed to take her, and others stranded at intervals all the way up the building. One of them, a round, wooden door painted crimson, had a staircase which wound its way around the outside of the building and ended outside the door. Others bore no apparent means of access at all.

Bess was instantly enchanted by it.

A large sign over the narrow ground-level door proclaimed simply: "The Motley." A fitting name, considering the patchwork appearance of the place. The grass-green door helpfully bore three brass knockers: one large one placed high up, though within Bess's reach; one a little further down; and one only a foot or so from the floor. Drig went up the pair of steps, took hold of this last and pounded mightily upon the door. The sound produced was not the dull thump Bess was expecting, but a burst of shrieking laughter.

The door opened immediately. Revealed in the entrance stood a goblin taller than Drig – almost Bess's own height. She was of comfortable proportions, with deep brown skin and a mass of greying hair. She wore an earthy-brown dress with a neat apron, a long coat of riotous patchwork, and a large hat of soft purple velvet. 'Aye!' she shouted. Her eye fell upon Drig and then upon Bess, and her generous mouth stretched into a beaming smile. 'Driggifer! Ye've brought me a customer! What a fine fellow ye are.' She bent down to bestow an appreciative salutation upon Drig, and then stepped back, opening the door wide. 'Whishawist, then. 'Tis a fine, cold morning and no doubt ye'll be wanting big fires and warm chocolate and all the what-not.'

'Morning, Maggin,' said Drig cheerfully. 'All the what-not and more, if you please!'

These prospects cheered Bess, and she lost no time in following Drig into the inn. The hall was as mad in character as the building's exterior, with mismatched furniture sized for goblins of all proportions. It was cheerily lit up with curious lamps in many hues, and strewn with rugs and cushions. Bess felt at home at once, and could not reproach herself for having accepted Drig's offer.

Drig tucked his bubble pipe into a pocket of his jerkin, and smiled up at Bess. 'The Motley's the best spot for miles, especially if you're one of the leggy folk.'

Bess could well believe it. Maggin led them to a staircase at the rear of the hallway and disappeared up it. Bess had some difficulty following, for it spiralled tightly and was not so roomy as she might wish; she was obliged to duck her head to keep from hitting it upon the next stairs up. She emerged two storeys farther up onto a small landing. Its ceiling was higher, to her relief, and she was able to stand fully upright. Its walls were painted dark green and crammed with pictures, embroidered cloths and other knick-knacks hanging from large brass hooks. Directly ahead of her, a glass door was set into the wall. At least, it *appeared* to be fine, clear glass, but Bess could see nothing through it.

Maggin produced a matching glass key and presented it to Bess with a flourish. 'I'll just need yer name, dear, fer the book.'

'Elisabeth Bell.' Bess took the key, and smiled her thanks.

Maggin beamed. 'What-nots to follow,' she promised, and disappeared back down the stairs.

Bess unlocked the strange glass door and went through into a narrow room with a very high ceiling. The walls were all wooden, but an enormous window set with greenish glass overlooked the street below. The room was furnished with a wooden bed, a pair of armchairs and a cupboard, together with a set of shelves. All were sized to suit Bess, a little to her relief, and everything was bright with the lively colours she had admired below.

'It will do,' Drig decided, having surveyed the room. He walked to the fireplace in the far wall and flicked his fingers at it, upon which gesture the neat bundle of firewood promptly burst into flame.

'Well, now!' said Bess, smiling broadly. 'If this ain't the nicest room I have ever had for me own!'

Drig seemed delighted with this praise. 'You need not concern yourself with the matter of payment, for it is taken care of.'

Bess was quick with her thanks, for that question had been troubling her. But Drig waved this away. ''Tis part of our agreement.'

'My thanks, nonetheless. But what am I to do here?'

Drig took out his pipe again, though he merely put it to his lips and stood there in thought; no bubbles flowed from its bowl. 'Mmp, well. His Maj—the *Gaustin* will be about someplace. By your account he will lose no time in calling the Market, so we'd best wait for that. And then, sooner or later, he will come here.'

'Oh? Why should he do that?'

'The Market crosses Gadrahst from border to border. Every town and village participates, and more besides – you'll find stalls set up in the middle of the woods. If the *Gaustin* is looking for something in particular, he will come through every one of the bigger towns, at least.'

'Won't he send retainers to do the searchin'?'

'Oh, yes. I intend to be one of them.' Drig smiled smugly. 'But he'll show. He was never one to leave underlings to do everything for him. Most involved, our *Gaustin*. And if he is in an urgent hurry, all the more so.' He put his pipe briefly to his lips, only to remove it again a moment later. 'And the Motley, you know, is a popular spot.'

Bess considered. 'How will we know if he's the right one? After all, there *is* a lookalike wanderin' about.'

Drig waved his pipe at her. 'He will recognise *you*, will he not? We could not expect an imposter to have the faintest idea of who you are.'

'Aye. True.'

Drig cackled. 'You are useful for all manner of things, Elisabeth.'

'Bess, please. Elisabeth's a right lengthy nonsense.'

Drig bowed acceptance. 'As you wish.'

Bess was left to amuse herself for the rest of the day, and she did so with alacrity. She spent happy hours exploring Gorrotop and meeting some of its residents. Most were as friendly as Drig and Maggin, with but one or two exceptions, and Bess enjoyed herself enormously. The town was lively, eccentric and powerfully interesting from end to end, and Bessie was well entertained. She wandered abroad until some hours past sundown, enjoying the plethora of merry lights that winked into being once darkness fell; the snatches of music, laughter and song she encountered as she wandered the streets; and the delicious, if strange, foods she purchased with the coin Drig had given her. She retired to bed at last in a state of high satisfaction, happier than she could ever remember being before.

She had planned to spend the following day furthering these explorations, but upon rising the next morning she found the Motley in a bustle of high excitement. She made her way down to the dining parlour at the back of the house, and found not only Maggin but Drig and a few other guests assembled around a veritable feast.

'Bess!' greeted Drig. 'You are in fine time.'

'Have a seat, lass, and eat yer fill,' invited Maggin. 'And ye'd best hear the news at once.'

Bess obeyed this invitation, though she had neither time nor need to reach for any food. The moment she sat down in the chair her hostess indicated, the plate before her filled itself, with naught but an odd shimmer in the air to indicate that anything unusual was happening. Generous portions of eggs, ham, fresh bread, brightly-coloured fruits and many other delicacies appeared, heaped so high upon the plate that Bess was taken aback.

'Help yerself to what ye like,' Maggin said with a wink, apparently noticing Bessie's confusion.

Bess quickly got over her surprise, and began to eat. 'What is the news?'

'The Market!' said Drig happily. 'You were perfectly right! It was called at dawn, and will soon be underway.'

'Oh!' said Bess. 'Mighty quick work indeed! But how was it called? I heard nothin'.'

Drig merely pointed at the window behind Bess. She turned, and saw what had escaped her notice before: every tree and lamp-post upon the street behind the Motley was decked in purple-and-green flags, streamers and ribbons. They fluttered in the wind, displaying glittering traces of gold in the mild sunlight.

'Them ribbons?' she enquired.

'Aye,' said Drig. 'They appear when the Market's called. Folk are preparing, even now.'

Bess felt a thrill of excitement. The bright banners held the promise of colour and liveliness beyond anything she had ever experienced before. What wonders might she discover at such a Market?

Her feelings were broadly shared, for there was a holiday atmosphere at the breakfast-table, and Bess's fellow guests soon departed on Market business. Bess's own anticipation was in such high degree that she scarcely noticed the food she ate. She emptied her plate absently, her mind fixed upon the vivid visions of her imagination, and was recalled to herself at last by Drig's voice encouraging her to rise from the table.

'Maggin would be grateful for your help, I believe,' Drig said, and Bess looked an enquiry at the innkeeper.

'Aye, that I would,' confirmed Maggin. Bess agreed readily enough, by no means unwilling to earn her keep by the only means she knew.

But her expectations proved to be misplaced, for Maggin did not set her to cleaning. Instead she led Bess outside, where a trio of stout goblins had just erected a wood-framed market stall directly outside the Motley. They were laying a crimson awning over the top as Maggin and Bess arrived, and Maggin clapped her appreciation.

'Very good, boys! That will be all! Bess and I will see to the rest.'

The goblins departed, tipping their hats to the ladies as they did so. Bess noticed that Maggin's was by no means the only stall going up in the vicinity; more were being constructed as far up and down the street as she could see.

'I hope ye've an eye fer this kind of thing,' said Maggin. 'Ye see the competition! We've a deal to do if my stall's to stand out.'

Bess understood, and fell to with alacrity. The morning passed rapidly by as she helped Maggin to assemble a staggering range of wares in an appealing array, and afterwards decorated the stall with streamers and ribbons in shades to match the awning. By the time they were finished, Maggin declared herself highly pleased.

Bess took stock of her handiwork, and smiled her own satisfaction. Maggin had a surprisingly large quantity of goods to display. Many were edible: Bess had set out towering stacks of raised pies with golden crusts, each lavishly decorated with jewel-coloured fruits, and sweetmeats of every conceivable kind were packed in delicate boxes or set out upon wide oaken dishes. Maggin had also arranged fragrant salves in glass pots, clear bottles filled with bubbling potions and an array of embroidered cloth knick-knacks. Everybody stockpiled goods for the Market, she explained. One didn't wish to be caught short, for the Market came but rarely, and without warning. It drew customers from all over Aylfenhame, and anyone suitably prepared might make enough gold to make for a fat and easy year to follow.

The salves caught Bess's eye as she had set them out, and her heart had leapt with a hope she later recognised as unreasonable. But her discreet enquiries confirmed that none of the dainty glass pots contained anything so rare as fairy ointment; they were but treatments for work-roughened hands, or goods more along the cosmetic lines. Maggin demonstrated the use of one set upon Bess herself, by smearing some of the scented violet salve upon Bess's thumbnail. Bess watched in amazement as the nail seemingly absorbed the colour and turned a pretty violet hue.

'It will last nigh on a month, that,' said Maggin proudly. 'Ye'll find others sellin' the like, but none so long-lasting.'

As a sample of the Market's probable delights, Bess considered it highly promising.

It took the residents of Gorrotop (and, presumably, beyond) most of the day to set up their stalls to their satisfaction. By late afternoon, the Market was well underway. As the sun began to sink, lanterns lit up in a range of colours, adding more liveliness and delight to the scene than Bess could have imagined.

Drig took her out into the streets directly, leaving Maggin happily installed beneath her eye-catching crimson awning. The innkeeper was already doing a brisk trade, Bess noted as she waved farewell, and she looked delighted.

'How long does the Market stay?' Bess enquired as she followed

Drig through the chattering crowds of shoppers.

'As long as it's wanted. When everything is sold, away goes the Market.' Drig had lit up his pipe once more, and Bess was able to follow the streams of coloured bubbles as much as the slight figure of Drig himself. He had swapped his regular hat for another, which he called his Party Hat. It was even more fantastically oversized than the last, very broad at the top and broader still at the brim, and covered over in sumptuous purple velvet. To Bess's puzzlement it contained a little door set into the base, and three windows spaced above. Bess had thought them merely decorative until, to her immense surprise, the door had opened and a tiny vole-like creature with cloverleaf-green fur and a long striped tail had crept out. This little animal now rode upon the brim of Drig's hat, its nose lifted and quivering as it inhaled the delicious aromas of the Market.

She and Drig had agreed upon their shared intent: they would scour the stalls of Gorrotop and, should there be fairy ointment somewhere available, be sure to snatch it up at once. But Bess soon felt in danger of forgetting this mission entirely, so enchanted was she with the Market. She marvelled anew at her position. Had it truly been only a few days since she had been a lowly housemaid? At this moment, perhaps, she would be preparing somebody's bed for their night's rest, or taking a plain meal with the other servants in the kitchens. Instead she was deep in Aylfenhame, free to experience the delights of the Goblin Market, and her future was hers to decide.

She wandered Gorrotop in a state of high enjoyment, frustrating Drig with her eagerness to pause at every stall and examine virtually everything that she saw. A stall selling flowers caught her attention particularly, for though they were clearly living blossoms, their petals looked like fine velvet or glass. More enchantingly still, each one emitted soft motes of light from their centres; the sparks of colour drifted lazily into the air, twinkling like tiny stars. Bess stared so long at these that Drig grew resigned, and offered to buy one for her if it would encourage her to move along.

'Why, no!' said Bess, laughing. 'What would the likes of me do wi' such a pretty thing? I'd have nowhere to put it.'

Drig shrugged. 'As you please, but do let us continue. At this rate, it will take us a week to search Gorrotop alone.'

Chastened, Bess could not but admit the justice of his argument. Their progress after that was faster, and Bess became more adept at resisting the allure of sweetmeats and sable-winged songbirds; gowns which looked wrought from cobwebs and starlight; shadowy cloaks with deep hoods, radiating a warmth Bess could feel from the street; pies offering a change of flavour with every mouthful; flourishing miniature gardens contained in glass bell jars; toys of cloth and wood which danced and told jokes; and so many more delights that her head spun with the wonder of it.

It did not seem conceivable that fairy ointment could be absent among such an array, but so it proved. Bess and Drig examined every stall selling salves, ointments or potions of any kind, and made enquiry after enquiry, but to no avail. The Market ran throughout the night, and their errand kept them busily employed until such a late hour that Bess became too weary even to appreciate a stall of hats even more fantastical than Drig's. And still they failed to discover any trace of fairy ointment.

'Ah well,' said Drig heavily, as they made their way with weary steps back to the Motley. ''Twas too much to hope, I dare say, that it would be so easily found. Otherwise why would his Ma—the *Gaustin* have to call a Market?'

'But the Market goes far beyond Gorrotop, no?' said Bess, trying to ignore the pain in her feet; she had earned herself at least three new blisters this night.

'Oh, 'tis across the whole of Gadrahst by now. Tomorrow we will get as far as Hogwend, and see what we can find.'

Bess thought of Grunewald. Was he out somewhere under the bright moon, striding the Market as she was in search of the ointment he needed? Had he yet discovered any? Before the Market had begun, she had not doubted that she would encounter him eventually, if she was out in the streets every day. Now that she had witnessed the crush of shoppers for herself, and heard Drig's account of the flabbergasting extent of the Market, she was not so sure. How would they contrive to discover Grunewald's whereabouts at all? And if they did not, how could they know when he had completed his errand?

'Why is the ointment so rare?' she asked instead, struck with an alternate thought.

''Tis twofold, that,' said Drig. 'The ingredients are most difficult to find, or some of them are. It's the mushrooms. Finicky things.' He paused as the clover-furred creature atop his hat slid over the brim and almost fell off; Drig caught it with a practiced gesture and settled the tiny animal back atop its perch. The creature squeaked in a fashion Bess interpreted as derisive, whisked back inside the hat and shut the door behind itself. 'The snowfoots only grow in winter, if it snows enough, and the velvet queen parasols — well, they grow wherever the Queen-at-Mirramay has lately trod. And seeing as there's no Queen-at-Mirramay anymore, those are getting mighty scarce. And then it is no easy task to combine them in the right way. There's few as can manage it.'

Bess thought back to Grunewald's request of Isabel, and her failed attempt at the task. If Drig was correct, the ingredients she had been offered had been incomplete after all; Grunewald had given her snowfoot boletes, but Tafferty had been correct to point out that the parasols were also required.

'What became of the Queen?'

But Drig would not vouchsafe much of an answer to that question. 'Died,' was all he said, and curtly. He would not be drawn to elaborate, and soon fell silent altogether.

Bessie let him be. She was weary, and growing eager to be returned to her comfortable room at the Motley for some slumber. The swarming crowds around her blurred into an indistinguishable mass of people and colour, and the noise of the market filled her ears in a roar. She blinked, trying to focus her tired mind; she could not merely drift after Drig, and rely on him to deliver her safely home.

It gradually dawned upon her that the noise had grown distant, and she was no longer surrounded by shoppers. In fact, all about her was darkness, and there was no sign of Drig. Heart thumping, she spun about, thrust into abrupt alertness in her consciousness of sudden peril. She could see nothing, save a haunting wisp-light drifting somewhere above.

'A fine piece of merchandise,' said a low voice from close by.

Something about the tone invoked a sudden, piercing fear in Bessie, and she shivered. 'Who is there?' she said sharply, irritation building along with the fear.

Nobody replied. Bessie waited, in silence as well as darkness, her heart pounding so fiercely she could hear the blood rushing in her ears. She could not shake the creeping sensation that the *merchandise* spoken of was herself...

She roused herself from her stupor of fright with a strong effort of will, and began to walk. The wisp shed no useful light, and she blundered about in near darkness. She found a wall only by dint of walking into it, and quickly changed direction. Another wall, and another. She was enclosed in some tiny space, like a cupboard, but no door could she find.

When the floor disappeared beneath her, she fell with a shriek.

Bess landed heavily upon something painfully solid, and for a moment she lay dazed and blinking in sudden, bright light. 'Take the hair,' somebody ordered. Myriad tiny hands grabbed at her loose locks and pulled, hard. Bessie shrieked again, this time with anger, and shot to her feet.

She was surrounded by goblins, most of them smaller even than Drig. She had fetched up inside some kind of caravan covered over with lengths of torn and tattered fabric. To her horror, the walls were hung with neatly-coiled ropes of hair.

'Yer *not* havin' me hair!' she shouted, grabbing the length of her tumbling black locks and gripping it tightly. She had few vanities, but her hair was one of them. These little nasties wouldn't get so much as a single lock of it!

She cast a quick look around the caravan, and saw absolutely nothing that she could use as a weapon. Very well; it would have to be flight, then. There was a door, but it was sized for the convenience of the goblins, and Bessie suffered some doubts as to whether she could fit through it.

No way to find out but to try. She laid about with her fists and her feet, knocking away the creatures who attempted to swarm up her skirts, and ran for the door.

She fumbled with the catch. To her irritation, her hands were shaking too much to easily unlatch it, and she was set upon from behind by at least three of the wretched goblins. Hands grabbed at her hair again, and a swift, sharp pain told her that they had succeeded in parting her from some of her hair.

Fury rose in a choking surge, and she abandoned her attempts to open the door by civilised means. She began to kick it instead, and though she sorely hurt her feet, she finally succeeded in breaking the latch.

But the door blew violently open before she had chance to capitalise upon her success. On the other side stood Drig. He had lost all semblance of charming friendliness; his face was dark with malevolent rage, and he positively crackled with a fierce and disturbing energy.

The goblins clinging to Bess's dress fell away at once, babbling something incomprehensible. Drig spoke a single word by way of reply, a revolting syllable evocative of dark places and vile, crawling things, and a chorus of pained shrieks went up behind her.

Drig grabbed Bessie's hand and pulled. Either she shrank for a moment or the door enlarged; she could not tell which, only that she slipped through it easily and found herself restored to the bustling crowds of Gorrotop's market.

She turned, but saw only throngs of shoppers; of the caravan there was no sign.

Drig looked her over in silence, the malevolent look gradually fading from his face.

'Unscathed, I think,' he finally said.

Bessie dusted off her gown, taking a moment to collect herself. She was badly shaken by the experience, though she would never admit to it. Grunewald's attitude might have been cavalier and dictatorial, but he had not been wrong to question her safety.

'All well wi' me,' she said to Drig, once she had properly composed herself.

He flashed her a swift, fierce grin, and she knew that he saw everything she wanted to conceal. But he merely bowed with a tip of his hat, and sauntered off. 'Homeward we go,' he called over his shoulder.

Bessie gladly followed in his wake.

Bessie woke upon the morrow feeling largely refreshed, though she remained a little unnerved. The hair vendors had been disturbing, but she had little doubt that there was worse to be found at the market. It was galling to have to acknowledge, even to herself, that she needed Drig's protection.

When breakfast was over, Drig led Bess out of the rear door of the Motley. Stationed outside was a neat open carriage with space for two passengers. Its seats were upholstered in green velvet and its frame was painted a rich maroon; this looked far too fine to Bess's eye, but Drig clambered aboard with scarcely a glance at the velvet, and stuck his booted feet up on the seat with blithe unconcern.

The carriage was drawn by a pair of ponies, or something like.

They resembled Tatterfoal more than a little, which intrigued Bess more than it alarmed her, for they seemed docile enough. They were barely of a size to carry Bess, had she chosen to ride one; their coats were thundercloud-grey darkening to black, and their manes and tails were bright white. As Bess took her seat in the carriage, one of them tossed its head. At once, a flurry of incorporeal, bone-white moths erupted into the air and flew frantically away. Its mate snorted impatiently and pawed the ground, and a jet of stormy cloud-wisp streamed from its nostrils.

Drig had taken a seat with his back to the horses, but Bess was not left to wonder long how the carriage was to be guided without a driver. As soon as she was settled, Drig called out, 'Hogwend, dear ponies,' and the horses stepped instantly into motion. Bess had nothing to do but sit at her ease while the neat vehicle wound its way slowly through the streets of Gorrotop — for though the sun had not yet fully risen, the roads were crowded with carriages and shoppers afoot — and at last cleared the town. The horses picked up their pace as soon as they reached the open countryside, and Bess made the most of her opportunity to see a little more of Gadrahst.

The environs did not appear especially prepossessing, she was forced to admit. In the thin, dawning light, she could not see much. The weather was not disposed to show her the best of the Goblin Lands, for the sky was heavily overcast and the air filled with a sodden mist. On either side of the road, Bess saw fields, bare and dark at this season. The one feature of the landscape which pleased her eager eye was the row of trees lining one side of the wide dirt road they were travelling upon. The trees were as varied as the buildings in Gorrotop, and no two were alike. Some were but a few feet tall, others of a towering height. Though some had shed most of their foliage in the manner of the trees of England, others bore a full crop of leaves, and in rather more colours than the shades of green, russet and yellow Bess would expect to see in the autumn.

She amused herself in examining each tree as closely as she could, for Drig did not seem inclined to talk. He sat sprawled with the party hat over his eyes, sucking idly upon the stem of his bubble pipe. In this fashion the journey to Hogwend passed, and fairly quickly. Bess saw the town on the horizon, a huddle of buildings adding colour and life to the grey sky. It, too, was decked in the glittering streamers which adorned Gorrotop, and Bess's heart lifted at the sight.

Drig spoke. 'I have a notion we may be seeing the *Gaustin* sometime this morning.'

'How could you possibly know that?'

Drig's mouth stretched into a lazy grin. 'Goblins have ways.'

'I enjoy nothin' so much as your mysterious pronouncements, I assure you. It adds such a delightful zest to the mornin'.'

Drig snickered. 'Well, I might have been summoned.' He tapped one of the jewels that decorated his long ears: a dull grey disc inset with a large purple gem.

'Aye?' she said. 'Somethin' happens to the jewellery when his Maje—the *Gaustin* wants you?'

Drig lifted the brim of his hat to look at her, his darkling eyes glinting with amusement. 'Too quick on the uptake, my dear Bess. Yes, indeed. The gem glows.'

Bess nodded wisely. 'A glow! Mighty useful. Especially when you are the one wearin' it, and it happens to be positioned quite out of your sight.' His ears were long enough that she doubted he could see the gem at all.

Drig blew a stream of blood-coloured bubbles at her. 'It grows warm, too, if I am slow to answer.'

It occurred to Bess that the flesh around the jewel appeared disordered. She leaned closer to improve her view, and noted signs of blistering. 'Warm, eh?'

Drig shrugged. 'I was asleep at the time.'

Clearly the *Gaustin* was in a hurry. Bess was unsure what to make of this mark of Grunewald's impatience. 'We had best get you some salve,' she said firmly.

Drig laughed at that, and thrust a hand into a deep pocket fixed to the front of his trousers. He withdrew a large ointment-pot, took off the lid and applied some of the pale green contents to his ear. 'As you see, I am well supplied.'

From this, Bess concluded that the damage to Drig's ear was by no means unusual. But the carriage drew up and stopped, preventing her from pursuing the topic, and Drig jumped down with a lively energy at odds with the lethargy he had hitherto displayed. 'He'll be somewhere about,' he announced. 'I can feel it. Not close yet, but soon.'

'That's a function of your ear-ring, too?' said Bess as she descended to the street.

Drig nodded once. 'And now, to shop!' he said grandly. 'For fairy ointment, and mushrooms! The *Gaustin* will have emptied his supply of the boletes by now, and will also require the parasols.'

Some of Bess's zeal for shopping had worn off over the course of the previous day, but she fell to her task with largely unimpaired enthusiasm. Hogwend resembled Gorrotop in most particulars, and certainly in the eagerness with which its citizens participated in the Market. After some two hours' searching, Bess's thoroughness was rewarded when she spotted a scant handful of the snow-white mushrooms Drig had described, almost buried in the midst of a pile of velvet gloves. They bore the scattering of silver motes which marked them as snowfoot boletes, and Bess was quick in securing them. She tucked them into a pocket of her skirt, handling them with great care, for they were delicate.

She had just completed this transaction when she heard a low, cultured voice speak from directly behind her. 'I would know that shabby excuse for a cloak anywhere, and the hair—! The locks of some wild creature, I make no doubt! Come, baggage, turn about.'

Bess turned to find Grunewald standing barely two feet away, his pose nonchalant and his hands buried in his pockets. He was dressed differently from the last time she had seen him: he wore long dark trousers and tall top-boots, his creamy cravat stark against a black shirt. His wine-red velvet coat was of no fashion she had ever seen in England, though it was sumptuous indeed, its hem sweeping the floor. A row of buttons adorned the front, though they insisted upon changing their configuration every few moments; Bess saw gilded buttons shaped to resemble roses, and then half of them adopted the appearance of coiled snakes painted in stripes. They were purple moths, and then white gems; the neat, smoky-hued caps of mushrooms, and then fiery stars. This fascinating changeability threatened to mesmerise Bess; she blinked, and forced herself to look into Grunewald's face instead.

He stood staring down at her with an amused smile, though she thought she detected signs of annoyance as well. 'Good mornin', your Maj—I mean, *Gaustin*,' she said, and bobbed a curtsey. 'Mr. Drig said nothin' about me?'

'Mr. Drig appears to have said very little to the purpose,' he said coolly. His eyes narrowed. 'At least to *me*. But he appears to be keeping you remarkably well informed.'

'Not at all!' said Bess brightly. 'Nothin' could be more mysterious. I beg you will not trouble yerself with the idea that he might be tellin' me anythin' useful. Besides, there was nothin' much to be said. An infant could ha' put the pieces together.'

'You underrate yourself, baggage,' said Grunewald – or the King of the Goblins, as she was now certain was his true title. 'Most people are frighteningly self-absorbed.'

'How cynical.'

'No doubt. I am entitled to a little cynicism, however. Do you have any notion at all what manner of life it is? See these energetic shoppers, now.' He nodded at the streams of people passing them by upon either side. 'This guise is well enough known, and if any of them were paying the smallest attention they would know that their liege-lord walks amongst them. But see how they pass me by!'

Even this speech failed to attract the attention of any among the crowds. Bess watched as several goblins, a pair of brownies, an Aylir and other creatures she could not name swept past without pausing. 'You are disappointed to be denied your fair share of worship!' she said, struck with a keen sense of the tragedy of his plight. 'I can understand it! It must be terrible to stand for three minutes together without bein' so much as bowed to. Here, I will do my little part.' She offered him a low curtsey, her head lowered with becoming humility.

Grunewald tangled a hand in her hair as she rose and pulled back her head, gently but firmly. He scrutinised her face, his expression unreadable. 'You are impertinent. *And* disobedient.'

'No, no,' Bess demurred. 'Well, perhaps a mite. Shall it be another curtsey, to make up for it?' She could not have said what moved her to speak so to him; only that if king he was, he contrived to be the strangest monarch she had ever heard of. There was naught of majesty about him, naught of grandeur, and nothing of superiority either. Irritable he might sometimes be, but he spoke to her as an equal, and had done so since the moment he had taken her up in his carriage.

'Heavens preserve us! No,' he said, releasing her hair. 'I have scarce seen such a graceless curtsey in the whole course of my life.'

''Tis these cursed garments. 'Tis hard to be a lady in grace, when I am weighed about wi' such rags! Your Gentship has the right of it.'

'Put you in silks and jewels and you would still be an infernal baggage. Indeed, it has been soundly proved already. What made you decide to discount all my warnings?'

Bess inclined her head. ''Tis an honour to be thought so. And, as you see, I am still all in one piece.'

Grunewald's head tilted. 'I think you are displeased with me.'

That surprised Bess. He gave off an appearance of lazy inattention, not unlike Drig's; she had not thought he could discern so much of the feelings she had not consciously displayed. 'A little,' she admitted.

'It is because I would not bring you with me? You appear to have contrived marvellously in spite of my churlishness.'

''Tis not that. I would have asked Mrs. Aylfendeane, if Drig had not found me. One way or another I was comin' here.'

'Then what is it?'

'You've hurt Drig's ear. More'n once.'

Grunewald's eyes narrowed once more. 'He has complained of it, has he?'

'Not in the least! Nothin' could exceed his nonchalance in walkin' about wi' a blistered ear. He is quite used to it. I am to imagine he's left in such a state tolerably often.'

Grunewald's eyebrows rose. 'If Idriggal does not feel himself to be ill-used, why should it trouble you?'

'Drig's feelin's change nothin' about right and wrong,' said Bess firmly. 'Speakin' as one who is used to a fair amount of ill treatment meself, I cannot help standin' up for your retainers.'

Grunewald folded his arms and stared at her, his eyes hard. Bess could not but admit that the effect was intimidating, but she refused to be cowed. She folded her own arms and drew herself up, giving him stare for stare until he finally spoke.

'If you mean to class me with the likes of *that* family…!'

By *that family*, she supposed he meant the Adairs. 'Not so much,' she said, obliged to be fair. 'But I ain't lookin' forward to the day when I find out that you are of a type wi' them after all.'

She allowed that to sink in, watching his face closely. His expression did not change. She judged she had pushed her luck as far as was reasonable, and sought another subject. Delving into her skirt pocket, she produced the bundle of mushrooms and held them out to him.

His eyes lit up. 'You have found it?'

'Not the ointment,' she cautioned. 'Just a few mushrooms.'

He unwrapped the bundle enough to observe the frail, dried boletes that lay within, and nodded. 'Thank you, baggage. That is of some little use to me.'

'We'd best get on, if we have the whole of Gadrahst to search.'

One of his brows went up at that. 'We?'

'Aye. Seein' as I am not urgently occupied at the moment, I can offer you my services as shoppin' assistant.'

His mouth twitched, but he did not smile. 'We do not, in fact, have to search every corner of Gadrahst. That has been done.'

She blinked. 'Already?'

'Do you imagine I have naught but Drig to assist me?'

Bess imagined no such thing; the Goblin King must have retainers without number. 'Well then, I will be on my way,' she said cheerfully. 'It was nice seein' you, my Gent.' She curtseyed.

Grunewald's hand shot out and grabbed her wrist. 'Not just yet, baggage. You'll come with me a while.'

'You do have work for me! And no wonder. Retainers I am sure you have aplenty, but none of them are quite like me after all.'

His eyes glinted with amusement. 'I am increasingly persuaded that there is no creature alive quite like you. Come.'

Bess allowed herself to be led. She resented the grip Grunewald retained on her wrist, for a little while, but the crush of the crowds was such that she soon adjusted her ideas. If he had not maintained a link with her, she would in all likelihood have been swept away in the rush of market-goers.

Drig joined them, looking cross. His face registered a flicker of alarm upon seeing Grunewald with Bess, but he quickly hid it. He offered no word of greeting to his master; instead he held up his bubble pipe in his hands, in two pieces. 'Smashed,' he grumbled as he fell into step beside them. 'Some great, lumbering oaf of an ogre. Impossible to avoid! So trying!'

Grunewald let go of Bess long enough to snatch the pieces from Drig's hands. She could not see what it was that he did to the chunks of glass, but moments later he was able to restore the pipe to his retainer, whole once more. If he was angry with Drig for conveying Bessie into Gadrahst, he said naught of it.

All of this apparently surprised Drig as much as it astonished Bess, for he gaped at his healed pipe in amazement before he remembered to thank his liege lord. Grunewald's hand immediately closed around Bess's wrist once more, and she was obliged to trot to keep up as he strode faster through the crush, people melting out of his path. His posture was rigid, and he made no reply to Drig's gratitude. It was as though he was annoyed by the kindness of his own gesture, and wished to have it forgotten as speedily as possible.

'Here we are,' he said some little time later, and halted before a particularly large stall selling, as far as Bess could tell, nothing but jars. Great, weighty things they were, wide at the base and securely stoppered with wedges of dull grey metal. But as she looked, something shifted in the nearest jar, and she discerned coils of roiling mist contained within the clear glass. A moment's scrutiny revealed that every jar contained a similar complement of vapour. It was *fog*, she swiftly realised, for she had seen more than enough of late to recognise it. Some of the jars contained the thick, white fog with which she was familiar; others housed mists in shades of rain, storm and wind, and even in rainbow.

All of this was fascinating, but Bess could imagine no reason whatsoever why Grunewald would desire to bring her here.

But he had not. He had stopped not in front of the fog vendor, but a little to the left. In between the jars of fog and another stall selling, according to the impressions of Bessie's nose, scents, there was another stall. It was tiny, barely four feet in width; wedged as it was in between two such large, dominating shop fronts, Bessie had missed it altogether. It was covered over with an awning of patchwork leather in shades of fenberry and moss, which looked handsome indeed, but it did not appear to house any goods. Bess looked an enquiry at Grunewald.

He ignored her, instead addressing the stallholder. 'Attend to the lady,' was all that he said.

The stall was minded by a goblin rather taller than Drig, his skin almost black in hue. He had a shock of night-dark hair and large eyes the colour of amber stones. His garments were made from the same patchwork leathers as his awning, and over his tunic and leggings he wore a sturdy apron. He bowed to Grunewald, suggesting that he at least recognised the red-haired gentleman as his monarch. But his manner lacked the deference Bess might expect; he flashed Grunewald a cheery smile and said, 'Right ye are, Lordship,' and turned to Bess.

Goblin society was odd indeed, she thought. Their king acted nothing like a ruler, and his subjects barely remembered to show him even common deference. But in spite of that, Drig's loyalty to Grunewald was above question, no matter how many times his ears sprouted blisters in response to his lord's importunate summons. It was a curious puzzle.

As was Grunewald's intentions in bringing Bess to this stall. 'You must forgive me,' she said to the stallholder. 'My powers of readin' minds have unaccountably failed this mornin', and I have no notion what my Gent is fixin' to achieve wi' this.'

She received a grin in response, and the goblin pointed at Bess's feet. 'Off wi' those,' he said.

Bess supposed that he meant her shoes. They were gone in a trice; so worn and stretched were they that they slipped off easily. The goblin wrinkled his nose in distaste as he looked at the tattered old shoes, even their colour now indeterminate. He made a faint gesture with one hand, and the shoes promptly disappeared.

'How's that?' he said then.

Bess blinked. She could hardly suppose that Grunewald had intended to vanish her shoes and leave her in stocking feet; but as she opened her mouth to express her confusion, it occurred to her that this was not, in fact, the case. She looked down.

Her feet were clad in boots so fine she was struck speechless. Wrought from cherry-red leather, they were strong and sturdy in make and yet an experimental flex of her feet proved them to be soft and comfortable as well. The toes were a little pointed, and she felt small heels underneath. They rose over her ankles and laced with mossy green ribbon, each one bearing a bunch of hawthorn berries at its end – apparently real, though surely they were not.

On top of all of this, the boots were *warm*. A chill morning in early November, and she was not obliged to bear the discomfort of cold feet! And she could no longer feel her blisters; had they healed?

Bess could not speak.

Grunewald observed her reaction, and nodded once at the stall-keeper. 'Thank you, Hastival.'

The goblin tugged his forelock to Grunewald, and winked at Bess. Then he turned to another customer, and Grunewald walked away. He did not trouble to collect Bess beforehand, and she was left standing in shock.

Drig grinned at her. 'Oh, you have impressed my Gent, right

enough.'

Shaking herself, Bess hastened to catch up with Grunewald. 'I don't understand,' she called after him.

Grunewald glanced sidelong at her as she drew alongside. 'I am desolate at having confused you.'

'What was that about?'

'Your attire is a disgrace. I am ashamed to be seen with you.'

This reply was flippant, and Bess was persuaded it was nothing to the purpose at all. But Grunewald said nothing more.

'Hastival is the best shoe-maker in Gadrahst,' said Drig, trotting beside her. 'He fits the shoe to the customer.'

'Don't every shoemaker do that?'

'Not like Hastival. Those are *your shoes*. They are perfect for you in every way. They'll do everything you need, whatever the occasion. You will probably never need to buy another pair.'

'Ever again?'

'Never, and not ever. You'll see what I mean.' He waved his pipe at the crowds, sending a stream of cheerful green bubbles flying, and added, 'Any one of these people would give their first-born child for a pair of Hastival's boots. And you are wearing the very best that he can make.'

Bess tried to thank Grunewald, but he ignored her attempts and strode on oblivious. In truth, she hardly knew how to express her thoughts, for she felt that the gift held significance beyond the merely practical. *I would stop walking around in someone else's shoes,* he had said not long before. Now she had her own, and there could be no doubt that they would take her wherever she wanted to go.

Well, and well. If he would not listen to her thanks, she would find some other way to express her gratitude. There must be some fashion in which she could be of use to him; at the very least, she could bend all of her efforts towards finding the fairy ointment he sought, or discovering some other means of identifying the imposter whose actions disturbed his peace.

# CHAPTER SIX

*Oh, Hastival is sought-after! Right enough! Carelessly bestowed them boots might ha' been, but fer a lass like Bessie, they meant the world. I don't even think Grunewald hisself knew what he 'ad done fer her — a lass as was overlooked an' abused by all the world before.*

*Well, tha' Grunewald is an odd fellow. I think even he cannot rightly decide whether he's more kindness or cruelty. Anyroad, he 'ad a problem on 'is 'ands. That Tatterfoal was roamin' the Wolds every night while the Markets were on in Gadrahst, and the infernal nag was gettin' bolder. It got to be that travellers were loath to set foot abroad at night, and who could blame 'em? One glimpse o' Tatterfoal is enough to stop the heart, wi' folk o' the timid persuasion.*

*Not tha' the person ridin' the beast 'ad yet shown hisself overmuch. Grunewald 'ad caught a glimpse o' the fellow, an' Lyrriant o' course, but naught much else 'ad been seen o' him besides. What, then, was he doin' tearin' about wi' Tatterfoal? I sent out all o' my best to keep an eye on 'im, wi' some hopes they'd learn a mite or two about his intentions.*

Grunewald gave up on the Goblin Market. If it had failed to furnish him with fairy ointment in its first day, it had failed entirely, for he held out no hope at all that such a thing might happen to surface later. He left his servants scouring the stalls in his stead, in case he was mistaken, but he did not consider it necessary to supervise them himself.

'There is but one person left to entreat,' he said to Drig on the afternoon of the second day. He had returned with them to the

Motley, and he, Drig and Bessie now sat before a lively fire in Maggin's parlour. She had secured the room for their privacy on Grunewald's account, ushering out the sparse few of her guests who had chosen to remain there at such an hour; the majority were still out enjoying the Market.

Bessie sat at her ease with a cup of chocolate in her hands. The fire was warm, her chair was comfortable, and she had not yet ceased to revel in the glory of her new boots. She sat listening drowsily, flexing her toes from time to time with a frisson of hidden glee.

Grunewald did not elaborate upon his statement; apparently it was not necessary, for Drig nodded thoughtfully and said, 'She will not lightly help you.'

'She is compelled to assist me,' said his master coolly. 'She is gravely in my debt, and she knows it.' Grunewald had thrown off his coat and sat in his waistcoat and shirt-sleeves, his cravat loosened. He, too, cradled a cup of chocolate, though his delight in it clearly did not equal Bess's. As a high lord in these parts, she supposed he had long since grown used to such luxuries and they could hold little wonder for him now.

Bess listened carefully, intrigued to learn more of the reluctant woman they discussed. Was she a witch, like Mrs. Aylfendeane? Why would she dislike being of use to Grunewald, and what had happened to place her in his debt?

But little more of her was said. Silence fell for a short space, and then Drig asked: 'She is not still in Mirramay, is she?'

Grunewald grunted, an inarticulate sound which Bessie interpreted as a negative.

'So we are to Aviel?'

Grunewald sighed deeply – and then his eyes flicked to Bess. He had, perhaps, forgotten her presence, so quiet had she been. He spoke again, but this time in a tongue she could not understand. It was a lisping, faintly guttural language, and Bess found it interesting to listen to, in spite of its utter incomprehensibility. Drig responded in the same tongue, and their conversation proceeded for some minutes.

Then, as one, they fell silent and both looked at her.

Bess's eyelids had been drooping shut, lulled as she was by the warmth, comfort and peace of the parlour. But she opened them wide upon noticing this joint scrutiny, and waited. Clearly they had been speaking of her; what had they discussed?

'There is some debate, dear baggage, as to what to do with you,' said Grunewald. 'Drig is in favour of bringing you along.' One side of his mouth curved into an amused, half-sardonic smile; he was well aware, Bess guessed, that Drig had some ulterior motive in mind for wishing to keep her close.

'But you are not?' she said in reply.

'I am in favour of depositing you back into the ditch I hauled you out of. Or one similar, for I do not think I could find precisely the same one with any accuracy.'

Bess nodded sleepily, and took another mouthful of chocolate.

'You accept this probable fate with equanimity.'

Bess smiled upon him. 'You ain't really contemplatin' it.'

Grunewald's eyes opened wide. 'No? Why do you say that?'

'I dunnot think your heart is cold enough, for all that you pretend.'

Drig chuckled at that, but Grunewald sighed in annoyance. 'I tell you one thing for certain: if you dare to use the word "ain't" in my hearing one more time, straight into a ditch you shall go!'

'That's fair,' Bessie agreed.

Grunewald muttered something inaudible, and drank the rest of his chocolate off in one gulp.

'I hate to seem overly curious,' Bess said, 'but whereabouts was it you was absolutely not thinkin' of cartin' me off to?'

Drig glanced sideways at Grunewald, who made a carelessly dismissive gesture accompanied by a roll of his eyes.

'We are to Aviel,' said Drig. 'The King's Court, that is. There is one there who may yet be able to craft the ointment.'

'How fascinatin',' said Bess politely. 'And just what is it you'd wish me to do there?'

That stymied Drig a little, for he could hardly own out loud that he had yet to request his favour of Bess. 'The lady is of a stubborn nature,' he said after a moment. 'You may be of use in persuading her!'

'And I am noted for my powers o' persuasion, to be sure. They have always operated powerfully upon his Gentship here, for one.'

'Do you mean to say that you do not wish to attend us?' said Grunewald, a little sharply.

Eagerness had availed Bessie little before; she suspected

Grunewald of harbouring a contrary streak. Instead, she made a show of scepticism. 'What would the likes of me want wi' the King's Court? You said it yerself: I am a disgrace in these rags. 'Ceptin' the booties.' She stretched out one leg to admire her beautiful cherry-red boot yet again, smiling complacently.

Grunewald grunted.

'Besides, I am not sure as I have the time,' she continued. 'I need to be settin' about buildin' a life for meself somewhere in these parts. Won't happen by itself. I'll need to seek work.'

Grunewald glowered, his teeth set. 'Dreadful girl!' he complained. 'Drig, she could out-manoeuvre you any day.'

Drig grinned at Bessie. 'Do I not know it?'

Bess watched as Grunewald struggled with himself. She could not imagine why, but she sensed that he could by no means cast her off so easily as he claimed — or what was he doing sitting at his ease in the parlour with her, when he could have departed for Aviel more than an hour since?

'I do not require assistance with Hidenory!' Grunewald growled. 'She cannot refuse her aid.'

'But it is so much nicer when people help of their own volition, is it not?' said Drig coaxingly. 'A willing Hidenory is always so much better than a resentful one. She might make you fairy ointment, but she'd poison it before she gave it to you.'

'Hidenory will despise the baggage,' Grunewald predicted. 'This bundle of rags is the last person that lady would ever listen to.'

'Well and well. Bess is looking for work, did you not hear? I am sure we can be of use to our English friend, and set her in the way of some suitable mode of employment in Aviel.'

Grunewald merely sat looking at Bess, his eyes half-closed. She was not fooled by this posture into thinking him careless in his scrutiny, for she felt herself closely studied, and by a mind full awake. 'Very well, baggage. You have your offer. Out of the kindness of his tiny heart, Drig would like to assist you in this life-building business of yours. Shall you have it so?'

Bess pursed her lips. 'Reckon I could go along wi' that for a time. Only I'll not be a maid again! 'Tis to escape that fate that I left England.'

Grunewald made no outward show of satisfaction, but Bessie felt a slight lessening of tension in the room. He jumped up with alacrity and collected the coat he had carelessly thrown across a nearby chair. 'Then let us away, and at once. There is no time to lose!'

Bessie could not account for his sudden hurry, when he had been content enough to lounge before. But she made no objection. 'I'll collect me things,' she said, and darted away to her room.

When she came down, Grunewald and Drig were waiting for her in the hallway. 'Is it far to Aviel?' she enquired.

'In a manner of speaking,' said Grunewald.

'It is rather far, but it will not take long,' added Drig.

Bess grimaced, and sighed. 'Very well. Just how much of my guts am I likely to be retchin' up this time?'

'How refreshing you are,' said Grunewald with vast amusement. 'I had no notion how wearied I was with fine ladies and sophisticated company. Mr. Green's life has been sadly devoid of such plain speaking.'

'I should not ha' mentioned vomitin', I suppose,' said Bess, demurely smoothing her cloak. 'But seein' as you'll be watchin' me do it in but a short space of time, it can't be of much use to avoid speakin' of it now.'

'The second time will not be so bad,' said Drig with an encouraging smile. 'Besides, our Gent is a better hand at the Whishawist than I. You will hardly feel it.'

'Tis of small matter either way,' Bessie assured him. 'I'll lose all my fine chocolate, which is a blow; but I dare suppose you are plannin' to feed me again at some point after.'

'Stale bread and water,' Grunewald promised. 'That is what you deserve, for your sauce.'

'How fortunate that none of us receives our just desserts!' Bess said devoutly.

Grunewald's eyes gleamed amusement for but a moment, and then he was all business. She thought he might take hold of her arm again, as he had before, but nobody moved so much as a step nearer to her. 'Here's off,' was all that Grunewald said, and in a conversational tone.

It was enough, for the Motley dissolved around Bess and the night rushed in.

In spite of Drig's confident prediction, the sensations of disorientation, dizziness and nausea were much the same as before.

Bess realised with dismay that the outcome was likely to be identical, too – until all of it stopped, all at once. She was able to breathe, and swallowed some of her panic.

She received the impression that their passage was not complete, not least because she remained buried in a darkness so deep she could see nothing. She felt, by some obscure sense, that their progress had been interrupted; an idea strengthened by Drig, who uttered two syllables in an alarmed tone only to be shushed by Grunewald.

Bess waited, breathing slowly. The darkness was unnerving, and the patently disturbed reactions of Drig and Grunewald did nothing to soothe her. What had occurred?

Judging from his call for silence, Grunewald must be listening for something, but no sound reached Bess's ears at all. After some little time spent in breathless anticipation, a soft, greenish light flared and Grunewald's face materialised in the darkness before her. He was frowning. He met Bess's gaze for an instant, and she lifted a brow in a silent question.

He made no answer. A second, paler light bloomed: Drig held up a glowing bauble, and by its light he peered up at Bess. 'Hmm,' he said. 'What are we doing here, Gaustin?'

The two lights together were strong enough to illuminate their surroundings, and Bess glanced curiously around. She perceived a tunnel with rounded, darkly gleaming walls. Each was covered in deeply-graven carvings, though she saw no lanterns or windows; why the images existed in such a dark place, Bess could not imagine. She looked more closely at the nearest patch of wall, and saw what appeared to be a trio of goblins engaged in sharing a pipe. Nightmarish creatures crept up behind the oblivious smokers, teeth bared; the inevitable outcome of the tableau was clear.

Bess looked away, half fascinated and half sickened. What manner of place was this?

'Don't look at the walls,' Grunewald recommended. 'These are the Darkways. Built by my grandfather, whose tastes were a little strange.'

'What are we doin' here?' said Bess, tired of waiting for an explanation.

'We passed someone,' said Grunewald shortly. 'It felt… strange to me.'

'Someone who should not be down here?'

'Indeed.' Grunewald uttered the word in a clipped tone which clearly heralded the end of the conversation. Bess had no chance to enquire further, for the sickening whirl of passage resumed without warning and her thoughts shattered into confusion once more.

Some minutes passed, as far as Bess could judge; perhaps it had only been a few seconds, and the extent of her misery only made it seem longer. She came to herself again to find that, to her relief, full light had bloomed around her, and the Darkways with their disturbing carvings were gone. A moment's investigation revealed that she had not again disgraced herself, and her garments were clean. This pleased her immeasurably.

She was once again surprised by her surroundings, though this time she experienced less of horror and more of wonder. They had emerged in a room of small proportions, but it was sumptuous in all its particulars. The floor was of dark marble, and low benches piled with richly-upholstered cushions were fitted against every wall. Those walls appeared to be made from glass, or perhaps some kind of semi-translucent crystal; they gleamed with an odd iridescence, a rainbow of purplish colour which only partially obscured the vast hall which lay beyond. Bess glimpsed soaring crystal columns and an extravagantly high ceiling.

'This is Aviel?' she asked.

'Pretty, no?' said Drig. He took off the party hat and flicked it up into the air, whereupon it rose by three or four feet and promptly disappeared. Drig drew a new hat out of nowhere, and set it onto his head. This one featured a peaked crown and a narrow brim, and was covered in ebon-black velvet.

'Very fine,' Bess commented.

Drig grinned at her, swept off the hat again and made her a flourishing bow. Revealed underneath was a tiny ball of glowing light, which contrived to remain floating an inch or two above Drig's head even as he bowed. A will-o-the-wyke, Bess realised as Drig replaced his hat, concealing the wisp from sight.

'You have contrived to keep your insides on the inside,' said Grunewald, looking Bess over. 'I congratulate you.'

Bess beamed. 'Indeed, and I have scarcely ever been prouder of meself.'

Grunewald's white teeth flashed in a grin, but he did not pause to converse further. He strode away at once, disappearing through a high archway into the vast hall beyond. Drig fell in beside Bess as she followed.

'This place may seem strange after the Darkways,' he said.

'They could hardly be more different.'

'Mm. Wasn't built by goblins, this bit. Ayliri construct. There's no one to beat them for beauty, has to be said.'

The hall was larger even than Bess had imagined, and well-lit with a white light turned faintly purple by the prismatic crystal. The chamber was filled with a vast assortment of people: goblins of many tribes, judging from their differing heights and skin colour, mingling with hobs, trows, a scattering of Ayliri and the occasional vast bulk of a troll or even a giant. There were other creatures aplenty for which Bess knew no name. All were fabulously dressed, and the array of colour dazzled Bess's eyes.

'How is it that the King's Court is Ayliri-built?' said Bess in confusion, as she trotted to keep up with Grunewald.

Drig, unexpectedly, laughed. ''Tis a matter of some debate, that. Most folk would have it that the place was taken by conquest – by his grandfather.' He nodded at Grunewald. 'And to be sure, that particular Gaustin was of a blood-thirsty tendency – as you might guess from the Darkways. But –'

'But it was a gift,' interrupted Grunewald, without either slowing his pace or turning his head. He spoke with the emphasis of strong irritation, and received startled bows in response from several courtiers. 'People enjoy the narrative of Darklings versus Aylir, but in truth there is no such thing as a "Darkling" – it is merely that some fae are blessed with excellent night vision and are, by consequence, frequently nocturnal. This apparently unsettles those with inferior vision, for some unaccountable reason I have never been able to grasp. Meanwhile, there has never been any real rivalry between the Goblin Court and the Queens-at-Mirramay. On the contrary, we have always been allies and excellent friends – yes, this was true even· of my grandfather. His supposed blood-thirstiness was more for show. He always said it deterred those who might be inclined to howl for his head. He may well have had a point.'

Grunewald strode heedlessly through the throng of courtiers, talking on in the same irritable manner and ignoring every attempt to catch his attention. A trio of trows lifted their dark pipes as Grunewald approached and began to play a kind of fanfare, but their

Gaustin cut this off with a dismissive wave of his hand. His relentless stride did not cease until he arrived beside an unassuming woman, her back stooped with advanced age. She wore shapeless, ragged black robes, with the hood pulled up to cover most of her wispy white hair. 'I have brightened the place in recent years,' he continued without pause. 'King of the "Darklands" I may be, but I grow tired of gloom. Hello, Hidenory. I need hardly tell you that I have missed you with a fervour beyond telling.'

The old woman looked up at him with a sour expression. Her face was remarkably ugly, Bess could not help observing; her skin was spotted and mapped with a thousand wrinkles, and her bulging nose sprouted multiple boils. Her teeth were crooked and discoloured, like a collection of ancient gravestones knocked askew. 'Grunewald,' she said flatly. 'Thank goodness. I could not have borne your absence an instant longer.'

Grunewald smiled beatifically. 'I felt it instinctively. You will also be delighted to learn that I have discovered a means by which you may repay me for my infinite kindness in releasing you.'

Hidenory's sourness increased tenfold. 'How wonderful, for I have nothing at all pressing to do.'

Grunewald waved a hand with an odd, twisting gesture, and the purplish light which bathed the walls developed instead a yellowish tinge. As an approximation of sunlight, it was close enough, though the quality of the light was odd. There was, Bess thought, something faintly sickly about it. 'Of course,' he continued without pause, 'One must consider just how many delightful refreshments I deprived you of by removing you from the tea table. I can only imagine how much you were enjoying the party! My interference was the very heights of boorishness!'

Hidenory's lip curled. 'Your point is made, I assure you. In what way may I be of service?' She gave an ironic little curtsey as she spoke. Then her eye strayed to Bess, and she seemed to notice Grunewald's companions for the first time. 'What have we here? I cannot remember the last time I saw a human in the Halls of Aviel.'

'I found one in a ditch,' said Grunewald, smiling. 'I thought it a presentable example, and made free to bring it along. Make your curtsey, baggage.'

Bess did so, but Hidenory paid no attention. 'Found in a ditch?' she repeated. 'When? You have been gone but half an hour.'

Grunewald went very still. 'Half an hour?'

'It is certainly not much more.'

Grunewald said nothing for a moment. His face had hardened, and a muscle twitched in his jaw. 'Are you certain that it was me?'

Hidenory blinked, and stepped back. She looked Grunewald over from head to toe, and her brows rose. 'Mm. Have you also changed clothes in the last half an hour?'

'I have not.'

'If that was not you, I must say he was a more convincing example of His Majesty than you are. That waistcoat. What possessed you?'

Grunewald glanced at the vibrant peridot-green silk confection he was wearing, and his face twisted with annoyance. 'This is serious, Hidey.'

She shrugged. 'A prankster. A disturbingly convincing one, I grant you, but—' Her eyes narrowed, and she stepped back. 'Unless you are the prankster.'

Grunewald sighed deeply, and rubbed at his eyes. 'The waistcoat is not so very uncharacteristic as all that, is it?'

Hidenory said nothing, but her posture and expression were expressive of suspicion.

'Oh, confound it.' He took Hidenory's elbow and steered her away from the clusters of courtiers, into a secluded nook in between two vast pillars. Bess and Drig followed. 'You owe me,' Grunewald continued, 'because I released you from the Teapot Society, where you had been acting as host for several months. It took us many attempts to discover a way to liberate you, do you not recall? For being a contrary and stubborn woman you would not settle merely for being replaced; nothing but the disintegration of the entire enchantment would do.

'In the end it took a volunteer host and a dose of fast-acting poison. One of my retainers took your place at the head of the table – I cannot, at this moment, remember which servant it was – and seeing as he (or she, I can scarce recall) had taken a lethal dose of spear-root only moments before, he promptly died, and so ended the enchantment. Is that sufficient in detail? I can hardly imagine any prankster would be apprised of all of that.'

Hidenory looked convinced. 'Then who did I see?' she demanded.

'I do not know, but there is more to this,' Grunewald said grimly. 'And I require your help in uncovering the imposter.'

'Perhaps that was who we passed!' said Drig in sudden enlightenment. 'In the Darkways.'

'What was he doing here?' Grunewald said sharply. His question was directed at Hidenory, who had fallen into a thoughtful – and suspicious – silence.

'You invited me to return to England with you,' she said.

'He invited you, not me! I suppose he did not happen to mention why he required your presence?'

'Nothing so direct, no. But he did question me as to my familiarity with the county of Lincolnshire. He did it in that infernal "casual" way that you have, when you do not wish me to suspect that the answer to your question is important. I tell you, Grunewald, he was most convincing.'

Grunewald's nostrils flared with anger. 'He knows me.'

'Oh, assuredly. He has studied you. He has all your mannerisms, your speech, your posture, your manner of walking. It is a consummate performance.'

Grunewald fell into deep reflection, his hands thrust into the pockets of his coat. His face was grim. 'I cannot catch him,' he finally said. 'I must know who it is! More and more, I receive the sense that if I could but glimpse his true face then I would know. I must know! If he knows me so well, I must surely know him.'

Hidenory examined her yellowed, splintered nails. 'I perceive we are returning to the question of what I am to do for you.'

'I need fairy ointment.'

Hidenory sighed. 'An obvious course of action, certainly, but more difficult than you know.'

Grunewald made an exasperated sound. 'I know that it is hard to make, and that the ingredients are well-nigh impossible to assemble besides! How much more difficult can it be?' His eyes strayed to Bess and lingered on her face, though he neither spoke nor made any obvious sign of what was passing through his mind.

'I have attempted seventy-seven times to make fairy ointment,' said Hidenory flatly. 'You may imagine how many velvet queen parasols I wasted in the process. Do you wish me to waste all of yours as well? I achieved nothing but a foul-smelling mess.'

Grunewald's eyes flickered. He opened his mouth; nothing came out, and he closed it again with a faint croak.

Hidenory looked amused. 'You fully expected that I could but turn around twice and produce a whole cauldron-full, I suppose? Your faith in my skills is flattering, but misplaced. My abilities at Glamour know no equal, I flatter myself, but as a crafter I fall sadly short.'

She received no response to this sally, which told Bess more than anything else how hard he had taken the news. He merely rubbed at his eyes, looking weary beyond words, and when he finally spoke his voice was strained. 'Hidenory. I feel the gravest trepidation about this business. Tell me! Do you know of anyone else who could brew it? Or any conceivable way I could contrive to buy some?'

'I fear the art is fading,' said Hidenory, with what sounded like sincere regret. 'Perhaps it is because the Queen is gone, and it is now all but impossible to acquire the materials. Whatever the reason, I would be surprised to learn that any such thing still exists in Aylfenhame.'

Grunewald's shoulders sagged, and he gave a growl of frustration. 'I cannot catch the devil while he rides my Tatterfoal. I cannot seem to prevent him from taking the wretched nag either, and if I am not to see what lies behind the Glamour then tell me, Hidey! What is to be done?'

Bess cleared her throat, earning the startled and slightly irritated attention of both Grunewald and Hidenory. 'I can't help thinkin' that the number of candidates must be small,' she said. 'Someone as knows my Gent particularly well; has the wherewithal to get hold of Tatterfoal, and ride such a beast besides; and, if you are right about who we passed in the Darkways, someone as can use the Goblin-roads as well. Cannot be too many people like that, surely.'

'And,' added Drig, 'those are considerable powers of Glamour at work. There are not so many Glamourists who can boast of such skill.'

Silence followed these remarks. Judging from the matching blank expressions on Hidenory and Grunewald's faces, they were casting about in their minds for a person who matched this list of specifications – without much success. 'I can think of no one now living,' Hidenory pronounced.

'Nor I,' said Grunewald heavily, 'but I shall enquire.' He nodded at Bessie. 'Sound thinking, baggage. I have permitted alarm to disorder my thoughts.'

It did not seem characteristic of Grunewald to become alarmed.

The theft of Tatterfoal was no small matter, to be sure, and the use of his visage must be disconcerting; but thus far, she had not heard that the imposter had inflicted any harm, or caused any real mischief. What was it that Grunewald feared?

'I would also like to know what he wanted with you,' Grunewald said to Hidenory. 'And, indeed, what he wants with Lincolnshire.'

'Seems like he is looking for something,' Drig offered. 'Riding around half the night in the Wolds, and questioning Hidey about Lincolnshire?'

'Indeed, but with such scant information it is perfectly impossible to imagine what he could be after. If he appears again, Hidey, I charge you to find out from him.' She opened her mouth to speak, but he waved a hand to cut her off. 'Yes, how will you know that he is not me? The moment I see any of you, I shall say something perfectly absurd, and you will suffer no doubts.'

'Shadowfire mushroom beetles,' suggested Drig. 'Heather-snouted newt eyebrows.'

'You are a font of ideas.'

Bess said nothing. What is to be done? Grunewald's question echoed in her mind, and she turned all her lively intellect upon that pressing matter. She was intrigued, and she felt all the force of Grunewald's urgency, even if she could not precisely understand its source. What could she, Bessie Bell, do to help? The conversation among her companions turned to mild levity as Drig continued to suggest ideas for Grunewald's inspiration, but Bess let it all pass by, her mind fully occupied in turning over an idea.

Bess was given a chamber of her own, among the sprawling maze of corridors dug deeply into the earth below the palace of Aviel. The room was small and comfortable, which was much to her taste. It lacked the dazzling splendour of the court rooms, displaying instead a plush, colourful cosiness that she found delightful. Nothing could be more in contrast to her former garret room at Hapworth; that chamber had been much the same size, but it had been stark and sparsely furnished, and shared with another girl. This snug little hollow was all hers, and it cost her some regret that she would be enjoying it but briefly.

Bess was served refreshment in her rooms soon afterwards, but she was not long left to the solitary enjoyment of it. A sharp tap sounded upon her door, and Hidenory entered without waiting for an invitation.

'Do come in,' said Bessie, without troubling to rise from her comfortable arm-chair. She might have offered more courtesy to a friend of Grunewald's, but she sensed at once that Hidenory's purpose was not friendly.

Hidenory shut the door behind herself, and looked down upon Bessie with amusement tinged with disdain. 'And what of you?' she said. 'What a charming surprise. His Majesty returns from England with a rag in his keeping! How unlike him! And this rag has lost no time in settling herself in all due comfort at his court. What can she mean by it, I wonder?'

Bessie nodded. 'Sound questions all, for what can the rag have in mind save somethin' proper shady?'

Hidenory merely raised her eyebrows.

Bessie's lips curved into a grin. 'What is it that you're suspectin', particular-like? If you're thinkin' I might be a confederate of that Grunewaldery-fakery, you are behind the fair. That has already been suspicioned, and dismissed.'

'That had crossed my thoughts, but perhaps it is nothing so complex; I daresay you are merely out for your own benefit, as indeed most persons are.'

'Hangin' onto the coat-tails of royalty, hm? Tis but a temporary state. I remain wi' Grunewald only until I have repaid the favour Drig asked of me. Once done, it's out into Gadrahst for me, and swift to makin' my own fortune.'

'Unless he should happen to want to detain you.'

Bessie swiftly saw the direction of Hidenory's thoughts, and was unable to suppress the bubble of laughter that rose up in her at the idea. 'Do you know what His Majesty calls me? Baggage. Tis not a name expressive of much affection, is it now? And as for me, well! He might ha' fished me out of a ditch, which is true enough, and I am grateful for it. But he has done little since but try to get rid o' me – exceptin' that memorable bit where he dragged me to the very feet o' Tatterfoal and scared me half to death. He makes use of his retainers wi' no thought for their comfort at all, and if he looks at me wi' some manner of interest, well; I would say it's the kind of interest a person might feel in some crawlin' creature never before encountered, and soon forgotten. I have no ambitions to become

Queen o' this mad Court, and the notion would never cross his mind; not if I spent a century hauntin' these walls.'

Hidenory listened to this speech without comment, and at its end her expression changed not one whit. Bessie felt that her interrogator was unmoved, but she dismissed the thought with a mental shrug. It mattered naught to her what Hidenory thought.

'I will be watching you,' said Hidenory, with an intensity which inspired an odd reaction in Bessie; rather than feeling in any way cowed by this threat, she felt an inexplicable urge to laugh. She suppressed the impulse, and merely watched in silence as Hidenory swept out of the room again in a swirl of ragged cloth.

The encounter had not been pleasant, but Bessie was more troubled by her inability to understand the witch's motive. Was it concern for Grunewald which led her to speak thus? They had, she judged, been friends, or something like it, for a long time indeed. Perhaps Hidenory endeavoured to forestall a threat to the Goblin King which he had not imagined himself.

Or perhaps she spoke out of some other motive. It was difficult for Bess to imagine that she possessed designs upon the position of Goblin Queen herself, considering her haggish appearance. But appearances could be but little relied upon, especially in Aylfenhame. Virtually anything might lie behind the witch's wizened façade. If she saw Bess as a competitor, that could certainly lead her to speak as she had done.

Bessie could not know, or guess, what had prompted Hidenory's visit. But she tucked the experience away, resolving to watch Hidenory just as Hidenory watched Bess herself.

That evening, Drig escorted her to the dining parlours, and she was able to mingle with Aviel's many residents. The food was reminiscent of the fare she had enjoyed at the Motley, and Bess partook of it heartily, enjoying her opportunity to observe the myriad guests at the King's Court and their sumptuous finery as she did so. Drig behaved as though he had something on his mind, and she wondered whether he was on the verge of claiming the debt she owed him, and putting forward his request. But he said nothing of any moment.

They encountered Grunewald again some little time later. Drig toured Bessie around the underlevels of Aviel, as they were called, but in time he led her back up to ground level and out into a large, glass-walled conservatory thick with flourishing vegetation. The conservatory was entirely empty, which surprised Bess, for it was a place of particular beauty. Flowers the size of her own head bloomed everywhere she looked and gleaming insects hung upon the air, filling the conservatory with a hushed, dreamy thrum. It was softly lit and scented with a heavenly aroma, and Bessie felt that she could gladly remain indefinitely.

But she understood the reason for its desertion when they rounded a corner and found Grunewald sprawled in a large armchair, his coat discarded and his cravat undone. A small table was poised at his knee, upon which sat a large decanter filled with something purple and probably alcoholic. He had already partaken of it rather freely, Bess judged, considering his air of boneless relaxation. But she doubted whether it had affected his wits, for the gaze he fixed upon her was as sharp as ever.

'Ah, baggage. At last. You do take your time.' He sighed, and then added, 'Pink-footed bottle larvae.'

'I am at your beck and call at all times, of course,' she replied promptly. 'What's more, I am blessed with an uncanny ability to know the very instant yer expectin' me.'

'Yes, perhaps I should have sent for you,' he agreed. 'But here you are, nonetheless. And Drig as well. Take a glass, will you? Starberry nectar, with honey vapour. Most pleasing.' He tapped the table, and two fresh glasses appeared: one for Bess, and a much smaller one for Drig.

But Drig bowed, and made a show of yawning. He had not seemed tired before, and Bessie mistrusted the sly look he threw at her as he straightened up. 'I am for bed,' he announced. 'Saving your Gentship's presence, of course.'

Grunewald flicked his fingers. 'By all means.'

Drig trotted off. Bess was not unwilling to stay, but while Grunewald had thought to provide her with a glass, it had not occurred to him that she might also require somewhere to sit. She waited as he filled her glass and handed it to her, then raised a speaking brow at him.

He patted the arm of his chair. 'Yes, I am improperly supplied with chairs. But this one is quite large enough.'

This was true, for the chair was vast, and each of its fatly stuffed arms was easily two feet wide.

'I think not,' said Bessie, in some surprise. She felt a faint flicker of alarm, for she had by no means anticipated such an offer from him; nor could she welcome it, not when it came from a gentleman in whose power she presently remained. Her treatment at the hands of Edward Adair flashed through her brain, and she had to resist the temptation to retreat a step or two.

But Grunewald took her refusal in good part; indeed, his eyes gleamed appreciation. 'You will stand, will you?'

'Given a lack of alternatives, yes.'

He grinned, and said in a different voice: 'Armchair. Well-stuffed. Crimson velvet.'

And an armchair appeared opposite. It was as vast as his own and as plush, but where his was upholstered in night-black silk, the new chair was covered in the rich crimson velvet he had requested.

Bess sat down at once. 'Very fittin', for a housemaid,' she complimented him. 'Wi' just the right degree of opulence.'

'You are no housemaid.'

'Some'd say I will always be a servant, no matter what I do now.' She raised the glass to her lips and received an inhalation of a heady honey vapour, followed by a sip of rich, sweet wine.

'You have spent altogether too much time at that wretched house,' he retorted. 'I advise you to give no credence to anything the Adair family might have said to you.'

'I never was much in the habit of doin' so.'

He studied her in silence for a time, his drink forgotten. Bessie bore this scrutiny without remark, savouring her drink and the remarkable comfort of her armchair. Truly, she was in danger of growing used to these luxuries.

'Why are you here, baggage?' said Grunewald at length.

'Seekin' my fortune, like any young woman in a fairy story.'

He smiled faintly. 'No doubt you have grand dreams.'

'Nothin' lofty. I want...' She paused a while to consider her words. What did she want? 'Freedom,' she finally decided.

'You were not made for the merely mundane.' A smile glimmered in his eyes. 'I shall enjoy watching you carve a path for yourself.'

'As shall I. At present I have little idea how I'm to go about it.' Something upon the table caught Bessie's eye: a rolled scroll, yellowed with age and tied with a sage-green ribbon. The sight disconcerted her, for she had not previously noticed it; how came she to have missed something so prominent? 'What is that?' she asked, pointing.

Grunewald appeared startled. 'That... was supposed to be hidden,' he said with some annoyance. He picked up the scroll and gently tossed it up into the air, whereupon it vanished.

'Secrets, is it?' said Bessie happily. 'How excitin'. I shall be sure to discover all about it.'

Grunewald's grin was a touch twisted. 'Doubtless it is impossible to prevent you. It is a scroll, baggage, upon which is written a partial account of an old conflict.'

Bess nodded encouragingly. 'And?'

Grunewald sighed. 'It misrepresents me.' His jaw clenched with anger and he glowered into his glass.

Bessie suppressed the urge to giggle. 'Truly? Someone somewhere wrote somethin' untrue about you and you are wastin' your time worryin' over it?'

Grunewald stared at her with narrowed eyes. 'You are dismissive.'

'Do you know how often I was accused of all manner o' things I had nowt to do with? Servants are blamed for everythin' that goes amiss. If I wasted my time carin' for the opinions of those as does the blamin', I'd have lain down and died long ago.'

Grunewald made an impatient gesture. 'All perfectly true, but this scroll was not written by just anybody. It is the official, and broadly accepted, account of my actions in the Times of Trial, and I took it — most reprehensibly — from the Royal library at Mirramay. This account has all the weight of truth behind it.'

'That is a mite more tryin',' Bessie agreed. 'What does it say of you?'

Grunewald sighed deeply. 'The conflict was between the King-and-Queen-at-Mirramay and one who sought to usurp their thrones. You know the sort of thing.'

'Indeed, I am delighted to learn that Aylfenhame has its share of such folk,' said Bess. 'I was startin' to think it much too charmin' to be real.'

'Mm. I cannot agree with you there, for it was a deeply unpleasant war, as all such conflicts are. It failed, fortunately, but —'

'It failed?' repeated Bessie blankly. 'And here I was thinkin' I was at last learnin' what happened to yer missin' Queen.'

'It failed. This was more than a century ago, or thereabouts.

Anthelaena survived that conflict. She broke some thirty years ago, when her husband vanished and her daughter... died.'

'Oh.' Bess felt unexpectedly subdued.

'Anyway,' Grunewald continued with some emphasis, 'According to official report, I supported Anthelaena and Edironal at times – and I also supported their would-be usurper. Here it is in the Chronicler's own writing. It bears the Chronicler's Seal, and as such, its veracity is beyond question.' He leaned forward a little, his eyes dark and intense. 'This has long troubled me. Anthelaena and Edironal were among my dearest and oldest friends! I could never have betrayed them. And yet, Aylfenhame believes it of me. Why? I had thought it merely a cursed deplorable effect of my position; after all, what would you expect of the King of the so-called Darklings but self-interested trickery?'

Grunewald said this in a light tone, but Bessie sensed that the injustice of it troubled him more than he wished to admit, and had done so for a century. She began, dimly, to perceive that there were reasons for his flippant, cynical attitude.

'But,' she said with a flash of insight, 'A Royal Librarian must be proof against such flimsy reasonin', no?'

'Exactly! I knew you would see it. The ordinary intellects of Aylfenhame know nothing of me, and may freely believe whatever they choose. But the Chronicler? And worse... Anthelaena?' He shook his head. 'Anthelaena never fully believed it of me but... she doubted. And she had never doubted me before. I wanted to know why.'

'So you stole the scroll.'

'Indeed. It occurred to me to wonder how recorded history remembered me, and I found a way to penetrate the Library. I did so for other reasons and other information, but I took the opportunity to explore this problem as well.' A spasm of something like regret crossed his face, which Bess did not know how to understand. 'And the result! The Chronicler condemns me, in the dry, dispassionate voice of history itself. My misdeeds are confirmed, in ink and parchment.' He snatched the scroll out of the air once more and stared at it, as though to do so would force it to give up its secrets. 'It has troubled me ever since, but the more so of late. This business with my fetch has caused me to reconsider the problem.'

'Aye,' said Bessie. 'If someone can pretend to be you so

successfully now, might someone not have done so before?'

'Precisely. And I have seen, with my own eyes, how convincing an illusion it is.' He tapped the scroll absently against his cheek, his eyes faraway with thought. 'But what if it is not two separate souls, but one? In short, that the person impersonating me now and the person who did so before are the same person?'

Bess blinked, and said doubtfully, 'That could be the case, but what reason do you have for thinkin' it?'

'Two weeks ago, I would have called it impossible that anybody could so convincingly pass themselves off as me. Now, I must consider the notion that at least two people have successfully done so. I think it... of all things the most unlikely. It is not merely a matter of adopting my face, you understand. Tatterfoal would not be so easily fooled. No, this person wields some element of my powers as well – powers which are tied to my position as Gaustin. And that is... difficult indeed to explain.'

'Is it? How did you come to be Gaustin?'

'Goblin society is a fraction more complex than some, but... the position is essentially inherited.'

'So I assume, from your talkin' of your grandfather and such. Do you have any siblin's unaccounted for?'

'I have none at all. My father was late to wed, and my mother bore but the one child.'

The explanation seemed obvious enough to Bessie, but she hesitated to speak her suspicions out loud. The notion that Grunewald's father may have sired other children after all did not, in her eyes, lessen his character, but Grunewald may disagree.

'Are you sure?' she finally said.

His brow lowered, and his eyes glittered with some emotion Bess could not name. 'The notion has also been in my mind, baggage. I wonder if he is my elder?'

An interesting question indeed. If Grunewald had an elder sibling, would that person qualify as the rightful Gaustin? Did the principle of primogeniture apply among the Goblins? Considering Grunewald's question, Bess was inclined to think so. 'A right mess, that,' she commented.

Grunewald blinked, and then to Bessie's surprise he grinned. 'It is. But in some ways, I feel vastly relieved. An explanation at last! I need only prove it to be vindicated.'

'I congratulate you, to be sure,' she said with a smile. 'And how will you go about it?'

'That's more of a problem,' he admitted. 'But—' He broke off as Drig came in at a dead run, carrying his hat in his hands.

'Majesty!' he said breathlessly. 'You have visitors. The Aylfendeanes, out on the Lower Green. Urgent.' He turned at once and darted away again.

## CHAPTER SEVEN

Grunewald was on his feet in an instant, Bess only a moment behind him. She made to follow as Grunewald strode for the door, but he turned back and took hold of her arms. 'I mislike the looks of this. Will you stay, until I have made sure of my visitors and their errand?'

'Do you think me in danger, my Gent? Naught shall go amiss wi' me.'

'I should like to be sure of it,' he repeated. He did not wait for her response, but squeezed her forearms gently and then immediately walked away. Bessie was left to consider his words, his behaviour and his fears and decide whether she wished to be influenced by any of them.

But first, she turned back to the table upon which his discarded glass still rested. The plans she had begun to form were fresh in her mind; strengthened, if anything, by his confidences. She had a suspicion in mind as to the purpose of the Aylfendeanes' visit, if it was indeed they, and she would require a few preparations. She tapped the table-top firmly, mimicking Grunewald's earlier gesture, and said clearly: 'Small glass jar.'

She did not know whether the table's enchantment would function for her as well as for Grunewald; perhaps it was only for the *Gaustin*. But a jar appeared, rising smoothly from the solid wood of the table-top, and sat waiting to be collected. It was a few inches across, and fitted with a silver lid.

'Too big,' said Bess. She tapped the table again and said: 'Tiny glass jar.'

The first one melted back into the table-top and a second emerged. This one was more of the proportions Bess required, and she caught it up. It fitted neatly into a pocket of her gown, but she discovered a problem. The gown had not been equipped with pockets when she had received it; it was a discarded garment of the daughter of Hapworth Manor, and fine ladies had no use for such practicalities. Bess had fitted pockets herself. But she was no great seamstress; the work was clumsy, and the fabric had been taken from a chemise already worn through.

There was a great hole in the bottom of her pocket. She tried the matching pocket on the other side, and found a hole forming there, too.

Bessie spent a moment in thought. She had no other means of carrying the jar. She certainly could not adopt the custom of carrying a reticule, as gentlewomen did, without its exciting comments and questions she had rather avoid.

Bess tapped the table a third time. 'Gown, my size,' she said. 'Red. With pockets.'

Everything presently upon the table disappeared, glasses included, and red fabric began to appear. Bess gathered it up as the gown slowly emerged, and held it against herself. It was, she judged, perfectly sized to fit her figure, and of a practical style of which she heartily approved: the sleeves were long to suit the weather, the neckline was not too low, and it was made from warm, heavy cotton dyed a deep red colour. It even bore embroidered, leafy fronds around the cuffs and hem, which Bess felt was a pretty touch. Grunewald's table was blessed with a sharp sense of fashion.

Satisfied, Bessie disappeared behind a row of tall potted shrubs and changed her dress. She left her old, faded and worn gown in a careless heap, hoping she would never have to set eyes upon it again. The new gown was warmer, better fitted and altogether more delightful, and she felt like a new woman wearing it.

She went back to the table, rapped upon it one last time, and said: 'Sorry for all the work, but I need jus' one more thing. Cloak, wool. With hood.'

And a cloak emerged! With a wide hood as requested, and made from wool. She had not thought to specify a colour, but the table had chosen a shade of deep brown which matched nicely with her gown.

Not only that, it also thought to provide a pair of knitted gloves.

'You are without question the best table in the world,' Bessie said, donning the cloak and the gloves. For the first time in years – nay, for as long as she could remember – she felt warmly dressed. 'Thank you,' she said cheerily. She bent down, bestowed a kiss upon the obliging table, and then swept out of the conservatory.

Bess succeeded in following the route Grunewald had taken by the simple expedient of asking people. The corridors were full of courtiers – lingering, perhaps, in hopes of catching the attention of their *Gaustin* at some time or other – and Bess had little difficulty finding her way. Each person she asked assured her that Grunewald had given orders *not* to follow him. This Bess disregarded, with no thought save for a mild wonder at their collective obedience.

The lower green turned out to be at the end of a series of wide lawns situated behind the palace of Aviel. The moon was high, and by its light Bess could dimly perceive tall, ornately-shaped hedges separating each lawn from the next, and a variety of ornaments – statues and sundials and the like – littering the grass. In these she felt not the smallest interest, and passed them by.

The boat which had inexplicably taken up its residence in the middle of the Lower Green interested her fractionally more. It was of moderate size, though large enough to carry a fair number of people. A single, tall mast rose from its centre, upon which was hung an enormous sail which glittered in the moonlight. In the boat's prow stood an Aylir woman dressed in trousers and a long coat.

Gathered in a knot near the base of the boat were a number of people Bessie recognised: Grunewald, Drig, and Mr. and Mrs. Aylfendeane. Grunewald looked up as Bess approached, but instead of the expected scowl, she received a brilliant smile.

Mrs. Aylfendeane saw Bessie an instant later, and beamed upon her. She looked tired; her skin was paler than ever, and smudged with dark shadows beneath her eyes. But she was obviously in fine spirits.

'Bess! I had hoped you were still with Grunewald. How glad I am to see you.' She bestowed a friendly salutation upon Bess, and her husband did the same. She did not appear to resent Bess's abrupt departure from her house, which somewhat relieved Bessie's mind. No one had ever treated her with such kindness as the Aylfendeanes, and she would be sorry indeed to offend them.

Bessie could imagine only one errand that could bring the

Aylfendeanes into Gadrahst so late at night, and send Drig scurrying to fetch his master with such a total abandonment of his customary lethargy. 'Tis a pleasure to be seein' you likewise,' she said with a smile. 'You have succeeded, I collect?'

Mrs. Aylfendeane laughed. 'I see what you mean, Grunewald!' she said incomprehensibly. 'I have been successful,' she said to Bessie. 'To my infinite surprise, and relief!'

'I never doubted ye could manage it,' said Mr. Aylfendeane, with a wink at Bess.

'Indeed, without Tafferty's help I should not have achieved it at all! Of that I am certain. And I have received the assistance of Sophy and Aubranael besides, for they were kind enough to travel into England with the express purpose of supporting my endeavour. I owe my success, in large part, to my friends.'

The attention of the group passed from Bessie, and she took the opportunity to surreptitiously observe Grunewald. His posture suggested that the precious delivery had been tucked away in his right-hand pocket, and she drifted a little closer.

Now to consider her options. She needed some of the fairy ointment Grunewald now possessed, if she was to carry through the secret plans she had been developing. But how to acquire it? She could not ask Mrs. Aylfendeane to make more; the materials must all be used, and she had no money to procure more. Nor did she imagine that Grunewald would willingly share his new supply with her, whether she shared her intentions with him or not. He had never been in favour of her interfering in his affairs, and what she proposed to do in his service would surely not be well received.

There remained one alternative.

Memories of Bessie's early years were not among the proudest of her life. Motherless and left much to her own care, she had been adrift upon the streets, and had learned one or two abilities which she had since striven to forget. It gave her no pleasure to dart her hand into Grunewald's pocket and extract the tiny wooden pot she found therein; nor to briskly whisk off the lid and remove a dab of the curiously cool-feeling salve it contained. The lid was replaced, the pot returned to Grunewald's pocket and her stolen dab of ointment secreted inside her glass jar, all in the space of barely fifteen seconds. The Aylfendeanes, deep in conversation with Grunewald, never so much as glanced at her. Only Drig's eyes flicked Bessie's way, but if he had observed her activities, he said nothing.

Having tucked her spoils away inside the deep pocket of her new cloak, Bessie was free to rejoin the conversation in all apparent innocence.

Mr. Aylfendeane said, 'Curse it, we almost forgot. When was the last time ye paid a visit t' Hyde Place, Grunewald?'

Grunewald's eyes narrowed. 'Not for a few days.'

'Oh, dear,' said Isabel. 'We feared that might be the case. You have been seen at home, you know, by more than one observer. The impersonation is holding, and no one has doubted that it was you in truth, except for Tal and me. Your *fetch* has contrived to take possession of your house.'

Grunewald thought that over, his eyes gleaming oddly. 'How ill-mannered,' he finally decided. 'And yet, how obliging.'

The Aylfendeanes cast him twin expressions of surprise. 'Obliging?' repeated Isabel.

'Why yes, for two reasons. Firstly, I now know where to find him, and may proceed at once to the great unmasking. Secondly, it will be simplicity itself to conceal myself within my own household staff, and by this means spy upon his movements. We shall soon know all, I assure you.'

The plan worried Mrs. Aylfendeane a little, Bessie observed, but her good sense saw the wisdom of it. Little more was said, and the company soon afterwards broke up. It was evident to all that poor Mrs. Aylfendeane had abandoned everything to the pursuit of fairy ointment, including her sleep, and her husband was fully justified in soon afterwards escorting her back into the boat. Bess watched this process in some confusion, unsure how a beached vessel could be expected to restore its occupants to England – until it rose into the air in a great gust of wind, and vanished in a cloud of white mist.

Bess took advantage of the flurry of departure to apply a faint smear of the ointment to her left eye. The jar was safely secreted once more before Grunewald turned to her. 'Interestin' conveyance,' she remarked.

'Quite a wonder,' Grunewald agreed. He shimmered oddly in her altered vision, as though two versions of himself walked together. But in the moonlight, she could discern little more. 'There used to be a great many, until the conflict I mentioned earlier,' Grunewald continued. 'But some of the lost wonders of Aylfenhame have lately returned, and the ferry's one of them.' He was in a fine flow of spirits, and Bessie recognised the effects of unexpected hope upon his state of mind. He escorted Bessie back into the palace, Drig wandering along beside them both with his bubble pipe in full flow. Bess thought Grunewald might mention the small matter of her total disobedience, but he did not.

He did, however, stop halfway back to the conservatory, and examine her with an arrested expression. 'Something is different about you, baggage,' he said, looking her over.

Bessie waited. She now received a clear view of Grunewald's face and form, under the soft but illuminating lights of Aviel's elegant passageways. She did not dare to close her right eye, in order to obscure the red-headed, green-eyed Glamour that he wore; but doubled up with that familiar visage was a second image, and quite different. The real Grunewald was as tall as his illusory persona, but instead of the pale, human skin he had chosen, his was ash grey. His features were not wholly dissimilar to his adopted face, but they were sharper and harsher, as though deeply graven in stone. His hair was white and long, tied back into a neat tail, and his ears bore the elongated points and curled tips of an Aylir. Only his eyes were the same: large and sharp and bright, bright green.

Those eyes — and ears — interested Bessie in particular, for it suggested to her that Grunewald was not of full goblin blood. He had an Aylir ancestor, she was certain of it. But had it been his mother, or perhaps a generation further back?

Unaware of her enlightened scrutiny, he examined her attire and finally said: 'Is your gown—?'

'Altered? Yes, considerably.' Bessie kept her face composed, showing nothing of her true thoughts. She wondered why it was that he maintained the façade, and whether she would ever know.

It took Grunewald a moment's reflection to guess how the change in Bessie's gown had come about, and then he laughed — rather relieving her mind, because he might with reason have been angered by her cheerful appropriation of his table's unusual properties. 'A fine ensemble,' he complimented her.

'A warm ensemble,' she corrected him with a smile. 'And I thank you for it. My fingers behave as fingers are supposed to, cold as it is.'

'Functional fingers! I am delighted to hear it. And now, I am away to England.'

Bessie nodded, unsurprised that he made no mention of taking her along. 'Are you certain you'll know the imposter, when you see his real face?'

'Fairly. It must be someone that I know — or someone I *should* know, if our shared surmise is correct. And if I do not, I will discover it by other, stealthier, means.' He paused, perhaps expecting Bessie to speak again, but she merely nodded. 'What?' he said with a teasing glint. 'No importunate requests to come along?'

'Take me along wi' you,' said Bessie obediently. She composed her features into a beseeching expression, and even contrived to flutter her lashes just a trifle.

'No.'

Bessie sighed. 'Why raise the topic, if yer only goin' to say no anyway?'

'It amuses me.'

'Disappointin' me is amusin' to you?'

'Excessively.' He grinned at Bessie's annoyance, his eyes twinkling. 'Or perhaps it's the way you smile at me when you are attempting to be winsome.'

*Attempting?* Bessie scowled at that, and folded her arms. 'Away wi' you, before you win yerself a beatin'.'

Grunewald gave a flourishing bow. 'Drig. See to the lady's comfort.' He gave the order without even glancing at his diminutive retainer, and then strode off.

Drig looked critically at Bess, and adjusted his hat – flat, wide-brimmed and berry-red, today. 'So I am to play nurse,' he said flatly.

'No! I am not in need of nursin'. But I have a better idea.'

Drig's sour look turned into frank suspicion. 'I am all agog to hear it.'

Bess beckoned him away to her room, though he followed with ill grace. Once the door was safely shut behind them both, she began with, 'Drig! I may need you to take me into England.'

Drig blinked, and his eyes narrowed. 'You barely tried to persuade our Gent,' he said shrewdly. 'If I didn't know better, I would say you wanted to be left behind.'

'His ways and mine must part for a time,' she said serenely.

'Then why England?' Drig squinted at her. 'You are planning something devious. I can all but smell it on you.'

Bess gave an affirmative nod. 'We are goin' to Hyde Place. Or I am, leastwise.'

Drig stared at her in horror. 'You are *trying* to intercept the *fetch*? What's in your mind, madwoman?'

Bessie beamed sunnily upon him. 'Many excitin' plans, Drig, but I'll need you to bring them off! Will you help me?'

'If helping you helps our Gent, then I must,' he said sourly. 'But I do not like it! You should know that!'

'Your objections have been heard,' said Bess merrily, 'and disregarded.'

Drig sighed deeply, took out his pipe, and sought comfort in a string of indigo bubbles. 'You will see us both killed,' he predicted.

'Never!' said Bessie stoutly. 'Trust me, Drig! We will untangle this mess yet, and our Gent will be mighty pleased wi' us both.'

# CHAPTER EIGHT

*Tha' Bess has a lion's heart, an' no mistake! Though between you an' me, she could mayhap be a mite too confident. Well, Drig's a goblin o' stout heart too, an' he were willin' enough to help. But Grunewald 'ad trusted Bess's safety to him, an' he were a touch worried. What manner o' mess might she get 'erself into, wi' no help but his? So he sent word to me. Oh, I knew Drig, right enough! I know most fae as sets foot in Tilby, or near-abouts.*

*As fer Tatterfoal an 'is rider, well! They kept up the mad antics fer three nights together, then vanished out o' Lincolnshire fer a time. After that though, they was back, an' the fog came in again wi' them. Afore all o' that — back in the summer a ways — we 'ad the Piper harin' about wi' his merry musical band, tryin' t' uncover two types o' people: them as was lost to the Torpor after the conflicts, like my good friend Sir Guntifer. And them as has Aylfenhame blood and don't know it, like the new Mrs. Aylfendeane. He can't spot it any more'n I can, but he can draw it to the fore wi' his enchantments an' his music. Such were the case wi' Isabel.*

*It entered me 'ead tha' the two things might not be unrelated. Some mad fetch of a Goblin King ridin' Tatterfoal all over the Wolds at a time when folk long slumberin' 'ave been wakin' up, an' folk like Isabel learnin' there's more to 'em than ever they suspected? What if Lyrriant ain't the only one interested in wakin' folk up? An' what if the Grunewald lookie-likie's fixin' to wake up a different class o' folk than the Piper? I 'ad to investigate.*

*An' my folk, they says to me, "Mister Balligumph, tha' Tatterfoal an' rider seems like they's lookin' fer somethin'..."*

Drig kept a watch on Hidenory's rooms. He had strict orders to inform Bess the moment Grunewald appeared, if he did at all.

Bess did not have to wait long, which reinforced her belief that the court of Aviel concealed a spy. Late in the morning after the Gaustin's departure, Bessie was wandering about the great hall of Aviel, on the watch, when a goblin even smaller than Drig sidled up to her and tugged once upon the skirt of her gown.

Bess looked down upon him, eager hope flaring in her heart. 'Yes?'

The goblin, yellow-skinned and sumptuously dressed, leaned towards Bess and muttered, 'Idriggal sent me to tell you: Hidenory's chambers.'

He departed before Bess could speak, and she left the great hall herself immediately afterwards. She had familiarised herself with the location of Hidenory's rooms, and she went directly there and knocked upon the door.

'Hidenory!' she called, and opened the door. 'I wanted to talk to you about – oh!' She made a show of surprise upon seeing Grunewald there, and then smiled warmly upon him. 'Grunewald! How gravely you were missed.'

Grunewald – or the fetch, as he indeed was – flashed the familiar, sardonic grin and said in Grunewald's own voice: 'Why, Bess! I had no notion that you cared.'

He omitted the gibberish upon which they had agreed, but Bessie no longer required this sign in order to discern the truth. Bess, indeed! He had been informed of her association with Grunewald, then, but had not learned of the Gaustin's odd nickname for her.

This version of Grunewald was fractionally shorter than he, she judged, though in other respects he was not vastly different in looks. His skin was a darker grey and his eyes bright blue instead of green, but his features bore a distinct resemblance to the Goblin King's. There was no sign of Ayliri heritage, however: his ears were as human in appearance as Bess's own, and his eyes lacked the distinctive size, shape and faint slant of the Aylir. Looking upon him, she did not think that she and Grunewald had strayed far from the truth when they had speculated about a family connection.

It took Bessie rather longer to realise that something else was different about this Grunewald. It was no he at all, in fact, but a she. With her white hair bound tightly back, and some manner of enchantment (Bess supposed) altering her voice, it was easy enough for her to pass for male. And despite the resemblance to Grunewald, there were differences enough to suggest that her mother had not been either goblin or Aylir.

Hidenory stood with her arms folded, looking sourly displeased about something. When Bess looked at her, Hidenory minutely shook her head.

'I am sorry fer bargin' in on yer conversation!' Bess said to Hidenory. 'I had some news from Tilby I thought you might find interestin', but I can come back when you're not busy.'

Hidenory looked puzzled at this mention of Tilby, as well she might; but as Bessie turned back to the door, she was rewarded by a word from the Grunewald-fetch: 'Stay a moment, Bess.'

The voice was convincing indeed; with her back turned, Bess could almost have sworn that Grunewald himself spoke the words. She turned back with an inquiring look, and found herself scrutinised with a familiar expression of intent interest; Grunewald had frequently examined her in the same way.

'I require your company,' the fetch said, in Grunewald's most imperious tones.

Bess congratulated herself upon a successful gambit. She had hoped that mention of Lincolnshire, and especially Tilby, would pique the interest of the fetch. But she must not appear too eager, for she had rejected the real Grunewald's teasing suggestion that she might wish to accompany him. So she lifted her brows, and said with some asperity: 'I am no subject of yours, Majesty! You cannot order me about as you do wi' your goblin-folk.'

Those eyes gleamed amusement, exactly as the real Grunewald's often did when he looked at her. She blessed the stolen fairy ointment, without which she would have been hard-pressed to discover that this was a fetch at all. 'How true. But I require you nonetheless.'

'For what?' Bessie said, setting her hands upon her hips. 'I am mighty busy wi' my own business, as you should well know, and I dunnot have the time to go harin' about wi' you. Do you not have retainers enough?'

The fetch folded his – or her – arms and looked down upon Bess with an uncompromising air. 'None that know Lincolnshire so well as you do. A denizen of Tilby is exactly what I need.'

Hidenory broke her silence to interject. 'Then Bessie is precisely the person to take with you! For she is a native of that place.' When Bess looked at her, Hidenory smiled brightly, with no obvious trace of the malice that could only lie behind such a statement. Bessie tried not to feel stung, for Hidenory must realise that this was not Grunewald. Only ill-nature could prompt her to send Bessie into England with a person of unknown motives, and dangerous abilities — even if she sought to protect Grunewald from Bessie's supposed machinations.

But it coincided with Bess's desire, so she smothered a flicker of anger and made a show of exasperation. 'If yer Majesty demands it.'

'I do, quite. But you will not go unrewarded.'

That interested Bessie a little, for the real Grunewald had never spoken thus to her. He had helped her and bestowed a gift upon her, but in both cases he had done so because he had felt so inclined; some whim or other had been behind his actions, and he had, primarily, pleased himself. He had not tried to couch his assistance in terms of reward for some past or future service. To do so altered their relationship at once, making Grunewald the power and Bessie the supplicant.

'If it must be so, then it must,' said Bess. 'But I trust yer errand shall not take a great deal o' time, for I have much to do wi' meself.'

Grunewald grinned and bowed extravagantly. 'You are kindness itself,' he said.

'Oh, beyond anythin'.'

Grunewald looked at Hidenory. 'I require a witch also.'

Hidenory's brows rose, and she laughed. 'I have told you already: I cannot help you. Ask Mrs. Aylfendeane, if witch you require. I am sure she will be obliging.' This last was spoken in tones of contempt.

Grunewald's eyes narrowed. 'I could compel you, if I so chose,' he said softly.

'When has that ever been thus? Persuade me and I am yours to command; force me and I shall fight you forever.'

'And you are not persuaded.'

'Not in the least. Ask me tomorrow, or the day after. I may be more kindly disposed.'

'I will,' promised the fetch, and he sounded as though he meant it. His green gaze returned to Bess; His hand darted out and took hold of her wrist. He gave a sudden, sharp tug, and Bessie fell sideways into darkness.

Bessie was proud of herself, for she endured this latest journey through the Darkways without disgracing herself at all. She was interested to note that the Grunewald-fetch navigated the route every bit as confidently as Grunewald himself, and without the smallest hesitation; if anything he (or she) was the more skilled, for Bessie emerged from the passage feeling only mildly nauseated. Grunewald would be highly irritated by that piece of information. She reminded herself to inform him of it at her earliest opportunity.

The fetch brought her into England in a spot she did not recognise. A manor house of moderately impressive proportions rose before her: a large, square property built from blocks of yellowish stone, with grand windows. She stood in the gardens a hundred feet or so from the house, surrounded by hedges and shrubs. Grunewald's fetch began walking at once up to the great front doors, trusting to Bessie to follow him.

Bess paused only to look about herself, though she scarcely knew what she was hoping to see. Nothing of any use met her gaze; the house sat inert, desultorily illuminated by the little watery grey sunlight that penetrated a heavy cloud cover. The gardens were quiet. She heard nothing save occasional, faint birdsong, and saw no one.

She followed the Grunewald-fetch into the house. 'Come,' he called to her, without looking back. Bess followed him through a silent, grand hallway, down a spacious corridor and into a library. He paused only to cast his coat onto the floor, and dropped into a deep armchair. There he sat, watching Bessie from beneath glowering brows. She could make no guess as to his thoughts.

Bess took a chair opposite, without waiting for an invitation. Her position here was precarious, and if she was to achieve her goal, she would have to adapt her approach – but carefully.

What she sought, primarily, was information. Grunewald's insistence on securing the fairy ointment was not in itself misguided, but she did not think he would achieve as much through its use as he expected. She had no doubt that he would succeed in catching another glimpse of Tatterfoal and his rider, for he was persistent, clever and powerful. But what would he learn from the imposter's true face, save a conviction that their theory about a blood tie was correct? He would be no nearer an understanding of who this person was, or what he – she – hoped to gain by impersonating Grunewald.

And it would be difficult indeed for Grunewald of all people to get close enough to learn anything more.

Bessie, however, had no real obstacles in the way of her doing just that. She was no one of importance; her movements did not have to be concealed, as Grunewald's would, because they were unlikely to be reported upon in the first place. Having no connection whatsoever to any part of Aylfenhame save Grunewald himself, she would not naturally be suspected of harbouring any ulterior motive that might be injurious to the fake Grunewald's cause. And if she could convince the lady behind the mask that she served her own goals in assisting the supposed Goblin King, she thought it unlikely that she would be viewed with suspicion.

Happily, Hidenory and the lady fetch had between them inspired her with an idea.

'What is it that you want of me?' she said.

'Why, information!' said the fetch. 'In the first place, my neighbours. How little one knows them, after all! We have met times beyond counting, at private balls and public functions and who knows what else. But on such occasions, one sees nothing beyond the appearance. Ladies and gentlemen all! Their lives wholly predictable! Their concerns identical! But one sees nothing of what may lie behind the façade.' He pointed one long, thin finger at Bess. 'But a servant sees all. Is that not the truth?'

'Aye,' said Bessie promptly. 'My former masters'd be shocked indeed if they knew the half of it.'

'Your former masters,' repeated Grunewald's imposter, in a thoughtful tone.

Bess wondered if the fetch was poorly informed, and decided to assist. 'I am in no hurry to return to Hapworth!' she said, with a strong shudder. 'The Adair family! So respectable, at least on the face of it!'

Grunewald-the-fetch nodded slowly. 'That is precisely the perspective I require. How does such a family behave in private?' He sat forward a little, his bright green eyes burning with eagerness. 'You have seen strange behaviour in that house, perhaps? Something out of place for a huma—for a high-ranking family? Or perhaps their guests! For is it not the case that they are a popular family, and much visited by their neighbours?'

Bess absorbed these questions, her mind working quickly to

discover the reason the fetch had for asking. She could not, as yet, guess at it; but the substitution of high-ranking for the word human offered her a hint. Was he looking for signs of some heritage other than human within the Adair family? It did not surprise her to imagine that others besides Mrs. Aylfendeane may have ancestors of Aylfenhame about which they might be ignorant. But why should this probable sibling of Grunewald's care anything for the ancestry of the wealthy families of Lincolnshire?

'I will tell you everythin' I know,' Bessie said, leaning forward in her turn. 'But I would know what you have in mind fer my reward.' She had imagined a new Bessie to present to this imposter; a version of herself far more grasping than she had ever been, with all the greedy, grand dreams which Hidenory had been so quick to attribute to her.

The fetch found this vision of an ambitious servant full convincing enough to swallow, for he smiled upon her with sunny enthusiasm – the kind of smile the real Grunewald would never think to direct at such as she. 'What is it you require, little Bess?' he said. 'Wealth? Jewels? Those may be easily bestowed.'

Bessie snorted in affected derision. 'Such baubles! Lovely – and then spent, and gone forever. No, I seek somethin' longer lastin'. I want a place at Court. A high position, if you follow me.' She smiled in predatory fashion, allowing her eyes to glitter with a calculation she had never felt.

Grunewald looked her over intently. 'I believe I understand you. You shall have it, my Bessie, I promise it! Only assist me as you can.'

'I shall be mighty pleasin', I assure you.'

'Then you may begin. Tell me of the Adair family.'

Herein lay the tricky part, for in truth, Bessie had little to impart beyond the commonplace. Servants saw much, to be sure, but she had never seen aught of the Adairs to suggest that they may be harbouring secret powers, or in possession of any blood heritage save plain human. Nor could she muster a recollection of any of their guests that might betray a hidden link to Aylfenhame.

But he need not know that. Moreover, seeing as she could not, as yet, understand the reasons for his inquiries, she saw an opportunity to cast some confusion over his endeavours by giving a great deal of information – all of it false. She trusted that the fetch would be occupied for some time in investigating her lies, and by the time her falsehood was discovered — if it was at all — she would be gone.

So she told him of late-night meetings between Mr. Adair, the elder, and his son. She told of half-overheard conversations among the family, hinting at secret endeavours; and of hearing Aylfenhame discussed, at times when they imagined themselves unobserved. She spoke of overnight visits from various of their neighbours, and circulated rumours of strange behaviour and whispered secrets on more than one part. All this she liberally interspersed with ordinary scandal and mundane gossip, the better to season her lies.

The fetch listened avidly, and questioned her closely about each person among the neighbourhood that she named. When she had at last exhausted her creativity, he sat in silence for some time, tapping the tip of one long finger against his lips.

'I thank you, Bessie,' he said at last. 'You have given me a deal to think about.'

'Happy to oblige,' she said cheerfully.

He sat in silence for a minute longer, and then abruptly said: 'You were born here?'

'In Lincolnshire? To be sure. I never left it before, until I went into Aylfenhame.'

'And have you ever chanced to hear word of the Hollow Hills?'

'Me Ma used to tell of them, afore she died. The In-Betweens, they was also called. Not England and not Aylfenhame, but betwixt the two. They used to say as how, if we was bad, the likes of Tatterfoal'd come out o' the Hills and take us away.'

'A charming children's tale.'

'Ma expected to scare me, but that weren't what happened. I always wanted to be snatched away to such an excitin' place, leastwise until I grew older and realised it weren't real.'

'Oh, but it is,' said Grunewald with a strange smile.

'So they're sayin' now. Some folk says the Piper's lot comes out o' there.'

'The Piper?' The Grunewald-fetch sat up, an eager light in his eyes. 'Say more of that.'

Bess told him all that she knew, which was little enough – though she omitted any mention of the visit the Piper's Rade had recently paid to Somerdale. Her information appeared to be of absorbing interest to the fetch, however, for he sat in avid attention while she spoke, and the moment she fell silent he said: 'There must be an entrance hereabouts! I had suspected as much! What do the tales say of that?'

'Not a thing,' Bessie replied.

This reply did not much disappoint her audience, though he appeared briefly disconcerted. 'It is of no matter,' he said thoughtfully, and she imagined he was turning over in his own mind some scheme for the discovery of the entrance, if there was one. But what lay behind his interest in the Hills, and how was it connected to his curiosity about the families of Lincolnshire? Bessie thought furiously, determined to find some way of enquiring without seeming to; but before she could hit upon a course of action, she found herself dismissed, with another dazzling smile. 'You may go. But not far, Bessie Bell. I will have need of you again.'

Bessie briefly considered making a bid to stay, but she was unwilling to push her luck too far. So she rose obediently enough, and took her leave.

'You will find rooms prepared,' he told her as she left.

Directly outside the door there stood a brownie, who bowed the moment Bessie appeared. 'I am to take you to your room,' said the little creature, whose ragged trousers and waistcoat had perhaps seen better days some years ago. But he only appeared as a brownie in her right eye; her left revealed a goblin of Drig's height and colouring. Somehow, she was not surprised.

Bess thanked her guide and followed him up to the first floor. She had been given a large, sumptuous chamber, which pleased both the real Bess and the greedy, luxury-loving character she had assumed. But she did not stay long to enjoy her surroundings. As soon as the brownie-goblin had left, she ventured out to explore the house.

Her wanderings revealed nothing of note. Hyde Place appeared to her in the character of a typical mansion, with nothing untoward to interest her at all. It possessed a full complement of human servants and a number of brownies; those she saw appeared perfectly ordinary to her, and her careful questioning of some few of them availed her nothing. She could not find out that there was anything unusual going on, as far as the servants were concerned, and they seemed wholly unaware that their supposed master was any different. True, his return had been sudden and unannounced, but by all accounts they were used to erratic comings and goings and thought nothing of it.

Bessie could well believe that.

The Grunewald-fetch did not summon Bess again that day. He left the house shortly after sunset, probably to retrieve Tatterfoal and resume his night rides. She was obliged to resign herself to the prospect of an unproductive day, for a search of Grunewald's study and his library uncovered nothing of either note or interest.

But soon after she retired to her chamber, there came a tap at the door. Upon her invitation, it opened to reveal the same brownie who had taken her up to her room earlier in the day. He swallowed nervously upon beholding Bessie, and looked furtively around.

'There is… someone to see you, Miss,' he said in a whisper. 'Outside, by the folly.'

'Someone?' she prompted, rising at once from the chair in which she had arranged herself. 'Who is it?'

'It is the bridge-keeper,' he said in a still softer whisper.

Bess knew of the bridge-keeper, of course. Everyone in Tilby knew of the troll who had, unaccountably, taken up his residence beneath the little stone bridge on the outskirts of the town, and set himself to the task of collecting the tolls. But she had never before met him, and she could by no means imagine what he might want with her now.

She wasted no time in collecting her cloak and putting on her wondrous boots. 'Where is the folly?' she enquired, when the brownie seemed intent upon a hasty withdrawal.

'Behind the house, and over the ha-ha,' he replied. These directions were not so minute as Bessie could have wished, but the poor creature seemed overcome by the demands of the evening, and withdrew without another word. Bessie was left to follow his instructions as best she could, in spite of the darkness and the fog which had, predictably, rolled over the grounds as the night drew in.

But when she stepped outside, she saw a light bobbing in the darkness — faint and dimmed by the swirling fog, but visible. Bessie followed it, and soon discerned another, and another. A string of wisps guided her steps into the grounds of Hyde Place, and before long she found herself at the base of what appeared to be a tiny, ruined Greek temple which loomed, incongruously, out of the fog.

Beside it she encountered a still more incongruous sight: a troll vastly taller than she and broad in girth, dressed in a neat waistcoat and with a tall hat set atop his riotous curls. He smiled as he saw her approach, setting the two curled tusks at either side of his mouth twitching in a manner Bess found more than a little horrifying, and bowed to her.

'Bessie Bell, I presume?' he said.

'Aye, sir! I am come, by yer request. But what can you be wantin' wi' me?'

He gestured, and the soft light of the wisps winked out save for one only. That one hovered over the bridge-keeper's head, illuminating part of his face in a faint, eerie light which gave his features a most unpromising cast. 'Stay but a little while, an' I'll tell ye everythin',' he promised.

# CHAPTER NINE

*Aye, I paid 'er a visit! I were curious to meet the young lady, after all I 'ad lately 'eard. Besides, 'er friends were right concerned when they knew what she 'ad done.*

*She might o' thought 'er movements would go unremarked, but she were dead wrong. The moment she were off wi' the wrong Grunewald, I 'eard of it. I 'ad word from Drig an' Hidenory both, an' soon afterwards a deal o' people turned up at the bridge wantin' all manner o' conversation wi' me.*

*But I 'ave got a little ahead o' meself. I must go back a step or two, an' tell ye what 'appened afore I met the little maid.*

Grunewald was to be disappointed by the results of his endeavours with the hard-won fairy ointment.

At first, his plans had been remarkably successful. The news that the fetch had commandeered his house had angered him, but only briefly, for he quickly realised that the knowledge was of benefit to him. If he knew where the other Grunewald was likely to begin his ride, he could all the more easily contrive to catch sight of him.

And so, he was hidden in his own stables at Hyde Place as the daylight began to fade. He watched as his fetch strode purposefully into the stable block, stopped in the centre and lifted his head. To Grunewald's horror, the fetch gave a perfect imitation of the goblin-call he himself used to summon Tatterfoal, on the rare occasions when he had reason to use the beast. And Tatterfoal came at once, his wind-swept, storm-tossed form materialising in between one breath and the next. The cursed creature was docility itself as the fetch climbed upon Tatterfoal's back and rode away.

Grunewald had enjoyed two or three minutes of unimpeded vision, for the fairy ointment anointed the lid of his right eye. He studied that face; noted its similarities to his own, and grew lost in wonder that he could possess a sibling he had never, in all his long years, heard so much as a syllable about. Why had his father never mentioned that he had sired another son?

Or rather... a daughter. This realisation was slow to come upon him, but it broke at last, and Grunewald was left speechless with amazement. And admiration! For his unknown sister's talents at the masquerade far exceeded his own. It was more than merely adopting his face, though that took skill enough at the Glamour. His probable sister – or half-sister, he was inclined to conclude – mimicked every one of Grunewald's movements and actions perfectly, and appeared absolutely masculine in the doing. Grunewald was seized with a fierce desire to know this person; to understand how and why she had contrived to remain unknown to him; and above all, to build some form of relationship with her. He had lived long indeed in the belief that he was without family; since the death of his mother, and then his father, his loneliness had grown until, at times, he could scarcely bear it.

And all this time, there had been a sister.

Why had his sister been hidden from him? Why had she hidden herself? And why was she indulging in this masquerade?

He left his hiding-place and wandered the grounds, ignoring the rising fog; he knew the gardens full well enough to navigate them without danger. But he had scarcely begun to turn over this new information before he realised that it availed him little. True, he now had some confirmation of his earlier suspicions, but what did that achieve? He had partially answered the most pressing of his questions, but in no fashion that could help him. He had expected to recognise some member of his own Court; some friend or enemy or colleague; someone whose character was known to him, and whose goals he might be able to guess. But such was not the case. He needed a vast deal more than a knowledge of his fetch's true face to proceed.

This realisation brought a renewal of frustration. He had to get closer to this sister of his, but how? Her knowledge of his movements and actions suggested that she had him closely under watch, by some means or other. It would not be long before she was informed of his return to Hyde Place. How could he disguise himself successfully enough to deceive her? And how, then, to gain her trust enough to learn of her intentions?

He had not long ruminated upon these points when he became aware of a tugging sensation, as though some invisible force sought to extract some internal organ. It was an unpleasant feeling, but a familiar one. One of his trusted retainers sought him through the Darkways. He fixed his attention upon the strange sensation, and pulled. A gaping, dark hole blossomed in the pallid fog, and a small figure tumbled through it to land neatly on his feet.

'Gaustin,' said Drig, and swept him a bow.

Grunewald blinked down at his henchman in growing anger. 'I left you with a task, I thought?'

'Indeed you did, my Gent: Stay with Bess. I have not forgotten.' Drig inserted his pipe into his mouth and sucked thoughtfully upon it, his hands tucked into the pockets of his waistcoat. A lone crimson bubble drifted from the bowl.

'And?' Grunewald prompted.

'I tried that, but she is a tricksy maid to be sure. She has wandered off.'

'She is gone?' he said sharply. 'How?'

Drig stared up at his master, his dark eyes unreadable. 'She had a mad, capersome plan to go dancing off after your impersonator. She wanted me to take her into England — a request I could not, altogether, refuse. I thought, this is madness and my Gent will be vastly angered. But at least I will be able to render her whatever assistance is within my power.' He took another puff upon his pipe, and Grunewald had to stifle a desire to choke him until he came to the point. 'Only, I did not receive the opportunity to be of use in any degree, for she is gone without me.'

'How?' Grunewald repeated. 'Bess has no way to travel, save on foot, and I can hardly suppose she jaunted out of the palace alone. Or that you could not easily have caught up with her, if she had.'

'No, indeed,' Drig agreed. 'She met you.'

'She did no such thing!'

'I know it, my Gent. She encountered your impersonator, and I imagine nothing could have pleased her more. She is gone with him.'

Grunewald experienced an uncomfortable sensation as of his

heart contracting with sudden, fierce tension. 'Are you certain?'

'Couldn't be more so. Hidenory was there.'

Hidenory. Had she encouraged this madness? He would put nothing past her. But what was Bessie about? She had wanted to find the imposter? Wretched baggage! She had been a step ahead of him, and had positioned herself so as to do precisely what he could not — get to know the person who wore his face.

'She must be here,' Grunewald said, and he contrived to control his voice such that it barely shook at all. 'I will retrieve her.'

Drig tapped his pipe, and a second crimson bubble squeezed itself lazily from the bowl. 'I sent word to Balligumph,' he said, apparently at random, 'about her plans — and again when she dashed off with the fetch. He is gone to Somerdale, and wants you to go there.'

'Not until I have reclaimed Bess.' He set off towards the house at a rapid pace, heedless of the obscuring fog.

Drig trotted alongside. 'He also says as how it's likely she's at Hyde Place, but not to disturb her.'

'Mister Balligumph may keep his opinions to himself,' said Grunewald shortly. 'I require none of his interference, or anyone else's.'

Drig made no reply, though he kept pace with his master. 'There is quite the gathering assembling at Somerdale,' he said conversationally, as though embarking upon a wholly new topic.

Grunewald was not deceived. 'Good,' he said roughly. 'I shall deliver Bess there.'

He had almost reached the house when the pounding ruckus of galloping hooves reached his ears, surging without warning from the muffling fog. He spun about, just in time to catch a glimpse of a vast, dark equine shadow of Tatterfoal bearing down upon him, its rider bent forward over the horse's back and reaching for him.

He had not time to react. He was seized by a pair of strong, bruising hands and hauled aboard the charging steed. Then they were away, blazing through the night. Grunewald was tossed over Tatterfoal's neck like a sack of grain, a posture he found so undignified as to engender in him the most violent rage he could ever remember experiencing. He roared his fury, but so engulfed was he by his temper that he could form no words; he merely spluttered incoherent expressions of inarticulate anger, the more so when his abductor entered the woods and his head came into painful contact with a profusion of narrow, whipping branches.

Silence, brother, said a dark voice in his mind. So shocked was he that he fell silent indeed, and at once. Had the words truly resounded in his mind? Such arts were the province of sorcerers, and rare indeed.

And he had been named as brother.

'Let me up,' he snarled.

I think not, my dear, purred the voice. I have questions to put to you.

'I can hardly hold a conversation with you under such circumstances as this!' Grunewald roared, though his face was pressed against Tatterfoal's hide and he could not imagine much of it had been intelligible to his sister. He attempted to reach Tatterfoal, but found the horse's inclinations set against him. Even his own steed was more inclined to credit this imposter as the true Goblin King than he.

We will manage, she said. Her voice in his mind felt icy-cool and insinuating, and it resounded with two emotions Grunewald could recognise: a hint of smugness, and a bizarre merriment. Twice you have looked upon me of late. Did you imagine I would not observe you?

'I gave myself away, on the first occasion,' Grunewald spluttered, remembering how he had lost his temper and gone galloping after Tatterfoal. He struggled to right himself, but her hand upon his back pinned him in a fiercely strong grip, and he could not move. Her other hand roamed over his coat, dipping into his pockets and searching the folds of his clothes; she searched for something, but he could scarce imagine what. A weapon?

I can sense you, she purred happily. Blood knows blood. Does it not?

'I sense nothing of yours,' he retorted. But he lied. Somewhere beneath the rage, he felt a sensation of shocked recognition. Something about her felt familiar to him, in a fundamental and undeniable way; as his father had done, and his mother.

I also know it when you lie.

Grunewald gathered himself, and with a supreme effort of strength and will, he hauled himself upright, throwing off her grip. His first impulse had been to hurl himself from the horse and vanish into the night, but he no longer wished to do so. Not just yet.

Instead, he stabilised himself upon the stallion's neck and twisted to look at his captor.

'Where have you been?' he asked. It was merely one of a thousand questions he wished to put to her, and he could not have said why it was the first that spilled from his lips.

The Torpor took me.

The Torpor. Like dying, insofar as the one claimed vanished from the earth. But it more nearly resembled sleep, and those who fell into it could return.

Still, it was uncommon, in the ordinary way of things. After the Times of Trial, as the Kostigern's war had been known, those who had lost too much and given too freely had sunk into it out of pure exhaustion.

But others… the Queen-at-Mirramay had shown both mercy and ruthlessness in her treatment of those who had aided the one who sought to usurp her power. All of the Traitor's known supporters had been condemned to the Torpor, and as yet, none had been known to have emerged from it.

'Supported the wrong side, did you?' Grunewald almost spat the words into her face. 'And using my visage! How obliged I am to you, sister dear! You knew, I suppose, that the Goblin King has been remembered by history as a turncoat?'

He could see little of his sister's face in the darkness, but he heard her laugh, aloud and delightedly. *Such was my aim, and how well I carried out the plan! It is my gift to you, brother dear.*

That puzzled him, and some of his anger faded in favour of confusion. 'You hate me. But you know nothing of me; we have never met.'

*The Goblin King*, she whispered in his mind, laughing. She said nothing else, as though this ought to be answer enough. But Grunewald could make no sense of it at all.

He felt such a conflict of feelings, he scarce knew where to begin. On the one hand, here was one who had sought to destroy Anthelaena, and she repented it not at all. That alone was reason enough for Grunewald to hate her in his turn. And she had done more. She had, with deliberate malice, implicated her own brother in her machinations, thus damaging his reputation abroad for a century and more. There were those who, to this day, mistrusted the Goblin King as a trickster, a turncoat, and a fraud.

But she was also his sister. His sister.

'I would not have us enemies,' he said, though the words threatened to choke him as he uttered them.

We can be nothing else. His sister rode Tatterfoal with blithe disregard for the darkness of the night, or the penetrating thickness of the fog. She sat tall and straight, radiating an arrogant pride and a ruthless confidence which could not help but impress Grunewald.

But her next words renewed all his desire to throttle the life out of her.

The little human maidservant. She is to your taste. How like our father, in that.

Grunewald blinked. 'What.'

She is in my care, she continued with terrible satisfaction, and her approximation of Grunewald's own mouth curled up into a delighted smile. She will be perfectly well, provided you do not interfere with my endeavours.

Grunewald's lip curled. 'How brave indeed, to threaten such a one.'

I am what you made me, she responded. All of you.

Grunewald growled deep in his throat. 'Is that why you arranged for this charming conversation?'

No. You wished to know who had stolen your face, your steed and the trust of your people? Now you know.

Grunewald had no opportunity to reply, for she administered a swift, sharp tug to the back of his coat, and he was dragged helplessly sideways. He fell hard, landing in the half-frozen earth with a grunt of pain. Tatterfoal vanished into the fog, and Grunewald was left to pull himself painfully to his feet, spit the dirt from his mouth and wait for his dizziness to dissipate.

The moment he felt stable, he reached for the Darkways and pulled.

Nothing happened.

Grunewald stood frozen in horror. He took a deep, calming breath and tried again, with the same appalling result. The path into the Darks was there; he could feel it. But no matter how he strained to bend it to his will, it evaded him. He could not draw himself into the Goblin Roads; they denied him.

What had his sister contrived to do to him? By what sorcerous arts had she barred him from the routes he knew as well as he knew his own face? He was the Goblin King! He owned those pathways!

Fear, anger and disgust warred within him as he looked around, searching futilely for some identifying sign that might enable him to discover where he had been deposited. He saw naught but the looming, indistinct silhouettes of nearby trees and the same blank white mist he was growing heartily tired of.

Disgust won, and with it he began to feel weary. He was far too old for this. He chose a direction at random and began to trudge, tucking his hands into his pockets against the chill night air.

He had barely travelled twenty paces when he heard a vaguely familiar voice calling through the night. 'Show yerself!' said the speaker – a male voice, and with an intonation he thought he recognised. 'I can hear ye clear enough, though I cannot see a thing in this dratted—'

'Tal!' Grunewald bellowed. 'The Ferryman! Damn, man, but I am glad to hear you!'

Silence for a few heartbeats. 'Grunewald?'

'Yes! And before you ask, I am the real Grunewald. I will gladly prove it, if you will only extract me from this thrice-cursed fog and take me somewhere warm.'

The dark shape of a tall, slender man clad in an enshrouding great-coat blossomed out of the mist, and then Tal stood before him. Isabel's husband – once the pilot of the Ferry they had used to deliver the ointment – looked him over with grim suspicion.

'Ye'll forgive me, but I cannot help askin' meself what the real Grunewald would be doin' blunderin' about in the woods o' Somerdale when he could ha' simply walked up t' the front door.'

'Am I in truth near Somerdale? Tatterfoal grows, if anything, swifter with age.' Grunewald took hold of the third button of his great-coat and tapped it, whereupon it came off in his hand, and transformed into Isabel's jar of fairy ointment. He showed this to Tal. 'You brought this to me yesterday. Isabel, bless her loyal heart, had probably stayed awake three nights in succession in the making of it.'

Tal sighed and gripped Grunewald's arm. 'Put that away. Ye look unsteady on yer feet. Are ye altogether well?'

'Not altogether. Take me somewhere warm, ply me with drink and for the love of Gadrahst, feed me. I will explain all.'

Drig had spoken truly, for Somerdale bustled with company. Isabel was the first to greet Grunewald when he entered her house, and she was as full of solicitude and concern as he would have expected. She soon had him wrapped in dry clothing, ensconced upon the most comfortable chair before the drawing-room fire and plied with all the food and drink he could desire. Her aunt, Eliza Grey, was also present; a knowing, cunning woman whom Grunewald did not much like, for he always received the impression that she understood more of his thoughts than he would wish, and found them amusing. He found the presence of Sophy and Aubranael more to his taste – and Drig, who had apparently returned directly to Somerdale upon Grunewald's abrupt disappearance and raised the alarm. Some strange, half-heard noises in the night had sent Tal and a few of the estate's manservants out into the grounds, though they had not expected to find Grunewald returned by that route.

Neither had Grunewald. He wondered whether his sister had intentionally delivered him to Somerdale, for some inscrutable purpose of her own, or whether it had been mere chance. Either way, he was both frustrated and grateful for it in equal measure. Grateful, because he had the peace and comfort to think as he needed to do, and comforts enough to quell the distractions of hunger, weariness and cold that had begun to plague him; frustrated, because he had fallen in with the blasted troll's plan against his will, and Bess was left to all the amusement and danger of unimpeded interference.

These thoughts whirled through his mind even as he related the evening's events, in between bites of the cold meat pie and sips of steaming tea he had been given. 'I must return to Hyde Place at once,' he concluded, when all was told and all was eaten. 'I haven't a notion what can have prompted the wretch to entangle herself in this rotten affair, but she must not be left in my sister's power much longer.'

'No notion, indeed?' said Isabel, with a strange look at Grunewald that he had no idea how to interpret.

'None,' he said with ill-concealed impatience. 'Not that it is of any moment whatsoever, for the present. My focus must be on retrieving her from it. But I will… require help.' This last was spoken with distaste, for he was unaccustomed to needing anyone's assistance and had no desire to become so. But with his access to the Darkways taken from him and his steed stolen, he had no effective means of rapidly removing Bess from his house. 'Tal, I must entreat you to lend me a horse.'

Tal favoured Grunewald with a considering look, but he made no response.

A different voice spoke from the doorway, and Grunewald sighed inwardly. 'Hold yer horses, yer Majesty! We are as concerned fer Bess's well-bein' as ever ye can be, but I am persuaded that yer sister's got some nefarious plot in mind.' Balligumph stooped to fit through the doorway and stood just inside it, the top of his head almost touching the ceiling. Grunewald merely cast him a sour look.

"Tis a trap, Grunewald,' said Tal flatly. 'Surely, ye must see that.'

'She cannot trap me.' Grunewald's lip curled at the very idea.

'And yet, she appears to have barred you from the Goblin Roads,' said Eliza Grey. Wretched woman. 'Her power to affect you is not so insignificant as you imagine.'

Grunewald could not but admit the justice of these remarks, though it galled him. 'What is it you suggest, then, my fine folk? Shall I leave the thrice-cursed baggage in my sister's power?'

'Yes,' said Isabel. He stared at her, surprised, and she smiled. 'We must not forget: she is no unwitting victim of your sister's. She volunteered herself for this predicament, and for my part I found her to be a capable, intelligent woman of sound good sense. Whatever it is she is attempting to achieve, she may be relied upon to carry it off.'

'You cannot possibly understand how dangerous any sister of mine could be. A daughter of my father's! And I believe her to be a sorceress.'

'Nonetheless,' said Isabel steadily.

She exchanged a look with Sophy, who nodded. 'Believe me, Grunewald, we are concerned for Bessie as well. But Isabel is right, and Tal. To ride in now would expose you, or anybody else, to danger, and would disrupt whatever it is that Bessie has in hand. We ought to have confidence in her. And besides...' She hesitated, and looked at Balligumph.

'We need 'er there,' said Balligumph bluntly. 'No one else can get anywhere near yer sister, exceptin' as she wills it. Only yer Bessie has managed t' pull that off. An' therefore, only Bess 'as the smallest chance o' findin' out what yer sister's fixin' to do in these parts. An' wi' no information, we 'aven't a clue what to do.'

'But,' said Grunewald coolly, 'She is not a spy.'

Aubranael spoke. 'Believe me, Green, I understand your feelings.

If it was my Sophy trapped at Hyde Place with such a person, I would be half-mad with worry! But—'

'That is naught to the purpose,' snapped Grunewald. 'Bess is not such to me as to—'

'—but,' continued Aubranael with stubborn persistence, 'the ladies are right. Besides which, she will not be unaided.'

'As far as I can tell, she is stranded there with no help at all!'

Balligumph folded his arms and cleared his throat, a powerful sound which cut across Grunewald's next words. 'Savin' yer Majesty's presence an' all? If ye'd cease yer grouchin' fer a minute or two, I will explain wha' the fine folk in this room 'ave come up wi' between ourselves.'

Grunewald fixed Balligumph with a baleful stare, but he fell silent. He was virtually powerless to do more than object, a feeling which he did not at all like. He had little to do, just at the present, but listen.

'Very good,' said the troll with a toothy smile. 'Well then, here is what we 'ave fixed upon.'

# CHAPTER TEN

'Yer a mite too big for stealth,' Bess observed, looking up and up at the troll. 'I dunnot suppose Grunewald means to return just yet, but he will soon know yer here if he does.'

Balligumph grinned. 'I 'ave folk on the watch fer 'im,' he said comfortably. '*Your* Grunewald, that is. The real one is snug at Somerdale wi' Mrs Isabel. Mighty concerned wi' your well-bein', he is.'

Bessie thought this unlikely, and said so.

''Tis the truth!' Balligumph protested. 'We 'ad to restrain 'im, near enough, to prevent 'im from ridin' straight over here, fog an' darkness notwithstandin', an' bringin' you out at once.'

'By this I am to collect that you're in favour o' my stayin' put.'

'Aye. Ye've yer wits about ye, an' I'll not lie. We need someone to keep an eye on this Grunewald-lookalike we 'ave on our 'ands. But ye'll not be left to do it alone. I 'ave brought ye a pair o' friends.'

A glint of something caught Bess's eye as he spoke, but it was not until he reached the end of this speech that she realised what it was she saw: a drifting bubble, almost the same hue as the mist. Only the faint gleam of wisp-light upon the bubble's shell had alerted her to its path.

'Ahoy, Drig,' she said.

A deep chuckle sounded in the night, and then a greenish wisp lit up a few feet from the ground, revealing Drig's face. He, too, appeared ghoulish in the faint, sickly glow, and Bessie thanked her stars that she was of a sanguine disposition. 'Ma'am,' he said.

'That's formal. When did I become worthy o' "ma'am"?'

'When you threw caution to the wild winds in order to help our Gent. It's my belief that the *fetch* has an eye to the Goblin Throne, and I'd liefer not have to accustom myself to a new *Gaustin*.'

The Goblin Throne? Nothing the fake *Gaustin* had hitherto said had implied as much to Bessie, but she imagined Drig to be a better judge of goblin ways than she could be. She tucked that idea away, to be investigated as the opportunity presented itself. 'Yer Gent has a fine mess on his hands,' she said. 'And he is not at all used to cleanin', poor lamb.'

Drig grinned. 'He has had too much time to become bored, and boredom soon leads to complacency.'

Bess nodded in agreement. 'You said a pair of friends?' she said to Balligumph.

The troll held out a dark bundle by way of reply, and Bessie instinctively put out her hands to receive it. The bundle proved to be warm, and perhaps a little frightened, judging from the way a small pair of hands clutched at her. 'BessBess?'

'Derri!' Bess beamed upon the brownie in delight, though she did not suppose that her joy would be visible in the gloom. She would have resisted all attempts to compel her to admit it, but she *had* been feeling a little concerned. The presence of two friends, however diminutive, eased her heart and bolstered her resolve. 'But should you be here?' she said to the brownie. 'Tisn't a lark, Derri-my-darlin'! There'll be trouble if you're caught prowlin' about around here.'

'Little danger o' that,' said Balligumph cheerfully. 'There's no less than two witches in residence at Somerdale this evenin', an' they have worked a wily bit o' magic on yer friend there. Brownie she is in truth, but to those as may feel suspicious, she'll seem a goblin in disguise. Such as the rest o' the fae-folk at Hyde Place.'

All the brownies hereabouts were goblins cloaked in Glamour? Bessie was not much surprised at it.

'I couldn't stay at Somerdale!' said Derritharn. 'Not when I knew you was here, and alone!'

Bessie was touched. 'You're the best friend I ever had, Derri. I just hope I ain't leadin' us all to disaster.'

'Drig an' Derri will be yer extra pairs of eyes,' said Balligumph. 'Yer task, fer the three o' ye, is to find out all ye can about the new master o' Hyde Place, an' what's really afoot wi' all this play-actin'.

Drig will arrange to get word to Somerdale, when ye need to report sommat, or if ye need help.'

'I have a report to make at once,' said Bessie. 'I had some speech wi' the *fetch* already. She was askin' a deal o' questions about the families hereabouts, an' whether any have been showin' signs o' bein' other than *human*.'

Balligumph's great eyes narrowed. 'Which families do ye mean?'

'Only the prominent ones, so far. The rich folk.'

The troll grunted. 'I 'ave a notion in mind what that's about, an' I like it not one whit. Take this as a warnin', Bess: Grunewald reckons as how this sister o' his was a staunch supporter o' the Kostigern – ye know who I mean by that? – an' is but lately come out o' the Torpor.' He stopped suddenly, and blinked at her. 'Wait. Ye know the *fetch* is a lady?'

Bessie cursed herself for that slip. 'Aye,' she said, but did not advance an explanation.

Balligumph squinted at her. 'Ye'd best tell as how ye know that, lass. It may be important.'

Bess sighed, and fished her jar of stolen fairy ointment out of her skirt pocket. Balligumph's eyes widened when she took off the lid, and held the jar up to the light. 'How did ye come by *that*?'

'I, um. Grunewald… gave it to me.'

'The real one?'

'Aye.'

Balligumph mulled that over, and his eyes crinkled at the edges. 'I believe I understand.'

'There is somethin' else,' Bess said hastily. She recounted the rest of her conversation with the *fetch*, and the interest Grunewald's sister had shown in the Hollow Hills – and the prospect of there being an entrance somewhere in the county.

Balligumph had no theory to offer on this point. He shook his great head, and grunted. 'I know naught o' what that may signify, but I am glad t' know it.' He patted Bessie upon the head; the gesture was no doubt a gentle one, from his perspective, but Bessie felt it as three great blows atop her skull which left her ears ringing. 'Ye're already o' more use an' importance than ye know, lass. Bless yer stout heart.'

'I have one question,' said Bessie.

'Aye.' The troll tilted his head in a posture of absorbed interest.

'How vile a temper is Grunewald in?'

Balligumph chuckled. 'Viler than vile, though he's hidin' it well.'

'He'll recover,' said Bessie wisely.

'He had better,' said Balligumph, with no trace of a chuckle. 'He needs t' keep hisself sane an' thinkin' clearly.'

'Some would say as sanity isn't our Gent's strong point.'

Balligumph grunted again, but Bess could not decide whether the sound indicated agreement or dissent. 'Ye'd best get on inside,' he said, making an away-with-ye gesture with his enormous, thick-fingered hands. 'Yer Gent-as-says-she-is will be comin' back sometime, an' besides, 'tis growin' mighty cold.'

Bess permitted herself to be ushered back in the direction of the house. Drig's night-eyes served better, in this endeavour, than her own, even with the assistance of his greenish wisp-lights. They were cautious, on the watch for any sign that Tatterfoal and his rider had returned; but there was no sign of either.

Bess took her friends and co-conspirators up to her room, taking the precaution of keeping Derri under wraps for the present. She released the brownie the moment the door was shut behind them, unwinding the folds of the oversized cloak Derri had been hiding inside.

'Well, now,' said Bess, hands upon her hips as she surveyed her little crew of spies. 'We've a deal of work to do, and had best get on. What manner of plan have the two of you in mind?'

'Drig has been teaching me how to pass for a goblin,' said Derritharn, fastidiously dusting down the skirt of her ragged dress.

'And you have learned nothing,' said Drig in disgust. 'Stop *fussing* over that dress. It is worthless, and therefore, no goblin worth the name would feel the smallest interest in its cleanliness or lack thereof.'

Derritharn looked faintly injured, but she obeyed. 'We are to mingle with the fae-folk here,' she said to Bess. 'If they know aught of the not-Master's business, we will soon know it too.'

'I am to appear in the character of a turncoat,' Drig said, with an evil smile which chilled Bess to the core. 'I'll be in good company in this house, I imagine.'

Bessie spared a moment's pity, faint though it was, for any goblin found to have transferred his or her allegiance to the *fetch*; Drig would not be lenient upon them. 'And I shall work upon the *fetch*,' she said firmly. She ignored the look of trepidation Drig thought it necessary to adopt. 'I shall wait in the drawing-room.' She swept downstairs without awaiting a response, leaving Drig and Derri to find their way to the kitchens.

The drawing-room was empty, as she had hoped. She ensconced herself in comfort before a lively fire, determined upon awaiting the return of Grunewald's sister, no matter how long delayed it may be. But the hour grew so far advanced, and Bessie's tiredness so extreme, that she was at last obliged to abandon her plan, and retire to bed. She had some hopes of hearing something of Drig and Derritharn's escapades among the servants before she closed her eyes in sleep, but she saw nothing of them. She lay in bed, her sleep-dazed mind struggling to refine the details of her newest plan in Grunewald's aid. At last she slept, trusting to the morrow to bring her the chance to carry it into action.

Her opportunity arose early indeed, for when she appeared at the breakfast table on the following morning she found Grunewald's *fetch* seated before an empty plate, a fresh newspaper spread before him.

'Good morning, Grunewald,' said Bess as she made her way to the dishes spread out temptingly upon a side-board.

'Bess.' The *fetch* fixed Grunewald's bright green eyes upon her, in a scrutiny she found disconcerting. Determined to show nothing of her unease, Bess devoted herself to the acquisition of a fine breakfast, and took her place at the table with a pleasant smile for her host.

'I have determined upon giving a ball,' said the *fetch*.

Bess paused in the act of slicing through a hunk of ham, and blinked at him in surprise. 'That is a sudden idea.'

'Is it? But nothing could be more likely. A single man in my position, in need of a wife? It is natural that I should open up my house to my neighbours.'

Bess perceived that Grunewald's sister had learned something of the role her brother had been playing in the neighbourhood, and its implications. 'Are you seeking a wife?' she said carefully.

'I am as intent upon matrimony as ever my neighbours could desire.'

Bess chewed thoughtfully upon a mouthful of bread. 'In that case, it seems a mite strange that you waited more'n a year to make your choice. And that you require yet another meetin' wi' these folk before you can decide upon who to ask. Have you not met them times enough already?'

The *fetch* frowned. 'I am indecisive.'

Bessie shook her head. 'That will not do, I am afraid. You'll be needin' a much more convincin' tale.'

'A tale?' A dangerous note entered the *fetch*'s tone.

'Aye.' Bess finished her eggs, and took a sip of tea. 'You should know somethin', afore we waste any more of each other's time.'

Grunewald-the-*fetch* sat back in his chair and directed such a perfect mimicry of his sceptical, incredulous look at Bessie that she felt a hint of doubt: was this indeed *not* Grunewald? But the evidence of her anointed left eye reassured her. Gracious, but the woman was a skilled actress.

'I am perfectly aware that you ain't Grunewald,' said Bess, looking the *fetch* squarely in the eye.

This was a gamble. Bessie had thought long and deeply about her predicament, and what she hoped to achieve. She had concluded two things: firstly, that to expect to live in the same house with the *fetch* for an unknowable period without ever once giving away the extent of her knowledge was unrealistic. She was but human, and by no means immune to error.

Secondly, Balligumph's notions agreed with her own. She needed to win information from Grunewald's impersonator, but it would be difficult indeed to do so whilst they were both maintaining a pretence. She must contrive a way to persuade Grunewald's sister to trust her — and subsequently, to confide in her. Even a very little confidence might make a significant difference.

But to deliberately cut through the deceit and expose the full extent of her knowledge was dangerous, and she knew it. How would the *fetch* react? Would she accept Bess's potential usefulness as a confederate, or would she find her too knowing, and remove her?

'I might ask,' said the *fetch* after a long silence, 'how it is that you came to discover that.'

'We had an agreement, you see,' said Bess apologetically. 'Grunewald and me. He was to give a sign, when he saw me, and I'd know it for him.'

'Ah.' The *fetch* gazed at Bess, narrow-eyed, and quietly closed the newspaper. 'You have given away your advantage in informing me, have you not? What can you mean by it?'

'Grunewald thinks you are after his throne.'

'Does he.'

'Are you?'

The fine red eyebrows rose, and Bess found herself subjected to a display of derision. 'You imagine I shall take you into my confidence, do you? I wonder why.'

Bess finished her meal, and pushed away her plate. 'The fact is,' she said with a confiding air, 'I have a fancy to rise in the world. 'Tis tiresome in the extreme, cleanin' up after the important folk.'

'You would like to be one of them, I suppose? Wouldn't we all.'

'I would. But Grunewald ain't likely to oblige me; not wi' my background.'

To her surprise, Bessie detected a flicker of emotion; something she had just said had touched the *fetch* more deeply than she had anticipated. But it was gone, too swiftly for her to identify what it had been. 'And?' said the *fetch*. 'I suppose you have some manner of service to offer me, in exchange for later favours.'

'I can help you wi' Grunewald, if you want him out of the way. Any trap needs bait.'

The *fetch* considered this for so long, and so silently, that Bessie's confidence began to bleed away. If her gambit had failed, she was likely to be in trouble. How undesirable, for Grunewald to regain possession of his house only to find naught left of Bessie but an unpleasant smear upon the carpet. That would be embarrassing.

But the *fetch* did not obliterate Bessie. 'If you deliver Grunewald, I shall see you richly rewarded.'

Bessie breathed again. 'I look forward to the fruits of your good favour. But there is more yet that I can do fer you. This ball you mentioned. What are you fixin' to achieve?'

Suspicion crept back into the *fetch*'s face, and he frowned.

'I dunnot need details,' Bessie hastened to add, with a wave of her hand. 'Just a notion as to what yer wishin' to get out of it.'

'I have been riding around the country in hopes of finding … something of importance. It occurs to me that the search may proceed more quickly if I bring the objects of importance to *me*. And happily, I have a fine, large house to accommodate the process.'

'Ah. So it is a large gatherin' of yer neighbours you're wantin'. The more, the merrier?'

'Among the families of breeding, certainly. What I seek is unlikely to be discovered among the low-born.'

'What you're wantin' is a grand society event, then, but it won't do to put it about that you're seekin' a wife. Mr. Green came here more'n a year ago, wi' another young man, and a finer pair o' bachelor gents you can scarce imagine. The whole town was wild for them for months together; aye, and folk far beyond as well. But Mr. Stanton left, and Mr. Green… well, he is still a bachelor. The mamas hereabouts gave up on *him* long ago.'

'You have some alternative idea?'

'If there is one thing folk love more'n wealthy bachelors,' said Bessie, choosing her words carefully, 'it's a prospective wedding. Supposin' Mr. Green lived more'n a year in these parts and overlooked every last one of the proper young ladies as was thrown in his way – only to become engaged at last!'

Grunewald's leaf-green eyes narrowed. 'Engaged?'

'There is nowt to pique the interest of yer neighbours like a sudden engagement.'

'I see. And to whom am I to engage myself?'

Bessie smiled. 'You may Glamour me into any role you choose.' She thought for a moment, and then added, 'Or not.'

'Engage myself to a servant? I would attract the contempt of all my neighbours, I suppose.'

'Which would do nothin' good to Mr. Green's reputation,' said Bessie with a smile. 'Derision you would certainly face, but also curiosity. They'd shun Mr. Green for certain, but first, they'd be fallin' over themselves to get a look at the schemin' wench as had contrived to catch him. Give 'em somethin' to interest them together wi' a nice scandal, and you'd be sure of bringin' everyone to yer house in short order.'

'And it would do you no harm whatsoever, would it?' said the *fetch*. 'What a coup for you!'

'It would amuse me more'n a little,' Bessie allowed. 'And it gives you a fine reason to hold a ball here, at short notice, when Mr. Green ain't never done so before.'

'An engagement ball.' The *fetch* stared unseeingly at the wall for some moments, and Bessie waited in mild trepidation for the result of her gambit. 'Very well,' came the decision at last, and Bess's heart leapt. 'You will assist me to the names and directions of all of the worthier families in these parts.'

'I dunnot know all the directions, but names I can do.'

'Let us begin at once. The invitations must be sent immediately, for I will brook no delay.' He rose from the table and left the room, motioning for Bessie to follow. She went with him to the library, whereupon he produced sheets of paper and a pen and said to Bess: 'Names.'

Bessie began with the Adairs. Having lived in Tilby for most of her life, and worked at more than one house in the neighbourhood, she was well supplied with information as to the inhabitants the *fetch* sought to meet. Indeed, her knowledge stretched farther abroad even than she had anticipated, and the task took half an hour to complete.

When at last her recollections ran dry, the *fetch* set down his pen and surveyed the long list with satisfaction.

'Word will spread,' Bess predicted. 'And more will come, even wi' no proper invitation.'

'Very good.' The *fetch* folded the list, and placed it inside a pocket of his waistcoat. 'You prove useful, thus far. Continue to please me.'

He left the room without another word, and Bessie enjoyed the pleasure of breathing freely for the first time that morning.

# CHAPTER ELEVEN

Grunewald sat in the parlour at Somerdale. The morning was but barely advanced, and he was not at all accustomed to such early hours. That must account for his being so out of humour.

Or perhaps it was the disobliging way in which his thoughts *would* keep straying to the wretched creatures who had taken up residence in his house. He could not account for the existence of a sister he had hitherto known nothing of; and Bessie's behaviour was no less unfathomable! He experienced the unsettling feeling of being wildly out of control: of his house, his connections, his kingdom and (in short) his entire life. It was as though a carpet had been abruptly pulled from beneath his feet, and all he had been able to do in response was tumble, helpless, to the ground. Whereupon every person of his acquaintance had taken an offensive delight in stepping upon him.

The one advantage to early rising, he reflected, was the peace and quiet it afforded, for few stirred at such an hour. It provided such an excellent opportunity for uninterrupted brooding.

He had scarcely formed this thought when the door opened, and Sophy stepped in. He ought, he decided at once, to have ventured out into the gardens, and accepted the soaking he would receive in consequence. A little rain would, in all likelihood, be less irritating to his nerves.

'It appears we are to congratulate you, Grunewald,' said Sophy, and waved a neat ivory-coloured card in his direction.

'I have not the pleasure of understanding you,' he said.

His tone could not deter Sophy. 'Why, you were the unhappiest of men! So long a bachelor! Could anything be more dispiriting? But now you are to satisfy the dearest wishes of *all* your friends.' She held out the card, and he took it, conscious of a sensation of deepest foreboding.

A few seconds' perusal was enough. The Aylfendeanes of Somerdale (and their guests) were invited to present themselves at Hyde Place on the evening of the thirty-first of October, in order to join with Mr. Green in celebrating his recent engagement.

Nothing else was said.

Grunewald suffered an almost overpowering desire to tear the invitation into pieces at once, and possibly to burn them. Before he could enact this terrible destruction upon the unoffending paper, he quickly handed it back.

'I look forward,' he said with forced calm, 'to meeting the lady I am to marry.'

'Indeed!' said Sophy, and fell into an armchair. 'It is to be hoped that she is a congenial young woman, and not *too* ill-favoured. Shall you object very much to an unusually prominent nose? In your situation – so long unwed! – you must not expect to carry off any great matrimonial prize.'

'I imagine I am to find her on the thin side, dark of hair and possessed of remarkably poor grammar.'

Sophy's eyes twinkled merriment at him. 'Yes, it must of course be Bess's doing. I wonder what her plan can be!'

'To cause as much trouble as possible,' said Grunewald shortly.

'I am sure it would amuse her very greatly if it did. But she has been clever. Here is precisely the opportunity for which we did not dare hope! In two days' time, we may see for ourselves what goes on at Hyde Place, and determine how we are to proceed. We may even succeed in taking some form of action against your sister, and liberating our Bess and your house at the same time.'

Grunewald had no response to offer. If Bessie's motive was unclear, his sister's was still more so. What could she intend by throwing open the doors of his house, and employing all possible means of inducing the entire neighbourhood to visit her there? Sophy's mood was sanguine, and her lively mind saw much to amuse her. But Grunewald felt too much foreboding to join in her merriment.

Did she indeed seek to claim the Goblin Throne? The possibility had crossed his mind more than once. Her commandeering of Tatterfoal, and her influence over the Darkways, both suggested it; and he had reason to believe that she had successfully subverted some of his people. That he was watched whenever he ventured to Aviel, he did not doubt.

But if it was his throne that she desired, why had she not made any direct move to claim it? He no longer doubted that she could mount a significant bid to depose him, if she chose, and he would be sorely pressed to defend his claim. But she had not.

And there remained the question of Tatterfoal. If Balligumph was correct, she had been riding across Lincolnshire, and perhaps beyond, in an attempt to wake others from the Torpor; fellow supporters of the Kostigern, most likely. People that he, and Balligumph, and Lyrriant, would rather not welcome back to wakefulness. But to what end?

The problem was a tangled one, and this latest move on his sister's part aided him but little in discerning her purpose. Sophy wandered away again, with a view to sharing the news with the rest of the household. After her departure, Grunewald sat for some time in thought, but with little result. He had not yet information enough to guess at his sister's mind; he must simply wait, for the present, in hopes that the spies they had inserted into Hyde Place would be able to bring more useful reports.

But to sit and wait while others exerted themselves on his behalf was intolerable. Worse, when the one who strove for his information was Bess. She should not be facing his sister alone – or at all, if he had his wish.

This decided, he rose at once and went in search of Isabel's husband. Contriving to speak with him alone was harder than he had anticipated, for it seemed as though the whole household was on the watch for signs of rebellion on Grunewald's part, and his desire to have a word with the master of the house drew suspicion upon him at once. It required all of his verbal dexterity to allay the suspicions of his fellow prisoners – no, no, *guests* – at Somerdale, and carry Tal away to the Orangery, which few had cause to visit at this time of year.

This accomplished, he proceeded to justify every one of his hosts' suspicions by immediately entreating Tal's assistance.

'I am worn half-mad with waiting,' he said without preamble. 'Tell me, man. Were it you in my position, could you sit and drink tea and merely *hope* that all is not badly amiss elsewhere?'

Tal sighed, and sank into a chair. 'Yes,' he said bluntly. 'But only because I was forced to. How do ye imagine I felt, only a few months ago? Knowin' that my Isabel was out somewhere in Aylfenhame, seekin' the means t' free me from a bindin' curse, an' without my aid? Considerin' my history, I could scarcely hope that she could contrive t' find my name without facin' *some* manner o' danger on my behalf. But I could do nothin', and go nowhere. I have never experienced such frustration – or such *anxiety* — in the whole course o' my life. Not even in the midst o' the conflict.'

Grunewald nodded. 'In war, at least you were able to take a proper course of constructive action.'

'Indeed. An' I dared not even show my fear, in case I should alarm Isabel an' make her burdens the greater.' A faint, crooked smile drifted across Tal's face. 'I had been hopin' ye would not think to ask my aid.'

'Unfortunately, I imagined that you would be unable to refuse me.'

'Though I fully understand the concerns o' my wife, I cannot leave you in such a predicament. What would ye have me do?'

'Little enough. I must see Bess, and to Hyde Place I go. But if you would make some excuse for yourself, and take my place for an hour or two, I should appreciate it very much. I can make you look like me.'

Tal nodded thoughtfully. 'But this is not merely to allay the concerns of Isabel and Sophy?'

'In part, but not wholly. I credit my sister with admirable guile, and considerable forethought. She has had me watched at Aviel for days, and I think it not unlikely that she may have eyes upon Somerdale as well. Eyes upon *me*, in short, wherever I may go. If she is to receive reports upon my whereabouts, I would like her to hear that I have remained comfortably shut up at Somerdale this whole morning.'

Tal readily agreed to this, and the business was soon accomplished. Grunewald left Tal ensconced in his former chair in the best parlour, scowling at a newspaper spread over his lap with every appearance of impatience and ill-humour.

Grunewald, meanwhile, let dissipate the vision of the pale, red-haired man he usually wore, and wove a new Glamour. He gave himself the weather-beaten appearance of a country squire much addicted to outdoor pursuits, together with a bulbous nose, twinkling grey eyes and a shock of greying brown hair. His garments became of the well-worn, practical variety adopted by such men, and he imagined a weather-defying hat for his head.

Thus equipped, he stole a horse from the Somerdale stables and set out for Hyde Place.

The morning was not yet far advanced, and he met few upon the roads. Rain drizzled unhelpfully upon him throughout the journey, for the sky was thick and grey with ill-promise; but he ignored these conditions, and rode with swift purpose to the house which, until recently, he had called his own. Less than twenty minutes' riding at a steady pace brought him to the handsome building he had grown to love, and he rode straight around to the stables at the rear and dismounted.

The place felt different to his senses, in some indefinable way. It was not so welcoming as it had been, though not precisely hostile either. Merely... strange.

He stepped into an empty stall within the stables, and adjusted his Glamour once more. A few moments later, a footman stepped out into the courtyard behind Hyde Place. He was a youthful, energetic lad with perhaps only twenty years behind him. His name was Matthew, and his semblance was usually adopted by one of Grunewald's most trusted retainers.

Grunewald-as-Matthew stepped into the house and walked quickly through the servants' quarters, as though employed upon some urgent errand. The cook aimed a somewhat waspish comment at him as he went past, which told him much, though he did not stop to converse with her. Grisha — shrouded in the semblance of a middle-aged, blonde-haired woman of comfortable size — was, under ordinary circumstances, a patient and good-tempered goblin of the Tykal tribe. That she could speak so to the person she thought to be Haglan, a fellow of her tribe and a friend of many decades, spoke of significant unease on her part. She knew, then, that something was amiss at Hyde Place, though perhaps she did not yet understand that her master's place had been taken by another. If his sister could fool

Tatterfoal, she could certainly fool Grisha.

Having successfully navigated the servants' quarters, Grunewald stepped out into the main part of the house – and paused. Where could he expect to find Bess? And where was his cursed sister? He ought to avoid the latter, until he had successfully removed Bessie. *Then* he may proceed with the second part of this morning's plan: that of ousting the pretender. He would take a great deal of pleasure in it.

His dilemma was resolved upon stepping into the great hall. He heard, faintly but distinctly, the sounds of somebody singing from the floor above. The voice was low and female, and he knew at once that it must be Bessie – though he could not have said how. He followed the song up the grand stairs and into the left wing of the house, and into the drawing-room. He paused on the threshold long enough to establish that she was indeed alone, and then he entered the room.

Bessie sat in the window with a pile of fabric in her lap. She was making a creditable appearance of sewing, like any good young lady of breeding, though he discerned at once that she had not set a single stitch of it herself. She was really employed in watching the front of the house, for the window overlooked the main gates. She was dressed in a gown he had not seen before: green velvet with a high collar of gold silk, and matching underskirts. It was almost of the present fashions in England, but not quite. Her abundant black hair was loose about her face, which most definitely did *not* coincide with English fashion. Her head turned as he entered the room, and she surveyed him with unruffled composure.

'Yer sister went away someplace,' she said without troubling to greet him. 'She weren't willin' to tell me her business, though I did ask.'

Grunewald felt peculiarly crestfallen. 'You know me, then.'

'Aye. Not that it ain't a worthy disguise.'

'I am delighted to win your approval.' He abandoned the Glamour that disguised him as Matthew, and resumed his usual appearance. With a slight cough, he added, 'Would you care to tell me what gave me away?'

'I would not.'

He blinked. 'That was, in truth, a request.'

'Or a command? I know it.' Bess grinned at him, and set aside her sewing. 'I have arts and ways of me own.'

'If it is to be mystery, so be it. I shall not entreat you.' Grunewald went towards her with his hands out, and felt obscurely pleased when she readily took them. He looked her over carefully for signs of anything amiss, but she looked much as he could hope: healthy, and whole. 'Very well. You have had a fine adventure, my baggage, and now we are to depart. Have you anything here you would wish to take away with you? You must fetch it, and quick.'

Bessie's brows rose. 'I ain't departin' yet. There's much left to do.'

'Indeed, and all of those things may be done by others.'

Bess took away her hands, frowning. 'Not so. Me and yer sister are becomin' fine friends, and Drig and Derri are makin' inroads wi' your servants – and hers. Most of 'em have no more notion it ain't you than Tatterfoal, but *some* are better informed, and they are workin' on those.'

'They may remain, if they so choose, after you depart.'

'I ain't leavin' my friends here alone.'

'There can be no cause for you to stay,' said Grunewald, beginning to feel irritated. 'In point of fact, there can be no purpose to any of your staying, for I intend to evict my dear sister. Her happening to have gone out this morning is of all things the most convenient, for she shall find the house closed against her return. And *you* safely out of the way of any trouble that may subsequently occur.'

'What foolishness. After all the trouble you took wi' chasin' her about, and findin' her mighty elusive at that. Now that she is fixed in one spot, and easily found, you would like to chase her off again? How then will you discover her purpose in these parts, or learn anythin' of use at all?'

'By other means.'

Bessie folded her arms. 'Oh? What might those be?'

Grunewald had no particular answer to make, but did not wish to own it. He folded his own arms in mimicry of Bessie's belligerent posture, and stared down at her. 'Very well, ma'am. For how long do you propose that I should remain locked out of my own house?'

'One more day. Tomorrow night, the best and brightest of your neighbours will arrive, and we'll see what your sister does wi' them. And I have some hopes that Drig and Derri may learn a thing or two beforehand.'

She spoke with calm decision, a manner which defeated all of Grunewald's hopes of winning her over. Her arguments were not devoid of sense; indeed, she repeated some of the same logic which had already been advanced by the Aylfendeanes and Aubranael, and which had, already, dissuaded him from dislodging his sister's grip on Hyde Place the moment he had heard of it. But it chafed him, nonetheless.

He dimly discerned that the source of his discomfort lay in the woman before him, and her unauthorised presence in his house. If *she* were not entangled in the business, he believed he might leave his sister to reign over Hyde Place for another day, and with pleasure.

'I will agree to that, provided you return to Somerdale with me.' He spoke this decision firmly, like the Monarch that he was.

Bessie merely cast him a look of deep scepticism, and her manner displayed how thoroughly unimpressed she was by this display of kingly power. Grunewald expected a tirade of renewed argument, but instead she spoke but one word: 'Why?'

Grunewald opened his mouth, and closed it again. Why indeed? 'It is of no use to remind you of the trifling concept of danger, I suppose?'

'You thought nothin' of that, when you came here. Why should you expect me to be cowed, if you are not?'

'Because this is *my business*. It is my responsibility to resolve this problem, as the *Gaustin*. But it is not yours! Why should you expose yourself to all the dangers of a tangled problem not of your making, when the outcome cannot possibly affect you?'

She grinned at that, her dark eyes sparkling. 'I've never had such a fine adventure in me life. Nor *any* adventure.'

'I know your sort,' he muttered grimly. 'Never happy unless you are daring some danger, and risking yourself in some new and thrilling way.'

She laughed at that. 'Now, my Gent. Be honest. If I were some pliant miss as would allow you to shepherd her gently away to safety, and then sit meekly at home wi' her sewin', would you like me anywhere near as much as you do?'

He narrowed his eyes at her, which had no effect whatsoever upon her merriment. 'I cannot imagine where you received the impression that I hold you in any favour whatsoever.'

Bessie nodded her agreement, a dimple of mischief lingering in one cheek. 'Aye, for I am sure you often ride to the rescue of damsels you ain't at all fond of. Now, since you're here you may be of use to me. Yer sister left but quarter of an hour ago, and I was watchin' to be sure she was safely off before I go lookin' around.'

'Do you imagine I am yours to command, baggage?'

'When I am engaged upon the King's business, yes.' She shook out her hair, twin dimples of laughter appearing in her cheeks once more. 'You heard that we are engaged, of course. I want to discover what plans have been fixed for tomorrow evenin', if I can.'

Grunewald abandoned all hope of persuading her, and fell in step beside her as she made for the door. If he could not convince her to abandon her interference in his business, at least he was at hand to ensure that nothing disastrous befell her in the execution of her self-appointed duty. For a time. 'When you say *we*,' he commented in a casual way, 'to whom are you referring?'

'Me and Mr. Green. I suppose the two of you will decide, at some point, which is to continue wearin' his face.'

Grunewald halted upon the threshold in shock. 'You do not mean to *marry* this fetch of Mr. Green!'

Bessie sighed deeply, a sound full of weariness. 'You are tiresomely excitable, my Gent. Of course I ain't fixin' to marry him. Your sister'd never have it, apart from anythin' else. We are playin' a fine game of stringin' each other along, and who knows where it will end? But *not* wi' marriage.'

Grunewald felt curiously chastened. Excitable? Him? He had, for ages past, suffered under a degree of *ennui* that wholly precluded his becoming excitable about anything. Had he emerged from that state at long last, only to make a fool of himself by growing excitable about foolish things? What was wrong with him?

They entered Grunewald's library, a room which appeared to have been adopted by his sister as her headquarters, for it was much changed. Bessie went at once to a pile of books laid haphazardly upon the central table, and began to search through them. He joined her. The titles intrigued him, and he took up many of them as she set them aside. They were guides to Lincolnshire. Some of them were geographical in nature, filled with maps and discussions of the local landscapes. Others were volumes from assorted peerages, and the pages of these bristled with strips of torn paper serving as bookmarks. Flicking through, he noted that his sister had marked every aristocratic family within a radius of fifty miles of Lincoln.

'Has she invited all of these families?' he asked of Bessie.

Bess glanced over the saved entries. 'Aye. Made a great point of it, too.'

Grunewald frowned, and replaced the volumes upon the table. What could lie behind her interest in powerful English families? If Balligumph was right and her behaviour mimicked Lyrriant's, perhaps she, too, sought to achieve more than waking those long lost to Torpor. He had discovered for himself that more families than Isabel's possessed a hereditary link to Aylfenhame, and sometimes the powers that came attendant with it; was his sister, like the Piper, trying to discover such families, and awaken their sleeping heritage?

This explanation threw some light upon her behaviour, but not enough. Why was she focused upon wealthy, even aristocratic, families? What manner of special interest was she taking in the privileged few, and what did she hope to achieve by attempting to gather them up?

'You have no idea, I suppose, why my sister is interested in such people?'

Bessie shook her head. 'None, yet. I will try for more today.' She moved away from the table and began searching in different places about the room. She met with little success, judging by the dissatisfied frown which marred her features.

'Has she spoken of me?' Grunewald asked.

Bessie looked up at him. 'She would like to get hold of you, certainly. That is where I'm to be of use, you know. But I dunnot yet know why, nor what her complaint is wi' you.'

Grunewald sighed deeply, for he could no longer avoid acknowledging to himself the usefulness of Bessie's venture. 'I wish you would attempt to discover it,' he said, with an unfamiliar feeling of diffidence. 'If you can do so at *no* risk to yourself. None whatsoever, do you understand?'

Bess smiled at him; not the mischievous grin he was used to receiving from her, but an honest, warm smile. 'I understand.'

He nodded and looked away, feeling oddly uncomfortable. 'You are not finding anything of use among these books, I collect?'

'She is too wily to write down anythin' of the sort I was hopin' for. I knew it, really, but I chose to hope meself mistaken.'

The door opened that moment, and Grunewald was instantly alert. He put himself between the door and Bessie, in case it should prove to be his sister returning.

Instead, Drig appeared. He grinned at his master, and made him so low a bow as to almost dislodge the towering plum velvet hat that he wore. '*Gaustin.*'

'Drig,' said Grunewald sourly. 'You have something to report?'

Drig eyed his master with amusement, as though he saw directly through Grunewald's unwelcoming manner to the cause. Which perhaps he did. 'Blood magic,' he said without preamble.

Grunewald blinked. 'What.'

Drig glanced at Bessie.

'It can be of no use attempting to hide anything from *her*,' Grunewald said — with, if anything, an increase of sourness. This display of ill-humour merely earned him an amused look from the lady, so he abandoned it with a sigh. 'Bessie is full worthy of our confidence,' he amended.

Drig's lips curved into a wry smile. 'Lovely. Well then, my Gent. Bess will have told you that most of your servants remain, only they are unaware that their master has been supplanted. Your sister has brought but three of her own supporters into the house, and your retainers are none too happy about it. And that's because we have got ourselves no less than two goblin sorcerers in the building, both with a flair for the blood arts.'

That surprised Grunewald. He thought fast, the pieces coming together rapidly in his mind. 'It begins to make sense,' he remarked.

Drig nodded.

Bessie had drifted back towards them, and now looked up curiously into Grunewald's face.

'The blood arts,' he said. 'You will not have heard of such things, I make no doubt.'

'Never,' said Bessie.

'That is because they are ancient arts – arts at which goblins tend to excel, by point of interest — and they have been long out of favour. The Kostigern made significant use of them during the Trials, and in the wake of that, few were willing to maintain the practice – or to own that they did. It is many long years since I last heard of them being used.' Grunewald began to pace, his mind full of new ideas which did little for his peace of mind. 'A great many things may be done with a person's blood. I shall not bore you by listing them all; I believe there is but *one* particular use which is of relevance here. With a sample of blood, even just a small one, it is possible to discover the blood links that tie families to one another.'

'Trackin' bloodlines?' Bessie said.

'Indeed.'

Incomprehensibly, Bessie giggled. In response to his inquiring look, she explained, 'You haven't spent much time wi' the grand folk if you ain't followin' my line of thinkin'.'

'I thought I had,' he replied, mystified.

She laughed out loud. 'In public places, no doubt. Ballrooms and the like. But in private, when they think no one is listenin', they talk about all manner of things which worry 'em a great deal. Do you have any idea how many secret *liaisons* are conducted between members of wealthy families? I cannot understand why, not considerin' how much they then have to fret and worry about who is the rightful son of *who*, and whether or not their legitimate heirs are their own blood or not.'

Drig grinned. 'Set a blood sorcerer loose among the elite of England, and much mischief may be had.'

Bess cackled with a vindictive delight which endeared her considerably to Grunewald. 'I would give a deal to witness it,' she said with high delight.

'But that cannot be her purpose,' said Grunewald. 'This is about *my* family.'

Drig and Bessie looked at him with twin expressions of inquiry.

'She seeks to prove her bloodline, and thereby, her claim to the Goblin Throne. It is *my* blood she seeks to draw, in order to prove her right to depose me. And if she is my elder, as she may well be, it will be difficult indeed for me to deny her right to do so. Furthermore! I am now aware, as I was not before, that my father enjoyed some form of *secret liaison*, as you put it, with some woman of whose existence I never heard of; someone, in all probability, human. Perhaps she was of these parts, which would explain my sister's choosing to settle here. She suspects that her mother was from one of these grand families, but knows not which it was. In which case, she need only use her own blood in order to discover the truth. That is why she has moved to draw so many of my neighbours to her; depend upon it.' His father had certainly possessed a taste for fine, sophisticated women, be they goblin or Ayliri. He could imagine it possible that he might have succumbed to the charms of a human lady, if she had been well-born, well-dressed and beautiful.

Drig exchanged a look with Bessie. 'But, *Gaustin*—' began Drig.

A fresh thought occurred to Grunewald. 'If I could be in possession of *one* sibling without being aware of it, perhaps there are more! The county could be awash in my half-brethren, for all I know. Perhaps that, too, is to be revealed upon the morrow.' The prospect did not displease him, even though it brought with it the threat of further challenges to his authority. He amused himself picturing these additional brothers and sisters that may prove to exist. Would they be people that he would like? But perhaps they would hate him, as his sister seemed to do. That thought depressed him again, and dissipated the happier flow of thoughts he had briefly enjoyed.

'Your sister seems interested in the Adairs, in particular,' said Bessie.

'Mm. Perhaps her mother was an Adair.' The thought was distasteful, but it made sense. That family was certainly well-born, and they were blessed with a great deal of beauty and grace. He could imagine his father, in a mood of particular loneliness, embarking upon an affair with an ancestor of Miss Elizabeth Adair.

It occurred to him that he still did not know his sister's name. 'Bear this in mind, baggage, when you speak with my sister,' he advised. 'She may let drop some hint in confirmation, if you are wily.'

'Wily is within my power. And now you had best take yerself off, my Gent. She has been gone some little time, and may return any moment.'

Grunewald looked her over. He could not detect any signs of unease about her, but he was learning that it was also within her power to dissemble; she would not openly display any discomfort, and especially not to him.

'I will return tomorrow night,' he promised.

'Ah! In another fine disguise, no doubt. I look forward to seein' what manner of appearance you next come up wi' for yerself.'

'I can have no hope of fooling you, it seems, and that destroys all my pleasure in the prospect.'

She smiled. 'I can pretend that my wits have gone to sleep, if it would make you happy.'

'Very.' He looked at Drig. 'Off with you, Drig. Find out more about these blood sorcerers, if you can.'

Drig bowed and withdrew, with a parting smirk over his shoulder.

Grunewald approached Bessie and stood over her, studying her face. He touched her chin very gently, ignoring the way her brows rose quizzically under his attention. 'I am grateful,' he said. 'Merely poor at expressing it.'

She inclined her head. 'I know it, my Gent.'

He tried again. 'You and Drig are achieving great things in my service, sour though I have been about it.'

'And Derri. Don't forget her.'

'And Derri as well. I shall find a way to express my gratitude to you all, in due course.'

Such an offer was not lightly made, and rare with him; so he was at a loss to understand why her face clouded over and her brow creased into a frown.

'I have said something wrong,' he observed.

She looked away, still frowning. 'In workin' wi' your sister, I am pretendin' to be a person I don't like. One with thought for nothin' but reward, and later advantage. I had been comfortin' meself wi' the reflection that there is naught of *that* wi' you. That I help you because... well, not for what I may later gain, anyhow. And now you are ruinin' that.'

'I never imagined you had any such motive.' This was not entirely true, for he had harboured some such notions early in their acquaintance. But he had soon got over that idea. Bessie constantly surprised him, and one of the many ways in which she did so involved her total lack of greed. Oh, she took pleasure in luxury; she would hardly be human, or mortal, if she did not. But she showed no sign of covetousness, no desire to gather it about herself by any means at her disposal. And she had never angled for any reward from him, or any advantage whatsoever. That was partly why he had been so wholly unable to account for her determination to involve herself in his affairs, for he could not see what she gained by it save for adventure. Perhaps, for her, that was enough.

Bessie did not seem convinced by these words, for she sighed, and made a shrugging gesture, as though to dispense with the thoughts passing through her mind.

Grunewald tried for a joke. 'I will be sure to treat you with the utmost callousness, if it will make you happy.'

She smiled crookedly at him, recognising the echo of her own earlier words. 'Very,' she said.

'Then we will consider it agreed.' He bowed before her, carried her hand to his lips and laid a brief kiss upon it. Before she could in any way react to this gesture he left the room, and soon afterwards, the house. He rode back to Somerdale in such a depth of thought, it did not occur to him until he arrived at the house that he had forgotten to restore his disguising Glamour.

Isabel was on the watch for him when he arrived back. He braced himself for a show of disapproval, or at least of concern; but to his dismay, she appeared to be in a state of distress.

'Oh, Grunewald!' she cried as he came in the front door. She came to him at once, hands held out. He took them with a frown, lightly squeezing them with an attempt at reassurance that she did not seem to feel. She gazed up at him with the air of a person who expects to be roundly chastised, her large eyes luminous with guilt and unshed tears.

'Good heavens, Isabel!' he said with mounting alarm. 'Whatever is the matter?'

Isabel bit her lip, and looked around as though to reassure herself that they were not observed. The hall was empty, but nonetheless she chose to lead him to the parlour and shut the door before she spoke. 'There is something I have not told you,' she began. 'Or, indeed, anyone.' She fell silent, frowning.

'It is a matter of some importance, I collect,' he prompted her. 'Do not keep me long in suspense, I beg you.'

'I am sorry. It is only, I am not certain that I was acting with sense in keeping the circumstance to myself.'

'It is too late to worry about that now.'

'So it is.' She sank into a chair and stared at him. 'You know that I went to considerable trouble to release Tal from the curse that bound him to his ferryboat.'

'I recall it with clarity.'

'Indeed. But I did not discover his name through any of my own efforts, or not precisely. All my endeavours failed, and I was at my wit's end; I had no notion where next to search. Only, it emerged that my journey had not gone... unnoticed. Someone, whose identity I could not discover, had become aware of my search and was watching my progress. And this person knew the name I sought. It was offered to me, in exchange for a promise of future aid...'

Grunewald began to feel a sense of foreboding.

'A voice spoke in my mind,' Isabel said, with a visible effort at self-control. 'I took the offer, of course; what else could I have done? I had no other means of releasing poor Tal from his slavery. At the time, it was easy to dismiss the prospect of the future payment as, in all likelihood, far off. I had no thought that I would be called upon so soon.'

Perceiving that she was too much disordered to speak with clarity or to soon come to the point, Grunewald controlled his impatience, but it required a strong effort. 'A voice in your mind?' he repeated, for the truth had dawned upon him the moment she had spoken those words. 'My sister? *My sister* gave you Tal's name?'

Her eyes turned upon him, but she did not seem to see him. 'I believe so,' she said. 'We were observed, it seems, when we brought the fairy ointment to you in Aviel, and the voice spoke of you as *brother*.'

'What were you asked to do?'

'Oh, dear. I am so sorry! I had almost nothing left, but I could not refuse to hand it over!'

Grunewald blinked. 'She asked you for fairy ointment?'

'Yes! She was most insistent about it, and really, considering that I had *promised* a payment for her aid, I could not refuse.'

This news bothered Grunewald more than he cared to show. His sister had been active in Aylfenhame some months ago; had somehow been informed of Isabel's endeavour, and had interested herself considerably in the business. That Isabel had been watched and shadowed during her journeys in Aylfenhame, and by one whose motives were so unknown as his sister's, troubled him greatly. That she had agreed to such a bargain did not much surprise him; Isabel had, by that time, been almost as much in love with the Ferryman as he had been with her, and she would have traded anything she owned for his freedom. But that his sister had been in a position to supply the lost name, when every other resource had failed, surprised him considerably.

'Isabel,' he said firmly. He was obliged to repeat her name before she could be brought to focus upon him, but at last she did. Her expression was woebegone; her eyes implored his forgiveness. 'You are not at fault,' he said. 'Though I wish you had confided in us before, I can understand your choice not to do so. But the matter is by no means as bleak as I see you imagine.'

Isabel blinked in surprise, and seemed to revive a little. 'It is not? But how can that be? I have been forced to support your sister, when all her efforts seem bent upon harming you!'

'I am obliged to you,' he said with a faint smile. 'I had no notion that my well-being was of such importance to you.'

That brought a watery smile. 'Oh, Grunewald, how can you talk such nonsense? Of course it is.'

He was surprised into momentary silence. Isabel had frequently behaved as though he discomfited her in some way, and he had most reprehensibly taken delight in teasing her as a consequence. He had long since assumed that he was not high upon her list of favourites, and endeavoured to ignore the peculiar pain that knowledge brought him. Had he been mistaken, or was Isabel simply determined to care for the well-being of every creature not absolutely known to be wicked?

Very likely the latter, he thought, knowing Isabel as he did. 'I am not much concerned at her possessing the remains of your ointment,' he persevered. 'To be sure, I had some hopes of going unrecognised at tomorrow's ball, and there can be no chance of that now. But I feel sure she would have discovered me anyway, no matter what disguise I chose to adopt. Therefore, her improved sight cannot much inconvenience me.'

Isabel began to look relieved.

'Consider further,' he went on. 'There is much good to be drawn from this. Firstly, we are given another clue as to her intentions. Mister Balligumph has previously posited that she may be seeking something, and this development appears to be in support of the idea. She wishes to be able to recognise someone that she expects to appear at her ball. Knowing this, we may be on the watch.

'Secondly, she has given us a clue, perhaps, to her identity. At present, we know nothing of her save that she is my half-sister; that she possesses some sorcerous ability, but we know not what it may be; and we theorise that she was associated with the Kostigern in ages past, but we have no proof of that. But if she alone, of all those you asked and searched among, recollected your Ferryman's name, then she must have known him. It follows, therefore, that he must have known *her*.'

'He will not remember! He remembers almost nothing from those years.'

'Perhaps not, but we may ask him. If he can recall for us even a little information, we must gain by it.'

Isabel nodded, and sighed. 'Then I must ask him.'

In order to ask him such a question, she must also confess to him that she had made a dark bargain on his behalf, and then neglected to tell him of it. He could well understand her distress at such a prospect.

Tal would forgive her, however. He would forgive her anything.

'There is one further ray of light in this business,' Grunewald said. 'You are released from the bargain that you made, and in truth you have been asked to do very little. I could scarcely have hoped for a lighter duty for you.'

Isabel's frown deepened. 'I hope that it may be so, but I cannot be sure. It was implied that I may be called upon again. I am not at all sure that your sister considers the debt to be paid.'

'She will be brought to consider it paid,' he promised grimly.

Isabel nodded distractedly, and rose from her chair. 'I had better speak to my husband directly,' she said. 'Such a duty cannot be too soon performed.'

He did not detain her, merely watched in silence as she departed the room. She left him feeling grim, troubled, and faintly melancholy in her wake.

And angry, that his sister should have chosen to so meddle with his friends. It was another offence he would bring to account, he promised himself.

He spent the remainder of the morning in thought, attempting to piece together the assorted hints and clues that they had assembled about his sister's past, and her recent activities. The picture did not become much clearer, no matter how he wrestled with the facts, and he was obliged at last to abandon the attempt.

But Tal sought him out, later in the day. The erstwhile Ferryman looked rather grim himself, and the habitual smile had gone from his eyes. But Grunewald did not interpret this as any sign of marital discord between him and his wife; no power in any of the worlds could accomplish that.

'I recall but little,' Tal said. 'But there are faint ideas – hints only.'

Grunewald nodded encouragingly. 'Anything. Tell me anything that you remember.'

'I recall...' Tal frowned in thought, and it clearly cost him an effort to fight his way through the cobwebs that had long clouded his mind and his memories. 'My Master, the Kostigern, had loyal supporters aplenty, but there were some few more favoured than the rest. More trusted. These I cannot remember with any clarity, but I do but faintly recall a female among them. Goblin blooded, I think? I seem to see greyish skin and white hair...' He trailed off with a sigh. 'Poor stuff, I know.'

'Not at all,' Grunewald said with a sinking heart. 'I fear you are on the right course.' The description, vague as it was, fitted his sister so far.

'I do not precisely remember her name,' Tal said. 'Nor cannot, in spite of hours of striving. But I think... something like Rasghah? Rathashgah?' He shook his head. 'That is all that I can offer you. I am sorry.'

'It is remarkable that you managed so much, and I think you have given yourself the head-ache in the attempt,' Grunewald said. Tal had been a beleaguered man indeed when Isabel had first encountered him; he had been nameless, lacking virtually all his memories, and bound to service as the Ferryman until his name should be discovered. That he began to remember anything at all must be considered a promising sign; a result, perhaps, of the freedom he now enjoyed.

Tal nodded, and rose from the chair he had sunk into. 'I do feel wearied,' he admitted. 'I had better take some rest before dinner.'

Grunewald did not detain him. He sat alone all the long morning through, lost in deep thought, and did not stir until Sophy came in to warn him of the approach of the dinner hour.

The day had been productive indeed, though in ways he had not been able to anticipate. But the only conclusion he had reached was that his sister remained several steps ahead of him; that he might guess at her intentions, but could feel no real certainty as to her plans; and that whatever may occur tomorrow night, it would behove them all to be prepared for trouble.

# CHAPTER TWELVE

'Tell me of my brother.'

The hour was far advanced, and with the ball to prepare for, Bessie had begun to think some time since that she would like to seek her bed. But the *fetch* had summoned her to the library after dinner, and had not yet permitted her to leave.

This would suit Bess's purposes admirably, if only the *fetch* would consent to entertain her invited guest with conversation. But she appeared to be in a brooding humour and sat in near silence, staring at the large fire that she had ordered lit.

And now, it seemed, it was to be Bessie who must talk. But the question intrigued her, and told her a little in itself. The *fetch*'s ostensible requirements for Bess had been satisfied; her knowledge of Lincolnshire, its environs and its families had been exhausted. That she was expected to serve some further purpose was clear enough, but Bess had been unable to determine what it might be.

'What do you wish to know?' she asked.

'Everything.'

And Bessie learned that as fascinating to Grunewald as his sister appeared to be, he was no less interesting to her.

She stretched out in her armchair, inched her feet closer to the fire, and began to speak of Grunewald's habits, his style of conversation and his treatment of herself. She kept her reflections general enough, unsure how much of his doings Grunewald would wish her to share. But the *fetch* was alert for any sign of concealment, and questioned Bessie closely and shrewdly. She seemed most fascinated by any part of his conduct which might be supposed to shed light upon his character, and Bessie was willing enough to expound.

She had not chosen to describe the occasion of her first meeting with Grunewald, for that obliged her to be open upon topics which reflected personally upon her, and upon which she would prefer to remain silent. But she was not to be allowed to escape. The *fetch* fixed her with a look of keen enquiry, her gaze raking Bessie from head to foot, and then said:

'But how came he to take up with *you?*'

This piece of implied rudeness was more than Bessie would willingly bear, even from one who imagined herself Bess's captor. She made no response save to lift her brows.

The *fetch* waved a hand. 'Gentleman do not wander the countryside in the company of servant girls. I have been long enough in England to know *that*. How much more can that be said to apply to a king! I cannot account for it. For he of *all* people to tolerate you; more than tolerate! I would say he was merely using you for some purpose of his own, but it is evident that there is more. He cares for you — sees you as a friend, perhaps more. How can this be?'

Bess took a moment to reflect. Here, apparently, was the source of the *fetch*'s fascination with Bessie; perhaps the true reason she had sought her company. But why? 'I do not know why you'd say that of him,' she replied. 'He of all people? He treats his retainers roughly at times, and I cannot respect him for that. But it ain't because he sees them as inferior. He treats *himself* roughly, and all about him, when he is in a certain humour. There's gentry enough as treats servants like they was dirt, but I ain't never seen anythin' of that in Grunewald.'

The *fetch* stared at her in wonder. 'How can that be?'

'I don't see why you suspect him of it.'

'Suspect! Hah!' The *fetch* drank down the dregs of brandy in her glass, and then hurled the empty vessel into the fire. The sharp sound of splintering glass made Bessie jump. 'He deceives you, somehow. He deceives us both.'

'Mayhap, but I cannot see why he would take the trouble of deceivin' the likes of me.'

The *fetch*'s eyes narrowed. 'You think him sincere, do you, in his regard for you?'

'Not in the least,' Bess said promptly. 'He calls me *baggage*, and baggage I am to him. But you are mistaken in thinkin' he ever meant to show anythin' that you are callin' *regard*.'

She spoke the truth as she knew it, but even as the words left her lips, doubts crept in. He had helped her, when he did not have to, but perhaps that did not mean much; though he could be cruel, she did him the justice to believe that he would not have ignored the plight of anybody in Bess's position. He had afterwards given her the gift of her boots, and a handsome and rare one it had been. But to the Goblin King, even the rarest and finest of goods could be nothing but trifles; she had seen that gesture as the careless charity of a man for whom luxury had become commonplace, and expense had long since ceased to matter.

These things, then, she could tentatively discount. But... he had come to Hyde Place. And if he was to be believed, he had come for her alone, because he believed her to be again in need of his help.

Where had that come from, if not some degree of interest in her well-being, and a willingness to promote it?

She put this problem aside for the time being. 'I cannot help thinkin', she said into the silence, 'that if 'tis insight into your brother's character you want, you'd be better off talkin' to him than to me.'

'You imagine it to be so easy.' The *fetch* spoke bitterly, her lip curling. It took Bessie a moment to realise that Grunewald's sister had spoken the words in her own voice, rather than mimicking her brother's. 'Are you lovers?' she added abruptly.

Bess's own lip curled with disgust at this most impertinent of questions. Forgetting the pretence of ambition she had previously adopted, she said, 'If you imagine me to be willin' to take up wi' a gentleman in exchange for his help, you are much mistaken.'

The *fetch* ignored Bessie's indignation. 'So it is not that, either,' she said in a musing tone. Her rage of a few moments before seemed gone, and in her mercurial moods Bess observed another similarity between the *fetch* and the Goblin King.

She seemed lost in thought, and it occurred to Bessie that she might be able to capitalise upon her odd hostess's distraction. So she said, in as conversational a tone as she could muster: 'What is it you want from him? Yer brother.'

The *fetch* shot a sharp look at Bessie, and smiled in a fashion which displayed too many teeth. 'What does any scorned and dispossessed royal sibling want, little Bess?'

'Power? Revenge?' Bessie guessed. 'To supplant him, mayhap. Or there again… maybe yer just wantin' his attention.'

'I want nothing to do with him,' said the *fetch*, with an expressive curl of her lip. She no longer mimicked Grunewald in anything save the stolen Glamour of his face, and it was strange to see the expressions and mannerisms of another imposed over Grunewald's features. Fascinated as much as she was appalled, Bessie watched the *fetch* intently.

'No?' she prompted. ''Tis a deal o' trouble yer goin' to wi' this ball, if it ain't to thumb yer nose at yer brother.'

The *fetch* waved this away. 'I confess, it amuses me to create trouble for him.'

'You are lookin' for yer family.' Something about the *fetch*'s bitterness brought this notion to Bess's mind. She seemed consumed by her resentment towards Grunewald, and yet irresistibly fascinated by him. Grunewald might be right in thinking that she sought to prove her blood relationship to him, and by now it seemed indubitable that his sister had her eyes on his throne. But that did not explain the ball. Disappointed by her goblin family, could Grunewald's sister be in search of her human connections? Could it be that simple?

The scorn in the *fetch*'s eyes quickly disabused Bessie of that notion. 'I know them,' she said shortly. Then she added in an undertone, 'As much as I ever wish to.'

What, then, were the blood sorcerers supposed to be for? That they were stationed here in readiness for the ball, it was difficult to question. Someone was expected to appear, someone with heritage that the *fetch* was in need of but someone whose identity she did not know. What was this person expected to do? Bessie wrestled with the problem, but she could not make it out.

'You wanted me to help you in trappin' yer brother,' Bessie reminded the *fetch*. 'I cannot help thinkin' you are mighty fascinated wi' him, for someone as wants nothin' to do wi' him.'

The *fetch*'s eyes narrowed, and she looked upon Bessie with malice. 'And I cannot help thinking that you lied, when you suggested that you might be of assistance to me in that. You care for my brother.'

Fine; Bessie had never been any good at dissembling. She folded her arms and returned the look, stare for stare. 'I had to say somethin' to get you to gi' me a chance.'

'A chance at what? Are you a traitor in the making, Bessie dear?'

'A chance at gettin' the two of you to talk to each other.' Bessie snorted. 'I think most of yer troubles are based on naught but misunderstandin', and I would be glad to see it resolved. For both yer sakes.'

The *fetch* rolled her eyes, and slouched in her chair with a palpable display of exasperation. 'Preserve me from peacemakers,' she muttered.

'He wants to know you,' Bessie persevered. 'All yer curiosity about him? Goes both ways.'

This sally was not without effect. Grunewald's sister studied Bess for some time in silence, with no sign of her earlier malice. Bessie read interest in her gaze, and maybe even... hope.

Then it was gone. Her face darkened into bitterness once more, and she shook her head. 'It is too late for that.'

'I am sorry for it.'

'Why?'

Bessie blinked. 'Why… because yer right, I do care about yer brother. And I have a notion I could like you pretty well besides, if you would stop wi' yer mad antics. As would he.'

This amused the *fetch*, for some reason, for that unpleasant smile spread across her borrowed face again. 'What a delight you are.'

Bess wanted to probe further, but she judged she had pushed her luck as far as she could; there was nothing more to be got from the maddening woman tonight, and she had already roused suspicion. So she rose from her armchair, saying firmly, 'I still think you should talk to him. But I am for me bed.'

The *fetch*'s eyes focused upon Bess, and she said, 'I would make a friend of you, Bessie Bell.'

'Would you, now? Why might that be?'

'For reasons of my own.'

Bessie shook her head. 'I made some show of seekin' rather more from the Goblin King than charity, but we seem to be droppin' pretences all around, so I'll tell you straight. As long as yer purpose is to cause him some manner of harm, then we cannot be friends.' She looked down at the vision of Grunewald, slumped in an oversized armchair. The pose struck her as dejected, which stirred a little pity in her. 'If it were not for that, I wouldn't say as it would be so hard for us to find some common ground.'

She could not imagine what she had said in that to cause offence or to invoke suspicion, but she seemed to have done both. The *fetch* sat up, and growled something inaudible. 'You are here for him, then?' she said coldly. 'Not for your own advantage, and certainly not for mine.'

'I never made any pretence of bein' here for yours.'

The *fetch* said nothing more, and after a moment Bessie quietly withdrew. The conversation had given her much to consider, though it had shed little real light. But Bessie now felt, that if she could only bring about some honest communication between brother and sister, much may be done.

But she had never met two such stubborn characters in her life. How could she possibly coax them to talk, when they seemed so irrevocably set against one another?

She was tired, but one task remained before she could rest. She summoned Derri, and had the little brownie pen a note to Mrs. Aylfendeane.

*'Tis my belief that the fetch is after her brother's throne, right enough, but how she means to bring that about I cannot discover. She ain't looking for her human family at the ball, at any rate. Grunewald says as the blood sorcerers are here to take a drop or two from him, but I doubt it, for she ain't a bit doubtful that he is her brother, and nor is anyone else like to be. No, it's something else. Someone important is meant to show up tomorrow, and the fetch has all her hopes pinned upon it. I plan to get in the way of her project, as I doubt not that it's something shady.*

*Please to bring plenty of useful friends tomorrow night. I'm thinking I will need the help.*

This she dispatched to Somerdale by way of Drig, knowing that it would find its way into Grunewald's hands before the morning. Then she sternly sent herself to bed. She would need her slumber, for the morrow promised to be a demanding day.

She could not sleep. Bess had never been disposed to worry, but the predicament she now found herself in was somewhat out of the ordinary way. She had taken it upon herself to champion Grunewald's interests, and she had done her best. Nor had her efforts been futile; they knew much more about the *fetch*'s doings and plans for Bessie's interference than they could otherwise have hoped to discover, and perhaps it would be enough to allow them to counter whatever scheme she had in mind.

But that *perhaps* haunted Bessie's mind as she lay in the darkness. Perhaps! For all her efforts, *maybe* was the best that she had managed to accomplish. She pictured Grunewald, deposed and forced to bow to his resentful sister. Injured? Perhaps even killed...

At length she was obliged to read herself a grim lecture. She would be of no use at all to Grunewald if she was worn out with lack of sleep before the ball even began, and what a wretched little cabbage she was being to so fret herself!

Having suitably cowed herself into submission, she slept.

And the day of the ball dawned.

The *fetch* woke earlier even than Bessie, and proceeded to embark upon the day in a high fever of anticipation; all her melancholy of the night before seemed forgotten. No debutante fresh from the schoolroom had ever looked forward to her first appearance with such an inexhaustible zeal, and Bess could hardly account for it. She did not suppose that the ordinary pleasures of a ball could in any way interest her hostess, let alone to such an extent. What, then, was she expecting to occur that could raise her spirits so high, and send her flying about the house in such a bustle of energy?

Drig and Derri shed some little light upon this question some way through the morning, when they contrived to appear in Bessie's room. She had been downstairs since an early hour, endeavouring to engage Grunewald's sister in conversation; for she had every intention of carrying out Grunewald's request, if she could. But every attempt was defeated, for her quarry barely consented to remain still for more than three minutes together. What she could find to so occupy her, Bess could not imagine.

At last she retired to her room, for some quiet reflection as to her plans for the ball. But she had not been returned more than five minutes before Derri crept out of the cold fireplace, and Drig sidled after her.

'We cannot stay long,' whispered Derri. 'We shall be suspected, if we are discovered here.'

'Or if we are long missed,' agreed Drig. 'All is bustle and chaos below, as you may imagine.'

Bess knew well the burdens shouldered by the servants upon the day of a grand ball, and this one was to be grander than most. On such days at Hapworth Manor, she had often been obliged to rise two hours early, and had not been able to seek her bed until long past midnight. 'I shan't keep you,' she agreed. 'What have you to tell me?'

'Mrs. Torig has had word,' said Derri. 'She is to expect several additions to the family party by tonight, and rooms are to be prepared.'

Mrs. Torig was the housekeeper. Bessie's fairy ointment informed her that the elderly, grey-haired lady with her soft-spoken ways was in fact a goblin, in all likelihood much more aged even than her human appearance suggested. She was a competent housekeeper and, Bessie believed, entirely loyal to Grunewald.

And she was to prepare rooms. That information was of interest to Bess. She had wondered before, whether Grunewald's sister had taken possession of Hyde Place purely in order to host the ball, and might afterwards relinquish it. But if she was fixing to entertain guests there, that seemed less likely.

'Is it known who these additions are to be?' Bessie asked.

Derri shook her head.

'Old friends,' said Drig. 'That is all I've been told. It is all that anyone yet knows, I think.'

'How many?'

Drig shrugged. 'Every room in the house not presently in use is to be prepared.'

That chilled Bessie a little, for it was a large house, and comprised a great many chambers. 'That had best be sent off to Balligumph,' she said. 'But I don't suppose either of you can get away?'

'I'll send a wisp,' Drig said.

'Good. I have little to report, meself, for she's as busy as a swarm of bees all by her own self. I cannot pin her down to any conversation.'

'We are having the same problem, with the servants,' said Drig. 'It's no matter. Keep your ears open, and be careful of yourself.'

Bessie could only agree to this, and Derri and Drig took their leave once more. Bess was left to her reflections, which were not much furthered by the news her friends had brought.

*Well, an' so the day came o' the grand ball! By that time 'twas all but certain wha' the fetch was up to – leastwise in the matter o' Tatterfoal. I reckon it all but certain, too, tha' she had a mind t' unseat her brother from the Goblin Throne, an' was fixin' to wake some o' her associates of old. She would need help to overthrow Grunewald, no mistake. He likes t' affect the appearance of a bored an' useless gent, but he ain't nothin' of the sort. None crosses the Goblin King lightly.*

*Whether she found them as she was lookin' t' wake, thas another question. I reckon she had, in point o' fact. Two o' the goblin servants at Hyde Place – them as Drig an' Derri encountered – were not long out o' the Torpor by then, or so I reckoned. An' thas what I made o' the news they brung. All those rooms to be prepared? The fetch was mighty certain of havin' a deal o' folk t' entertain. The ball was like to be a memorable occasion – an' mayhap a dangerous one. I made sure o' havin' as many o' my own folk attendin' as possible.*

Bessie wandered the house once more, late in the day, but to no avail; not a glimpse of Grunewald's sister did she catch. But when she returned to her room, she found that all was not quite as she had left it.

Laid out upon the bed was a fine ball gown. It was a deep purple in colour, a hue which Bessie found thoroughly agreeable, but in its fashion and construction it was odd indeed. It barely conformed to the prevailing fashions, insofar as it featured a high waist, a narrow skirt and short, puffed sleeves. In every other respect, it was different indeed. An overdress of purple silk floated over layers of dreamy, whisper-thin gossamer; the former was made from something reminiscent of butterfly wings, if such a thing could be possible, and the latter looked like the winds caught down and spun into gauze. The neckline – cut almost immodestly low – was adorned with gems that did not precisely resemble garnets, or rubies, or amethysts, but some hitherto unseen combination of the three. As Bessie drew closer to the lovely thing, she discovered that it even smelled delightful; an aroma hung in the air around it that she could not place, but it teased her nostrils with something dark and rich and seductive. An evening shawl of cloudy, silver-stitched gauze was laid next to it, and a pair of dark purple, silken slippers rested at the foot of the bed.

Bessie was very well pleased. She had nothing with her that would fit her for the ball, and had supposed that she must wear her own, ordinary gown and suffer it to be Glamoured. This was much better! She donned the luxurious garment with unabashed pleasure, revelling in the sensation of silk and gossamer against her skin, and the way the skirts whispered when she moved.

There was naught to be done with her hair. No lady's maid resided at Hyde Place, as Grunewald had no need of one; and Bessie, of course, had never had cause to learn the trick of arranging her own hair after the fashion of refined ladies. She merely caught it up loosely and pinned it, using an array of delicate silver pins she had discovered within her dressing-table. It was not fashionable, but her face and form were to be altered by Glamour, and so it could hardly signify.

But the hour of the ball approached, and Bessie saw no sign of the *fetch*. Nor did anyone else arrive to adjust Bess's appearance. The wan daylight faded, and chill night closed in; wandering the upper floors, Bessie felt grateful for the gauzy shawl, which proved to be more warming than it had any right to be.

When carriages began to arrive at the house and the great doors were thrown open to admit the first guests, she realised with a thrill of horror that she was expected to present herself as she was.

But not, apparently, just yet. She watched from the top of the great stairs, concealed from the sight of those arriving below, as the-*fetch*-as-Grunewald — but just emerged from wherever she had concealed herself – stepped forward to welcome her guests. There ought rightly to have been a lady of the house to perform this duty, but the *fetch* was either unaware of the convention or cared nothing for it. Mr. Green's reputation for eccentricity would be considerably enhanced by the close of the evening.

Bessie was pleased to observe that the Aylfendeanes were among the first to arrive, together with Sophy and Aubranael. There was no sign of Grunewald; if he still intended to come, he had chosen to appear separately from his friends.

More families arrived in a steady stream of guests. When there came, at last, a brief lull, the *fetch* looked unerringly up at Bessie.

Bess returned the bright, leaf-green gaze stolen from Grunewald, and made no move.

The *fetch* bounded up the stairs and stopped before Bessie. 'Will you not come down?'

'I am not ready.'

The *fetch* looked Bessie over, focusing in particular on the gown. 'You appear fully equipped to me.'

Bessie pointed at her face. 'All exceptin' that. Thank you for the gown, by the by.'

She received in response a dazzling smile, and a bow. 'What could possibly be considered amiss with your face?'

'The fact that it remains me own face, and no Glamour.'

'It is as serviceable a face as any I ever saw. Are you ashamed of it?'

'No!' said Bessie. 'But I have no right to be here, as meself. My former masters are attendin', are they not?'

The smile widened. 'You forget, Bess,' said the *fetch* in a low, purring tone. 'These fine folk are entering my world now, and the rules are made by me.'

Bess could not but admire the towering confidence of this attitude, but nor could she help feeling some scepticism as to its effectiveness with the cream of Lincolnshire society: gentry and aristocrats all, and well-used to ruling in their turn. Her opinion showed upon her face, perhaps, for the *fetch* let her satisfied smile fade into a frown.

But rather than turning autocratic, as Bess might have expected, and ordering her compliance, the *fetch* hesitated, and then said with all apparent sincerity: 'I need you present, Elisabeth Bell, and as yourself.'

It was an entreaty, an honest entreaty, and it surprised Bessie into speechlessness. At length she was able to say: 'But why?'

The *fetch* frowned more deeply. 'I know you are here for my brother, and I admire your loyalty to him. I do, though I think it sadly misplaced! But you are the only person in this house with whom I bear any *real* kinship. You alone can understand...' She left the sentence unfinished, shaking her head with a show of impatience and frustration. 'Will you oblige me? I swear that it will in no way harm you to obey.'

'I cannot understand you,' Bessie said frankly. 'How can I be said to bear any kinship wi' you? More so than your own brother?'

'It is a kinship of – of background and situation. Of circumstance.'

'You are no servant.'

The *fetch* merely smiled, rather wistfully. 'No. I was never that.'

Bessie shook her head in frustration. 'I need to know more, if I am to risk meself for your benefit.'

The *fetch* did not seem disinclined to confide further; she opened her mouth, and seemed about to speak. But a bustle went up below, a bustle of arrival. Glancing down, Bessie saw that the Adair family had entered the hall, with all the pomp and noise that could suit their consequence. The time for quiet conversation had clearly passed.

The *fetch* shut her mouth with a snap, an expression of acute irritation passing over her borrowed face. 'I swear it shall not harm you!' she said again. 'Remember: this is *my* world.'

With these words she was gone, bounding away down the stairs to return to her duties as host. Bessie was left to consider these inexplicable words as best she could, and to decide, if she could, whether or not to comply with the *fetch*'s request.

The decision was soon made. She could not help but fear the consequences of being recognised, by the very people who now occupied the hall below. But she would not cower in her chamber; to do so would be to agree with their categorisation of her as worthless. If the house's present host bid her welcome, then she had as much right to attend the ball as the Adair family, or any other.

Bess descended the stairs.

The shock, as she reached the hall and stepped into the Adairs' field of vision, was mutual.

On their side, it was the inexplicable surprise of recognising their erstwhile maid, dressed in magical finery and attending a society ball. Not that the elder Mr. Adair – nor, Bessie thought, his daughter – saw in the well-dressed, faintly fae-looking woman before them their former servant; she did not think either paid enough attention to their staff for that. But that Mrs. Adair realised Bessie's identity, she could have no doubt from the arrogant, cold stare she received.

And the younger Mr. Adair certainly knew her.

But Bessie's shock was, if anything, greater than theirs. For the fairy ointment that still anointed her left eye revealed something about the family which she could not possibly have predicted.

They were not all fully human.

No sign of other heritage was visible in the features of Mrs. Adair; nor, interestingly, in either of her two children. *There*, Bessie thought, lay a scandal for another day. But the head of the family was quite another matter. In Bess's right eye, he appeared to be of perhaps fifty years of age, grey-haired and dignified in the manner of wealthy middle-aged human gentleman. But in Bessie's left eye, he was fully Ayliri: tall and unbowed by age, his hair not grey but pale blond, his ears tapered and curling at the tips. It amused Bessie to recall her own lies to the *fetch* about the Adair family, and to realise that while the details of her fabrications may have been false, the substance was not.

Furthermore, when the *fetch* moved to greet him, she received the distinct impression that Grunewald's sister was surprised by what she saw – but not as Bessie would expect. She was… displeased. Something that she saw in Mr. Adair disappointed her expectations.

The younger Mr. Adair spoke. 'You have been imposed upon, Green,' he said, with sneering arrogance. 'That is no lady.'

'You have not engaged yourself to *her*, I do hope,' added Mrs. Adair, withdrawing her gaze from Bessie as though she might be contaminated by eye contact.

They received in response a stare so icy, so replete with all the disdainful superiority of long ages lived, of royal goblin blood, and of powers unknowable, that even the arrogance of Edward Adair shrank beneath it.

'How impertinent,' said the *fetch* at length, with a sharp, malicious smile. The *fetch*-as-Grunewald offered an arm to Bessie, who took it with a smile.

Mrs. Adair turned upon her heel. 'I will not stay an instant longer,' she announced.

'Ah,' said the *fetch* gently. 'I am afraid I cannot permit you to leave.'

Mrs. Adair ignored this and marched on towards the great doors without slowing her step one whit. Her children followed, Miss Adair spinning with a display of graceful indignation which Bessie could not but admire, whatever the ill-will that lay behind it. Their father, however, did not move.

Neither did Mrs. Adair, once she reached the door, for some invisible force appeared to prevent her from leaving through it. She walked directly into something solid, though impossible to discern, and stopped abruptly, with a little cry of surprise and pain. All her subsequent attempts to discover a way through were of no avail.

'I do apologise,' said the *fetch*, with blatant and smiling insincerity. 'But you see, it is to be an evening of marvels! A ball unlike any other! It would be too, too bad if you were to miss out on the festivities.'

Mrs. Adair looked as though she would like to protest further. But she looked, first, at her husband, and whatever she saw in his face evidently persuaded her to reconsider. Instead of bursting into an angry tirade, as she clearly wished to do, she forced an affected laugh instead, and said in a brittle tone: 'Well, Mr. Green. Your eccentricities grow more interesting hourly.'

This little exchange interested Bessie, and she wondered how much Mrs. Adair knew about her husband. That she was a little afraid of him was obvious; that the children would follow their parents' lead was equally evident.

The *fetch* smiled silkily. 'I pray you will proceed to the ballroom. You will find refreshments awaiting you there.'

The Adairs departed thither without another word, and the *fetch* proceeded to welcome the next wave of incoming guests. There came in another flow of lively, excited, chattering and *human* guests, shaking the chill from their hair, and the wisps of mist from the folds of their cloaks.

Bessie felt no right of interest in the arrivals as would justify her in retaining her place at the host's side, so she removed herself to a dark corner of the hall, and continued to watch. She knew who was expected to attend, for she had been deeply involved in the composition of the guest list. It interested her very much, however, to observe who had accepted the invitation; how they were treated by the *fetch*, and who appeared to be personally known to Grunewald's sister; and how they behaved. The majority of the families, she judged, were unaware that their host was anyone other than the Mr. Green she was pretending to be, and had no notion that anything untoward was occurring at the ball. They came merely to be merry, and to dance a great deal, and Bessie's anointed left eye detected nothing unusual in the majority of the great families of the neighbourhood. She knew, though, that the Aylfendeanes and their friends were in the ballroom already, and poised to further observe and question as opportunities presented themselves. If secrets were hidden anywhere within these visions of mundane humanity, they would be discovered over the course of the evening.

But two points of interest occurred. Late in the process of arrival, when the stream of guests had at last begun to slow, a gaggle of mismatched attendees appeared in a haphazard group. They *looked* full ordinary enough, in Bessie's right eye; but her left revealed that they were in truth a party of goblins, most likely of various tribes. Among their number was one lone Aylir, a woman with ice-white hair tinted with blue and a glitteringly cold, beautiful smile to match. Some signs of secret recognition she discerned, between these guests and the *fetch*. Were these among the associates Balligumph suspected her of having ridden to awake? If so, what was their purpose here, and why had they been drawn forth from the Torpor?

Soon after the arrival of this group, the noise and bustle of carriages drawing up outside and disgorging their beautifully-dressed inhabitants ceased. All seemed arrived for the ball, and the *fetch* may now consider herself free to abandon her post in the hall, and attend her guests in the ballroom.

But herein lay the second point of interest, for the *fetch* seemed disinclined to leave the hall at all. She paced up and down, glancing often towards the door as though still awaiting someone; someone much hoped-for, but who had not, thus far, appeared. The list of guests to be invited had been so long, and the flow of incoming dancers so chaotic, that Bessie could not guess at who had failed to arrive; and she certainly could not conjecture as to why the appearance of one family should be of such importance to the *fetch*.

Furthermore, she muttered to herself under her breath as she paced about. 'Not *them*,' she said, more than once. 'Not him. But if not them... who?' Bessie's questions went unheard and unanswered, and she was obliged to speculate for herself as to the meaning of this behaviour. The person referred to must be Mr. Adair, surely; the elder, with his unexpectedly Aylir appearance. He was the only person who had seemed at all out of the ordinary. But in what way had he failed to satisfy the *fetch*? What was he *not*?

At length the *fetch* was obliged to abandon her vigil, for strains of music began to be heard from the ballroom. Soon the dancing would begin. The *fetch* ceased her pacing. 'Come, Bess,' she said, offering her arm. 'It is time for the show to begin.'

Bessie found herself in the ballroom before one particular curiosity fully penetrated her awareness. She could have little familiarity with the music typically chosen for such events as this, but still it occurred to her that the melodies she was now hearing were something out of the common way. Indeed, even the instruments upon which they were played seemed somehow *other*. There was a violin, assuredly, but it sounded full strange – as though it might, perhaps, be made from glass, or its strings wrought from spider's webs. A pipe played; or three, or even more? And they were no ordinary pipes, for the tones ringing rich and pure in Bessie's ears teased oddly at her senses.

She could scarcely see the musicians in the crush of the ballroom. Indeed, she could not imagine how there was to be room enough for any dancing, for it seemed that every inch of the floor was occupied by a different pair of slipper-shod feet, a different silken train sweeping the ground.

But the *fetch*-as-Grunewald stepped a little forward, and cleared her throat. Nothing more was required. All of the guests ahead of them stepped aside, united in some deeply-felt but inexplicable impulse, and the way through to the centre of the room was clear.

At the far end, Bessie beheld the musicians. Not a one of them was human, nor bore a drop of human blood. Two were Ayliri: the fiddler's too-white skin gleamed like mother-of-pearl, and his long, ice-white hair was bound back in braids. There was a second fiddler, as dark of skin as the first was pale, his hair a halo of wispy, night-black curls decked with gems. These two were tall and proud of posture; they were dressed in waistcoats and knee-breeches of silks shimmering in too many colours, with spider-gossamer stockings clinging to their shapely legs and coats of leaves and moths' wings hanging from their shoulders. With them stood a trio of pipers, each much shorter than the fiddlers. Different creatures, these, with their overlarge hands and ears; their figures were gangling and ungainly, though they danced with a grace that would put the most elegant of debutantes to shame. They wore velvet caps and jerkins in riotous hues, and they played their pipes – odd, curling instruments of glass and silver and gold – with an infectious glee.

There were others, but Bessie had not the time to examine them all. The band of musicians was attracting a great deal of notice from the assembled guests, and excited chatter threatened almost to drown out the music.

The *fetch* led Bessie into the centre of the ballroom, released her hand, and bowed to her. Too late, Bessie realised what was intended.

'*No!*' she hissed in desperation. 'Whatever gave you the idea I'd know how to dance!'

The *fetch* merely grinned at her. 'But of course you do.'

She had not time for further objections, for the musicians struck up a new melody. These new strains caught hold of Bessie in a fashion indescribable, but instantly every nerve in her body longed to dance. This effect was universal, she judged, for every single one of the *fetch*'s guests ceased their chatter at once, formed themselves into pairs and began, in unison, to trace the steps of a dance unlike any ever seen in that hall before. Bessie was at no loss to follow the movements, though they led her to turn and whirl in an arrangement so complex, she could scarcely have learned it if she had tried. But all such reflections rapidly fled from her mind; there was only the music – the violin and the pipes, and the rustle of a hundred silken gowns keeping time; the glimmer of jewelled ornaments, glinting in a thousand colours; the perfumes of lilies and roses, of clear summer waters and chill, damping fog. Time passed, Bessie could not have said how much. She was barely aware, focused upon nothing save the whirl of the dance.

It came to a halt, so abruptly that Bessie was left gasping in shock as her feet stilled and the music died away. She required fully half a minute to collect herself enough to look about her and determine the source of the disruption, for such a delicious, terpsichorean frenzy could not have come to such a cease by itself.

She noticed, firstly, that changes had been wrought to the ballroom during the course of the dancing. The ceilings, previously bare of adornment, were now hung with trailing vines sprouting ethereal, pallid leaves, and flowers paler still. But these, in fact, were not *hung* there at all; they grew there, winding their way over the expanse of plaster in a fashion oddly possessive. Moths and butterflies in jewelled colours flitted lazily among them, and some had drifted down to rest upon the hair of the dancers below. Tendrils of vines coiled their way down the walls, and must soon claim all the ballroom for their own.

Bess saw little else, at first, but the crowds before her parted as they had done for the *fetch*, and a cluster of new arrivals stood revealed. Two pale-haired Ayliri women were dressed for the dance, in gowns of moss and rose petals anointed with dew. A third Aylir, a man, attended both of the women, for he had offered both of them his arms. He wore a robe of silk and starlight, and his auburn hair flowed long and loose.

With them stood four goblins: each, Bessie guessed, of a different tribe, for their appearance and height and attire were full varied. These, too, came prepared to dance, if she could judge by the finery they wore, the jewels punched through their ears, and the soft dancing-slippers upon their feet. Like their companions, they had dispensed with Glamour and stood as themselves, unabashed in such a throng of human company.

But the late arrivals were not all of Aylfenhame. One human stood among them; one human woman, whose finery was unquestionably worthy to stand alongside theirs, wrought though it was of mere human velvets and silks, and adorned only by the gems and embroideries of mortal earth. Her vivid red hair was built up high, almost in the fashion of the previous century, and it glittered in some odd way, as though strewn with diamonds. She was young, though perhaps a few years older than Bessie herself. That she was used to presiding was obvious from her straight-backed posture, air of confidence and the high tilt of her chin. Awed by this vision, Bessie closed her right eye; but she saw nothing altered with her anointed left.

Bessie had never seen her before, but her name was soon

supplied, for a whisper of awed surprise spread through the crowded guests. *Lady Thayer. Lady Cassandra Thayer. Lady Cass!*

Then came the *fetch*, walking past Bessie to greet this assortment of latecomers. In her alacrity, Bessie felt there could be no doubt: these were the people for whom the *fetch* had been waiting. Perhaps they were the ones for whom she had ordered rooms prepared – or, at least, those of Aylfenhame, for Lady Thayer stood a little way apart from them, as though she had merely chanced to arrive at the same time.

It took Bessie a little longer to notice the pipe the lady held. It was simple in design, straight and rather short, but it was made from delicate, iridescent glass. With a smile of mischief, Lady Thayer raised the peculiar instrument to her lips and played a brief, rippling tune.

The *fetch* had gone first to her apparent friends among the Ayliri and goblin arrivals, and had looked but briefly upon Lady Thayer. But this changed the moment she began to play that strange little pipe. The *fetch*'s head whipped around, and she fixed Lady Thayer with an intense stare. Her gaze took in the sumptuous red hair, every inch of her ladyship's finery and, most especially, the pipe that she held.

'Play again,' she commanded.

Lady Thayer lifted one delicate brow by the barest fraction, and stared back at her host – Mr. Green in appearance, if not in fact – with cool displeasure. 'I beg your pardon?'

To Bessie's surprise, the *fetch* grinned with swift, fierce appreciation. And then… bowed. 'My apologies. It would please me greatly if you would play that melody again, Lady Thayer.'

Her ladyship waited a few perfectly-judged moments before she graciously forgave the dictatorial manner, and granted the request. The melody rang out, clear and bright, and the *fetch*'s excitement grew. Swift as a snake, she stretched out a hand and seized one of Lady Thayer's. Something silver-bright and sharp flashed in the candlelight; Lady Thayer gasped in sudden surprise, or perhaps pain; and Bessie saw a glint of shocking red. Blood.

The apparent Mr. Green proceeded to shock his company by lifting his own hand, smeared with Lady Thayer's blood, to his lips. He sampled some of it, delicately, like a man urged to try some new delicacy of which he is suspicious. But as he tasted the blood, a terrible smile crept into being upon his face, and his stolen bright-green eyes flashed with eager triumph.

'It is you!' he cried. 'Everything is in agreement! Your hair! Your eyes! Your *music*. And the blood. The blood confirms it.'

Lady Thayer's cool confidence was gone, replaced by a mixture of anger and bewilderment. 'What can be the meaning of this!' she cried, cradling her wounded hand. 'Had I known I answered your entreaty of attendance only to be so treated, I should never have come!' And she turned, ready to sweep out of the ballroom in disgust. But the three Ayliri blocked her way, and the four goblins with them. She was forced to turn back to Mr. Green, which she did with enviable poise, as though she had chosen to grant him a further audience of her own accord. But Bessie saw the hint of fear in her eyes.

Mr. Green stepped forward and took both of her hands, careful of the pipe she still held as he did so. 'I apologise. But you cannot know how I have searched for you.'

Lady Thayer only favoured him with a look of strong reproof mingled with enquiry, and withdrew her hands.

'You are of a long, noble lineage,' he continued — or *she* in fact as well as appearance, for Bessie realised with a start that the *fetch* had let the Glamour that disguised her as Grunewald fade, and now stood revealed in all her part-human, part-goblin glory.

Lady Thayer inclined her head once, very slightly. If she was surprised by the transformation of her host into a part-goblin, she gave no sign of it save a slight widening of her eyes.

'I speak not of your human lineage,' said Grunewald's sister impatiently. 'Though it is not wholly irrelevant. Daughter of an impoverished earl; wife of a wealthy viscount. Oh, I have studied you. But further back! Decades of your years — more than a century. You have an ancestor *most* noble.'

Bessie received an inkling of the *fetch*'s meaning. She drifted closer, studying Lady Thayer intently with both of her eyes, and this closer inspection rewarded her with some few, small signs that she had missed: a degree of faint, fae otherness about Lady Thayer's green eyes, almost as vivid in hue as Grunewald's. The barest shimmer of otherworldly copper threaded through her hair. Her ears, so close to human as to pass all but an informed examination; but *then* one might discern a hint of strangeness in their shape and form.

Her Ayliri blood had not bred as strongly in her as in Mrs. Aylfendeane, but it was discernible, if one knew how to recognise it.

It was also evident in the music she played, for her melodies bore something of the strange allure of the Ayliri pipers and fiddlers.

But these observations were insufficient. The *fetch* spoke as though she referred to a particular ancestor; not merely the inherent nobility of Ayliri blood itself was spoken of.

'He is long lost to time,' said the *fetch* almost in a whisper. 'Even to me, once among his most favoured! And though I have searched, I cannot find him. *We* cannot find him. But with your help, all shall be changed. All shall be won.'

His Ayliri and goblin compatriots had, during the course of this speech, come to regard Lady Thayer with new interest. 'Can it be true?' said one of the women.

The man in the starlit robe frowned his disapproval, and shook his head. 'Your blood-magic leads you astray, Rasgha. There is nothing of *him* in this woman. Do you imagine he would so sully himself, as to lie with a human?'

The *fetch* – Rasgha, named at last – smiled maliciously at her doubting friend. 'Perhaps you were not so favoured as I, Torin. Perhaps I alone was trusted enough to receive this confidence. And do not think I do not notice, or will not remember, that slight.'

Torin glanced at Rasgha in faint surprise, as though he had forgotten her human heritage. Perhaps he had. 'He confided in you, did he?'

'He spoke of a dalliance, once. Once only. And he did not speak of a child, but I hoped... I *hoped*.'

Torin's lip curled. 'He, of all people, to dally with a human! Well I remember his disdain of them.' Torin's arrogant gaze swept over the assembled guests, whose chatter swelled with indignant protests at these words. He ignored it all.

'A most superior human,' said Rasgha, with a contempt that Bessie found puzzling. 'A woman of the highest birth, among the nobility of England and Ireland! And of the rarest beauty! Such a dalliance could bring him no shame. So he said.'

Torin shrugged his shoulders. 'We may make the attempt. At worst, it can but fail.'

The close, heated atmosphere in the ballroom abruptly vanished under an onrushing wave of cold night air. The dancers turned as one, Bessie with them, to seek the source of the sudden chill.

The outer wall had disappeared, or mostly so. Some vague,

flickering remnant of it shimmered still in Bessie's left eye, but it proved no impediment either to sight or movement. The vast expanse of the spangled night sky lay fully revealed beyond, and the ragged lawns below. These were barely glimpsed before the all-devouring fog gathered its might and descended upon Hyde Place, swallowing it whole in the space of a mere few breaths.

This development caused no small degree of alarm in the majority of the dancers, but Bessie observed with satisfaction and anticipation. Unceremonious, she elbowed and pushed her way through the chattering throng until she stood with a clear view of the frosted lawn.

Pale eyes glowed amidst the fog, and within moments, Bessie's straining ears picked up the sounds of oncoming hoof beats. Something dark and mist-ridden approached at a thunderous gallop.

## CHAPTER THIRTEEN

'My brother,' hissed Rasgha.

'Grunewald,' Bessie agreed, unable to restrain the smile which overtook her features at the prospect of his near arrival. *Now* they would see some fun. The show would begin in earnest.

Rasgha clutched at her arm. 'Do not desert me, Bess!'

Bessie shook her head. 'I told you. As long as you and he are at odds, *we* cannot be friends.'

The storm-wrought hide of Tatterfoal emerged from the mists, darker even than the night, and triumphant upon his back rode the Goblin King. He was a terrible figure, tall and shadowed upon a steed of nightmares, his hair wind-tossed and his leaf-eyes blazing fury. He rode his reclaimed steed to within a mere few paces of the crowd – the dancers knotted together now in fear – and halted. He did not dismount.

He spoke, and though his whole posture spoke of a boundless anger, his tone was icily polite. 'My dear sister,' he said. 'I would like you to return my house, my friends, and my Bess. Instantly, and without the smallest delay.' He paused, and added, 'Not necessarily in that order.'

Rasgha folded her arms, and she seemed somehow to swell in size and menace – though she was forced to look a long way up, to meet her brother's gaze. 'Your fortress is now mine,' she said. 'And I stand here amidst *my* friends, as well as yours. What is to persuade me to depart?'

Grunewald merely smiled, his eyes glinting like green ice. He said nothing, and Bessie was left in momentary confusion.

But not for long, for there came a stirring in the mists around him, and dark things crept to the fore. They were shadowy and insubstantial; some umbrous and benighted, others as pallid as the moon and the cloaking mists. The distant winds carried the sounds of their fellows on the approach: the howling of ethereal hounds, borne rapidly upon eager currents to their sovereign's side. One great, menacing hound approached Bessie and sniffed at her skirts, its eyes shining as cold and pale as Tatterfoal's. The ethereal goblin upon its back saluted Bessie with his insubstantial spear, and she promptly returned the gesture. She wanted to go at once to Grunewald, but to do so would bid fair to ruin the imposing tableau he had gone to significant trouble to arrange. Recognising the sheer artistry of his entrance and unwilling to mar its perfection, she remained where she was.

The assembled guests did not respond to this development with equanimity. Gladly would they welcome the interference of Aylfenhame, if it brought them all the delights of music and dancing and beauty. But the vanishing of the wall was quite another thing; it prompted a ripple of unease, and many dancers began to feel that they had danced long enough.

With the appearance of a second Grunewald, looking as bleak and terrible as death itself and mounted upon a nightmare, unease gave way to fear. When the Goblin Hunt rode in upon their ghost-hounds – armed, incorporeal and displaying all the menace of a dark, wintry anger – the ball guests broke and ran, almost as one. Bessie stood her ground, uninterested in the fate of such easily disturbed souls. Within a very few minutes, scarcely any remained of the hundreds of guests; Bessie noticed that the Aylfendeanes, Sophy and Aubranael, and Mrs. Grey lingered. And, more to her surprise, Lady Thayer. A few clusters of the braver, or more curious, remained also.

'The Hunt recognises their King,' said Grunewald in a terrible voice. 'Even if you do not.'

'Their king!' echoed one of the remaining guests. 'Here, what's this, Green? The greatest nonsense!'

This was ignored. 'You refer to my merely borrowing your pony!' retorted Rasgha. 'How ungenerous! Is it not to be expected, that siblings share between them whatever is their own?'

'I cannot be imagined to know,' said Grunewald, in a dry tone much more recognisable as his own. 'I never had any before this week.'

'No more did I, and for that I may thank our dearest *father.*' She spat the last word with withering contempt. 'And you as well, brother mine.'

Grunewald's brows rose. 'Do, pray, be clear, or we will make but a poor show for our gathered audience. For what are you thanking me?'

'For the outcast status I have enjoyed since the moment of my birth! It did not suit the prince any more than it did the king, I suppose, to acknowledge a family connection born of a mere human pauper? No noble lineage to render *that* liaison respectable!'

And Bessie felt, with sudden enlightenment, that she ought previously to have guessed one or two things about Rasgha.

*You are the only person in this house with whom I bear any real kinship.*
*You alone can understand.*

Those words of Rasgha's, spoken only a short time ago! They made sense now, as they had not before, and all of the *fetch*'s interest in Bessie which had yet remained unexplained now became clear to her. Grunewald had been wrong to imagine that his father's dalliance had been with a woman of high birth. Rasgha's mother had been as poor as Bessie! If Rasgha believed that her family had cast her off out of shame at her mother's low status, how much it must have intrigued and plagued her to see that same brother keeping company with Bess!

Grunewald's comprehension could not, it seemed, keep pace with Bessie's, for he made a fine picture of confusion atop his fearsome steed. 'What?' he snapped.

'Do not pretend to misunderstand me.' Rasgha, all wounded dignity and self-righteous outrage, stood her ground against Grunewald's bewilderment, her anger undiminished.

Grunewald merely blinked at her, befuddled. 'I have not the pleasure of understanding you,' he said, and it seemed that his confusion had dissipated some of his fury.

Rasgha growled her displeasure. 'You cannot deny that you have spurned me! Ignored my very existence, every moment that I have lived! While *you* enjoyed your rightful position as a prince of Ahglore and monarch-in-waiting, *I* was condemned to a beggar's existence! It cannot be justified.'

Grunewald's anger returned, swift and fierce. 'How can I possibly have spurned you when I did not know that you *existed*!' he roared. 'And before you mention father, I am not at all convinced that he knew it either! What a fine castle of ill-usage you have built out of nothing!'

Rasgha seemed struck dumb by these words, though in truth her demeanour spoke more of suspicion. 'That is a lie,' she said, after a moment's consideration.

'You call it so upon what grounds?'

'My mother said —'

'Very well,' barked Grunewald, cutting her off. 'Your mother has said one thing, and I have told you another. You may take her word, or you may take mine; I do not much care which. I only require you to surrender my house, my friends, and most especially *my Bess*, and without further delay!'

Bessie thought it vital that she should speak up at this juncture. 'Grunewald,' she said firmly. 'What did I say to you about tryin' to cart me about like a sack of potatoes? I'll not have it.'

Grunewald stared at her, his eyes narrowed. 'You imagine yourself free to leave, Bessie, and I *hope*, for my wretched sister's sake, that this means she has treated you well. But to *me*, she has threatened your safety, and I will not rest easy until you are liberated.'

This came as news to Bessie, and unsettled her a little, but she refused to permit any of that to show. 'Rasgha,' she said quickly. 'If you value my thinkin' at all, believe me when I say that I know him to be sincere. He had not the smallest notion of yer existence. What's more: if he *had*, I believe he would have been delighted to know you.'

Grunewald scowled. 'Do not trouble to speak for me, if you please. I can manage that for myself.'

A stinging retort rose to Bessie's lips, but it occurred to her that to enter into an altercation at such a moment could do no service to either, and she held her tongue. She responded only with a speaking look, which plainly said: *And you are making a fine mess of it.*

Grunewald's response was the faintest, barely perceptible grimace. *I know.*

'What is all of this in aid of?' he said to his sister. 'An attempt upon my throne? A ploy to overthrow my authority, and claim it for your own? You would be full revenged upon me!' This last was spoken with faint sarcasm, probably perceptible only to those who knew him well. Bessie wondered what he meant by it.

'I would make a finer ruler, brother,' said Rasgha. 'Though from your performance to date, that would be no difficult task.'

Grunewald dismissed that with a wave of his hand. 'More foolish hearsay? Your strategy entire is based upon nothing but whispers and moonlight. And I am to be proud of this connection?'

'I will yet see it done,' Rasgha growled.

Tatterfoal approached, step by implacable step, until the horse towered directly over Rasgha. 'You cannot have a hope,' hissed Grunewald. 'Blood may grant you the right to interfere – for a time. You may seize control of my steed, and my house, and the Darkways. For a *time*. But always, they will return to me. You cannot lastingly prevail. If you believe me to be so easily overthrown, even by one of my own blood, you can have no understanding of the powers, or the people, you were born into.'

Rasgha merely laughed, and seemed disinclined to make any particular retort.

Bessie thought, and disquiet stirred. 'I think she does,' she said, and there was no teasing note in her tone now. 'She's had two goals in mind, it's my belief. One: to wake up her cronies as had not yet risen from the Torpor, wi' the help of Tatterfoal. And some o' them are here.' She waved a hand at Torin and his friends, who watched the exchange with a mixture of perplexity and a palpable menace. Grunewald glanced at them in surprise, as though he had failed to notice them at all. Probably he had.

'Two,' she continued. 'He was lookin' for that lady.' And she pointed at Lady Thayer, who had not left, though she had taken up a position far removed from Torin. 'She is descended from some mighty noble lineage of Aylfenhame, we're to understand. And mighty important she is wi' that. She's to help yer sister find… *someone* powerful, who's to be of great use.'

Grunewald grasped the implications immediately. 'Old blood,' he said softly. 'Old connections. What did the Kostigern promise you, in ages past? My throne, in exchange for your aid? What a pretty bargain. But he failed to deliver. You are to raise him once again, are you, and hold him to the deal?'

'She shall make no use of me!' declared Lady Thayer. It was spoken with the confidence of absolute authority, which she was no doubt used to wielding. But Bessie could not help but wonder how far she could carry her point, if Rasgha, Torin and all their associates were to unite against her.

Rasgha looked upon Lady Thayer, and her eyes narrowed. Her expression was as cold stone; gone was any trace of warmth or humanity Bessie had ever seen there before. Worse, Torin's period of passive observation appeared to be over. He took a few steps forward, and as though this had been some manner of signal, his Ayliri and goblin friends began to move also — slowly, almost casually, as though they hoped to escape notice.

They escaped Grunewald's notice, fixed as he was upon his sister. But Bessie saw that she had not been the only one to observe their intentions. The Aylfendeanes moved likewise, and Sophy and Aubranael and Mrs. Grey. Each chose a target, and set themselves to intercept whatever that person's intentions might be.

Bessie's mind raced. What might they seek to do, while Rasgha held Grunewald's attention?

It must pertain to Lady Thayer; she seemed to be the key to Rasgha's plans. And she saw, in an instant, that if each of Rasgha's supporters was left to follow their own course unimpeded, they would soon surround that lady.

Bessie moved. Three steps carried her to Lady Thayer's side. 'You must leave,' she said in an urgent undertone. 'They will not leave you be. Run now!'

Lady Thayer looked as though she had too much pride to turn tail and run, and gathered herself for a stinging retort. *Aristocrats*, Bessie thought in disgust. Used to having the world laid out at their feet, they could not grasp that they were not in control of every situation.

But even had she run, she would have been too late. Grunewald's friends had succeeded in diverting some few of those who threatened the lady, but that could not last; and two of Rasgha's goblin friends abandoned all pretence at subtlety, and ran for Lady Thayer.

Bessie prepared herself to resist this onslaught, though scarcely knowing how. But a dark shape shot out of the darkness ahead of her — *two* figures, diminutive but ferocious. Drig and Derri fell upon one of the two goblins, and Bessie bestowed her most terrible smile upon the second as she took up a position before Lady Thayer. 'Ha! I wish you joy of yer attempt!'

Lady Thayer stepped out from behind Bessie. 'I think not,' she said to the goblin, cool and unruffled. The goblin struggled viciously, but it could not outmatch the two ladies. With quick efficiency, they disabused the creature of its notions of offering them any harm whatsoever.

'The ladies are ours,' called Sophy, and she sallied forth to engage the two Ayliri women, with Mrs. Aylfendeane and Mrs. Grey in her wake.

Mr. Aylfendeane moved to intercept Torin, offering him a courteous, but grim, smile. 'Ye'll not harm the lady, I thank ye,' he said. Sorcerous power gathered around him in a menacing shade. Aubranael busied himself with detaining the remaining goblins; though he possessed no magical arts, in strength and speed and dexterity, he was more than match enough.

Bessie began to hope that they might, between them, prevail; but her hopes were short-lived, for more approached, spilling forth from somewhere she could not determine. Trows were prominent among these new assailants, but she saw imps, pixies, hobs and goblins besides. Her composure suffered a check, for how could they withstand such a horde?

But she had forgotten Grunewald's incorporeal army. Grunewald gave a deep, tearing cry, and the Goblin Hunt sprang to obey. They howled in unison, a sound which raised the hairs upon Bessie's arms and sent a shudder through her. Drawing their weapons, they fell upon Rasgha's goblins, and battle ensued.

In the mass of struggling figures now surrounding them, Bessie lost sight of her own friends, and of Grunewald. She split her attention in two, devoting half of her awareness to Lady Thayer's whereabouts and the other half to Rasgha. If *she* was in Rasgha's position, she would welcome the chaos. It would allow her to do the only thing that could matter to her at this moment: to approach Lady Thayer, and wrest from her whatever it was she required in order to carry through her goal of finding the Kostigern. All things considered, Lady Thayer could only find it painful.

Rasgha levelled one final retort at Grunewald which Bessie could not hear; an insult, judging from the sneer which marked her face as she spoke.

Then she grinned, and laughed... and vanished. The shadows flowed in and claimed her, and nothing remained.

Grunewald cursed, loudly enough for his words to carry over the howls of his hounds and the clamour of goblin battle. He sat atop

Tatterfoal, twisting and turning in his attempts to discover where his sister had gone.

Bessie did not bother to follow his example. If he, from his vantage point and with all his powers, could not locate Rasgha, she could have no hope of doing so herself. Instead, she wound her hands into Lady Thayer's voluminous skirts and hung on tight. 'Watch yerself,' she hissed, directly in Lady Thayer's ear. 'Mischief is afoot, and I'm certain it's aimed at you.'

Lady Thayer hissed something inaudible, and then said clearly: 'Good *heavens*. I wanted only the music! I ought rather to have stayed at home.' She sounded more annoyed than afraid.

'Mayhap,' Bessie agreed. 'But what a lively party you would ha' missed. Look to yerself, now.'

And, almost upon cue, Lady Thayer suffered a sudden, swift tumble. Still clinging to her skirts, Bessie fell likewise, but neither of them hit the ground. The fog-ridden night dissolved into deeper darkness, and Bessie closed her eyes against the wave of disorientation and nausea which swiftly followed.

This time, however, she would not permit herself to be towed, inert and passive, through the Darkways. No goblin was she, but she had strength and will of her own. She wrapped herself tightly about Lady Thayer, determined not to lose her. In the process, she discovered Rasgha's hand, clamped tightly around Lady Thayer's arm.

She dislodged this grip by the simple expedient of setting her teeth to the tender flesh, and biting down as hard as she could. Rasgha shrieked with pain, surprise, and, Bessie was afraid, betrayal. This last caused her to feel some compunction, but she pushed that feeling away with some little resentment. She *had* warned the woman.

Then, summoning every ounce of will that she possessed, she wrenched herself sideways. She did not know whether she had attempted to move upwards, downwards, or in any other direction, for she had lost all sense of which way was *where*. But it mattered not. All that she sought to achieve was freedom from Rasgha's presence, even though it prove to be but brief. She had no opportunity to discover whether or not she had been successful, for her consciousness gave out, and she fell into the dark.

When the unpleasant sensation of uncontrolled, rapid movement ceased and full consciousness returned, Bessie was the first to rise to her feet. She was shaky, but unharmed; she had grown used to the Darkways, at last.

Lady Thayer had not fared so well. She lay in an inelegant heap amid reams of silk, her gown sadly disordered. She had been so unfortunate as to lose some part of her dinner, which could only annoy her when she came to herself.

Bessie glanced about, wary. They had emerged in a dim corridor, which was, to all intents and purposes, featureless. The wooden cladding upon the wall, the flagstones upon the floor and the muted lamps could offer her nothing by way of identifying features. She could be anywhere.

More importantly for the present, there was no sign of Rasgha, or of anybody else either. She permitted herself a moment's smug satisfaction on that score, for she had not been at all certain that her venture would succeed. Then she went to tend to Lady Thayer.

'My lady?' she said, and set about waking the woman by such arts as she had available. Her ladyship proved reluctant to rouse, but at length she opened her eyes and gazed, confused, at Bessie.

'Are we dead?' she said.

'Nowhere near.'

Lady Thayer digested that for a moment. 'Are we about to become so?'

Bessie looked around at the deserted corridor. 'I would say not, milady, for the present.'

Her ladyship nodded thoughtfully, glanced once at the ruin of her dress, and sighed. 'Then I think, all things considered, that you had better address me as Cassandra.'

Bess's brows went up. 'I beg yer pardon?'

'Unorthodox, I know. But you appear to have preserved me from an unpleasant fate, and it is not every day that one owes one's life to a... to another person.'

'I ain't saved you yet,' Bessie cautioned. 'I have no notion where we have ended up, and Rasgha's still about somewhere.'

'Very well. We shall not yet congratulate ourselves.' She rose shakily to her feet and stood, swaying slightly, one hand pressed to her head. 'Still, I believe you must have been remarkably quick-thinking and magnificent.'

'Perhaps a little,' said Bessie modestly.

Lady Cass visibly pulled herself together, taking a few deep breaths and squaring her shoulders. 'Excellent. We must first determine where we are, I suppose.' She glanced again at her ruined gown, her nostrils flaring in disgust. Then, with three quick movements, she tore a large section of her skirt away and threw it aside. All of the evidence of her earlier distress sailed away with it, and she smiled her satisfaction. 'Much better.' In spite of the tumble she had taken, her distress under it and the ruin of her gown, her dignity was unimpaired; she was every inch the aristocrat.

Bessie nodded once. 'This way or that way?' she asked, pointing to each of the two directions they could choose to move in.

Cassandra glanced down the corridor ahead of her, and then behind. 'I cannot possibly choose between two equally uninspiring options.'

'Then we will take this one.' Bessie picked a direction at random and began to walk. Cassandra followed.

A very few minutes served to convince her that she had not brought them anywhere useful. Featureless corridors gave way to more corridors the same, and she was forced to conclude that she had not contrived to carry them out of the Darkways at all. 'I have stranded us in the Goblin passages,' she admitted ruefully.

'No matter,' said Cassandra, brisk and unperturbed. 'It is worlds better than finding ourselves locked in any trap laid for me by that woman.'

'True, but it cannot be long before she finds us in here. We must get out, and fast.'

'I dare say. How did we get *in?*'

'Why… I dunnot rightly know. I decided to stop followin' the *fetch*, and swung us away.' Bessie looked around, frowning. 'Somehow.'

'If it is a matter of mere decision, I am sure we have enough of that between us.'

Lady Cassandra probably had decision enough to turn the stars about, if she chose. Bessie felt a pang of envy, its source mixed and not wholly clear. She quickly smothered it. She may not have been born with the right to command, but she would certainly choose to command her *own* fate, as far as that was possible.

Decision. Well.

'You had better lead, I think,' Cassandra instructed. 'Your familiarity with these parts is, I perceive, greater than mine.'

Wandering about alone had rarely troubled Bessie before; she was used to having no one else upon whom to rely. But she had never before been given charge of someone else's safety, and she felt the pressure keenly; perhaps the more so because the woman in question was of so elevated a rank. She felt poorly equipped for the duty, and had to smother a stab of fear as well as her envy. But that was nonsense. If she could manage herself without disastrous consequences — and she had, to date — then she could guide Lady Cassandra as well.

Now that she came to consider the matter, Cassandra could well be largely correct about the Darkways. These corridors were probably not physical passageways at all, or not in the sense that Bessie was used to. If she expected them to go on forever, they probably would. But if she preferred for them to end, then perhaps they…

…would. She turned a corner, and immediately perceived a doorway ahead of them. It appeared to be a little bit open, for light gleamed around its edges, illuminating it invitingly in the near darkness of the corridor.

Bessie's instinctive triumph quickly faded in favour of suspicion. Had that been too easy? Could she really have conjured an exit merely out of the desire to find one? If she had, where did the door lead?

'I had better see where it goes,' she said to Lady Cassandra.

Cassandra nodded once, and occupied herself with the inspection of her curious glass pipe — concerned, perhaps, that it had not weathered their impromptu journey well. Bessie felt a little hurt at this willingness to permit her to risk herself without support, and without the smallest protest. But Lady Thayer was an aristocrat. She was probably used to people risking life and limb on her behalf, and small wonder if she was more concerned about the fate of her pipe than with the fate of a mere servant.

*Nonsense*, Bessie lectured herself sternly, and pushed such unworthy reflections away. She approached the door at once, unwilling to show any hesitation. The door opened as soon as she set her fingers to it, and, heart pounding, she peeked inside.

The room beyond was a comfortable parlour, with furniture of mismatched proportions and riotously colourful upholstery. The walls were hung with tapestries, the floor covered in homey rugs. Shutters covered the windows, each one painted in a different rainbow colour.

To her relief, Bessie recognised the interior of the Motley. At first, this seemed to her too great a coincidence, but a little reflection reassured her. Where else in Gadrahst would Bessie choose to go, but the one place she had felt truly safe and at home? She had fetched up in Maggin's own parlour, she judged, for she had seen something of the room before.

The room was empty.

Bessie turned back to Cassandra, and was startled to see her poised with her pipe set to her lips. An odd time to be desiring music, she could not help thinking. 'Tis a place of safety,' she said. 'We can go in.'

When she turned back to the door, Maggin herself had appeared on the other side of it. She had observed the door and now stood blocking it, wielding a broomstick in one hand and a heavy metal bucket in the other. When she saw Bessie, her grim expression transformed into a smile, and she stepped back. 'Why, if it ain't Miss Bessie! What are ye doing walking the Darkways, lass? Is our Gent wi' ye?'

'Not at present, Maggin,' said Bessie, and stepped into the parlour. Cassandra followed, and received a curious stare from the landlady. 'We wasn't exactly expectin' to be in them passageways tonight.'

'Something amiss, is it?' said Maggin.

'Aye. Turns out our Gent has a sister, and she has some big ideas.'

It did not appear to Bessie that Maggin was much surprised by this news, and that fact intrigued her — and alarmed her as well, for how could a simple landlady be informed on such a point when Grunewald himself had not known? Thus far, everyone she had met who had known of Rasgha's existence and identity had been her allies and supporters. But she could not believe such a thing of Maggin.

She had not time to consider the question now. She began to relate the tale of Rasgha and Grunewald and everything that had happened in the past few days, but she had not proceeded very far with this narrative before she was interrupted by a tumult erupting behind her.

'Honestly, Bessie,' came Rasgha's voice. 'You are supposed to *close* your routes behind you when you are finished with them. I am not surprised that my disgraceful brother should have failed to nurture your obvious talent, but *I* could have taught you.'

Bessie whirled in horror. Rasgha had come through the door into Maggin's quiet parlour, and with her came Torin – and Drig, who quelled any fledgling alarms about his loyalty by running at once to Bessie's side. 'I tried to close it up for you,' he said to Bessie in an undertone. 'Failed.'

'Clung to my coat, the little wretch,' said Rasgha pleasantly, though the gimlet eye she fixed upon Drig was by no means friendly.

Then she looked at Cassandra. 'Lady Thayer! Excellent. Shall we proceed?'

## CHAPTER FOURTEEN

From atop his magnificent steed, Grunewald enjoyed a clear view of the proceedings. This did not help him greatly, however, for though he could guess where his sister would turn her attention, he had lost sight of her in the tumult. And now his vantage point proved his undoing, for he could not spur Tatterfoal through the throng to Lady Thayer's side, and to dismount would only bring him into the midst of the battle. He could never reach her in time.

When Lady Thayer tumbled sideways and vanished, he was watching. And he saw his Bess disappear along with her, black hair flying like a flag in the sudden, fierce wind of their departure.

If he had felt angry before, there was no word to describe the fury that now overwhelmed him. 'That is *quite* enough,' he said aloud. He gathered the force of his rage, took in a great breath and roared his displeasure. It emerged as a vast, echoing cry which sundered the skies and shook the ground beneath. It brought the combatants to an abrupt halt, and they stared as one at the terrible vision of the Goblin King in all his anger.

Grunewald himself felt curiously calm in the midst of it, though it was the kind of icy, controlled calm that made mockery of the word. He jumped off Tatterfoal's back, his mind already reaching for the Darkways which had been closed to him.

He could not sense them immediately, any more than he had done so before. But *that* he would not accept. He had regained control of his steed, and his home; the Darkways would follow. He caught up his rage and fashioned it into a spear; with this, he rended the fabric of the night until he glimpsed the shadows that lay behind. *There.*

He reached out, implacable in his determination, and caught up a tendril of that shadow in a crushing grip. It squirmed away from him, intent upon its orders from another; but he bore down, relentless. *He was the Goblin King, and no other; his Kingdom would obey him!*

All at once, the resistance vanished and he tumbled gracelessly into the Darkways. He paused in the pitch darkness, panting for breath. This point gained, what next? He did not know where Rasgha had taken Bess.

He closed his eyes and sought, not for any one of the many familiar pathways that he knew, but for Bessie herself. He concentrated upon the shape of her, and the tumbling mass of her hair that refused to remain neatly bound. He conjured up her scent, and the sardonic light in her eye when she looked at him. He thought of her smile, when he succeeded in making her laugh. Even those dreadful vowels of hers lived brightly in his mind; he imagined her voice in his thoughts. *You're bein' awfully slow, my Gent. The party will be over before we see any sign o' you.*

A flicker lit up in the darkness of his mind: a warmth and a light that could only be Bess. She was far away, deep in Gadrahst. He wished he had any means of guessing where in the Goblin lands his sister might seek to take her captives, but he had not knowledge enough of her habits. He could only drift after the light that was Bess, urging himself to greater speed as his lock upon her strengthened. In time, he sailed fluidly through the shadowed passages, gaining upon her as the seconds passed.

Still, the journey was intolerably slow. He knew it was taking *time*, more time than he wanted. Perhaps more time than Bessie had. Fear and rage warred within him, and he channelled both forces into more energy and more speed. He soared through the Darkways at a hitherto unthinkable pace, and as he flew there was room in his mind for but one thought: *Hold on, Bessie.*

Bessie held on to Cassandra, for Rasgha had wasted little time with chatter. She had withdrawn a most unpromising-looking knife from some hidden sheath and advanced upon Lady Thayer, weapon raised and ready. The blade was no kitchen knife, nor any clumsy working tool. Rasgha's knife was barely six inches long, the blade thin and rounded and gleaming a dull silver. Bessie could have little doubt as to its intended purpose.

Blood magic must require blood, and Cassandra's was the blood Rasgha had gone to such trouble to discover. How much of it was necessary in order to satisfy Rasgha's purpose was unclear. As was the question of whether Cassandra was likely to survive the experience.

If Bessie could help it, Rasgha would get none at all; not only for Cassandra's sake, but because her goal must be prevented at all costs. If she needed but a thimbleful in order to track down the Kostigern, that was well for Cassandra, but it could spell disaster for Aylfenhame. But how could she, Cassandra and Drig contrive to repel Rasgha and Torin? Torin alone must be more powerful than the two humans and Drig combined; he wore power and menace like a mantle. As for Rasgha... despite her earlier friendliness, Bessie doubted not that she possessed ruthlessness and cruelty in equal measures.

Bessie clung closely to Cassandra, unwilling to permit herself to be separated from her unlikely new friend. She tried to put her ladyship behind herself, but Cassandra would not permit it. They stood side by side, Drig poised a little way before them, and faced down their attackers. Bessie wished desperately that she had contrived to acquire a weapon of her own at some point during the evening; she was unarmed, and helpless in the face of that wicked blade.

Rasgha smiled at her. 'Dearest Bessie,' she said softly. 'You will not force me to harm you. I am sure you will not. In spite of your tiresome loyalty to my detestable brother, I admit I should be sorry to cause you any distress.'

Bessie merely stared at her, cold and unmoved. These protestations of concern could do Rasgha no good; there may be sincerity somewhere at their core, but they were hollow. Rasgha would not hesitate to hurt Bessie, if she considered it necessary. And Bessie would not step aside. That left her at the mercy of Rasgha's ruthlessness and that awful knife, and she swallowed. How much would it hurt, to be stabbed by such an object?

But Bessie had forgotten Maggin. 'Now, Rassie,' said the goblin woman. She strode to the fore and planted herself in front of Bess and Cassandra, her hands upon her hips. 'What a troublesome scrap of a thing ye were, when I had the care of ye! But I never thought ye could come to such trouble. Threatening my customers wi' violence, and in the Motley as well! I can hardly believe it o' ye.'

Rasgha blinked at her in confusion. 'Maggin? But what are you… the Motley! Am I here again?' She looked around herself as though she had no notion of where she had ended up. 'How came that about, I wonder?'

'Yon miss brought herself here, an' the lady,' said Maggin. 'Probably 'twas the only place in Gadrahst she thought o' aiming for.' Maggin winked at Bessie.

Rasgha focused upon Bessie for an instant. 'How curious a coincidence,' she said softly.

'Never mind that,' said Maggin briskly. 'I did not waste years o' care on ye, raising ye in secret and wi' no knowledge of his Majesty, only to see ye turn to such nonsense!'

Rasgha sighed, and pinched the bridge of her nose as though she was suffering a headache. 'The Kostigern used to say that to care was to weaken yourself,' she said conversationally. 'The only way to succeed is to rid oneself of all ties and all loves. I suppose he was right.' She looked at the stout little goblin woman, sturdy and belligerent, kindly and outraged. 'Maggin, leave be. I want only a little blood from this good lady! I shan't hurt her very much.'

'Aye, and what will ye do wi' that?' demanded Maggin. 'Nothing good, I fear!'

Rasgha appeared to be suffering some indecision. Whatever her resolve had been regarding Bessie, she suffered true doubts indeed about crossing Maggin – about revealing the true extent of her villainy before, perhaps, one of the few who had ever sincerely cared for her. For a moment, Bess hoped that it might be enough to turn her around.

But Torin had influence, too. He barked something at Rasgha in a language Bessie could not understand. His utterance was brief, but in the wake of it, all doubt vanished from Rasgha's face and she tightened her grip upon the blade. Bessie's heart sank, for those well-timed words had swept away all hope of deterring Rasgha.

Grunewald's sister pushed Maggin aside. Bessie had but an instant to observe her motion and guess at her intentions, and scarcely time enough to impose herself in the way of it. But she succeeded. Rasgha leapt forward; the knife flashed; Bessie jumped, almost too late. But no – she had been in time. She felt a stinging pain in her shoulder, and felt the warmth of flowing blood.

She gritted her teeth against the pain, and steadied herself. Well and good – she had deflected one attack, but another must soon follow. What more could she do?

Drig leapt in front of her an instant later, a dark knife glittering in each hand. He radiated a dark, cold anger, and Bessie doubted not that he would rend Rasgha in two should she attempt to inflict any more harm. But as skilled as he might be with those blades, he was scarcely one third of Rasgha's height – and she had Torin besides. He could not protect Bessie or Lady Thayer, much as she loved him for trying. She had to do something to protect herself.

Before she could gather her thoughts, she heard three notes played upon a piping flute. The brief tune rose into the air and swelled, filling the room with a commanding presence Bessie could put no name to. More notes followed, forming a rippling, mesmerising melody, and Bessie's mind blanked; she could not remember what she had been so intent upon, only moments before.

Rasgha faltered, shaking her head and blinking. The weapon, raised and ready moments before, now lowered in a hand visibly weakened and trembling. Torin, too, slowed his steps and stopped, staring at Cassandra with a vague, blank expression. Even Drig relaxed and began to sway, fractionally, in time to the music.

Lady Thayer played her pipes as Bessie had never before seen. The melody flowed, rippling, from her lips and her fingers with scarcely possible speed, but the lady never missed a note. Somewhere in the depths of Bessie's confusion, she was conscious of a distant sense of admiration. *What a musician!*

Not that the music was in any way beautiful. It was harsh in character – ugly, even. Cacophonic and disordered, it grated upon Bessie's ears in a fashion she found scarcely tolerable. But no matter how much she might wish to run away from it, she could not move.

Accordingly, she was slow to realise that they had arrived at an impasse. Cassandra's music kept Rasgha and Torin at bay, but it could only last as long as she did, and that could not be forever. Meanwhile, the strange melody lulled her allies as well as her attackers. The danger was only postponed, not removed, and she had placed herself as much beyond help as she was beyond attack.

The stalemate stretched, minute by minute, and gradually the strain upon Lady Thayer began to show. A fine perspiration beaded her forehead, and her eyes grew wide and a little wild. Bessie fought harder to escape the pull of the music, striving to move as much as a muscle under the enchantment. If she could find something – anything – to use as a weapon, perhaps she could contrive to eliminate at least one of Cassandra's enemies. But try as she might, she could *not* move.

The impasse was unbreakable. The music would stave off attack until Cassandra broke – and break she would, soon. When that happened, Cassandra and Bessie would be as poorly situated as they had been before, for Bessie's sluggish brain would not even oblige her by using the interlude to formulate a new plan. She could see nothing about her that might serve as a weapon, nor imagine any likely outcome to the situation than the fulfilment of Rasgha's intentions.

Unless...

Her befuddled mind conjured a single image for her perusal: an object, and a vague question.

*Yes,* thought Bessie. *That might do.*

Before she could follow the thought any further, something exploded into the room in a violent rush of shadow and a wordless snarl of rage. A frigid wind tossed Bess's hair into her face and chilled her skin.

Cassandra's music faltered for an instant – just long enough to permit Bessie to whirl about in search of the disruption.

*Grunewald.*

He stood in the centre of Maggin's parlour, and everything about him spoke of unconquerable fury. He was bone-white with it, his eyes piercingly green and his disordered, wind-swept hair bloodier in contrast. He stared back at Bessie, his eyes noting the blood that stained her sleeve, and grew still more terrible.

'Who,' he said in a terrible, quiet voice, 'Did. THAT?' The final word erupted from him in a thunderous roar that shook the walls, and Bessie flinched. Shadows gathered around him, spears of lightning sparkling at their core, and Bessie felt that she had never seen anything more terrifying in her life. The Goblin King's menace dwarfed even that of Tatterfoal.

He paused, listening, and then his gaze shifted to Lady Thayer. His eyes narrowed, and he shook his head, as though to clear it. 'Rasgha,' he said with a frightening smile. 'It was you, was it not?'

Rasgha glared balefully at her brother. Her expression showed nothing but a fury of her own, but Bessie discerned a hint of fear. Even *she* must tremble before such a vast and shattering wrath.

She did not speak; probably she could not, for Lady Thayer's music held her still. But her defiance was visible in every line of her body, and in the curl of her clenched fists.

Grunewald strolled around her in a circle, examining every inch of his wayward sister. He stopped in front of her once more, his brows lifting a bare fraction of an inch. 'So!' he said in a dangerously conversational tone. 'You would like to walk in my shoes, would you? Step into my place and my throne? Perhaps you imagine that it will be *amusing*, to give orders and be waited upon? To be flattered and courted? You can have no notion of what it means to lead.

'I am not, as you appear to suppose, so desperately determined to retain the role. You are unaware of how long I have been burdened with the duty. Had I known of your existence, and been able to esteem your character, I might perhaps have relinquished the role in your favour some years ago.'

This admission could not much surprise Bessie, but its effect upon Rasgha was powerful. Her eyes widened, and Bess could easily read the look in her eyes as pure shock. And, perhaps, chagrin.

Grunewald smiled congenially upon her, but the shadows wreathing his tall, thin figure roiled and flashed with lightning. 'But you made the mistake of expecting me to be exactly like *you*. You have shown me every one of your poor qualities and none at all of your strengths – supposing you to possess any. As a consequence, I will see myself dead before I will see you installed as the Goblin Queen. My people – *our* people – deserve better.'

His words faltered a little at the end, and his eyes began to develop a glazed look. Cass's music was getting to him. He clenched his teeth and shook his head once, defying the melody by pure force of will. 'That being the case,' he grated, 'there remains the question of what to do with you.'

Something shifted in the music, and Bessie received the impression that it was drawing to a close. Cassandra was growing tired, or perhaps she had something else in mind; Bessie could not guess. But she had only a minute or two to decide on what she was to do when the music faded. A glance beyond Grunewald revealed her only hope of constructive action: a large, sturdy bucket set down near the door. She spared a moment to bless the Motley's landlady for her habits of scrupulous cleanliness. She saw Maggin as well, still wielding the broom she had been carrying when Bessie and Cassandra had arrived. She exchanged a look with the landlady, and read a similar resolve in Maggin's eyes. The goblin woman looked first at Torin, then at the broom she carried. Then her eyes flicked to Rasgha.

Bessie understood, and held herself ready.

'I have the perfect thing!' continued Grunewald, smiling nastily. 'For you *and* all your wretched little friends.' He cracked his knuckles, his smile growing wider. 'Before I begin, allow me to assure you that I am very much going to enjoy this.'

Cassandra's melody rose to a crescendo and then cut out, so abruptly that Bessie was left briefly shocked by the sudden, heavy silence that fell.

But only for an instant. She leapt into movement, knowing as she did so that she was too slow. Her goal was Maggin's bucket, left standing by the door, but the way was not clear; she would have to get past Rasgha's friends to reach it.

As this passed through her mind, Torin spat an icy syllable into the air. Grunewald convulsed, with an agonised cry which tore at Bessie's heart. She wanted to run to him, but she must *not* be distracted. With a ferocious effort of will, she forced herself to ignore his distress and keep to her purpose.

But the Ayliri remained between her and her weapon of choice.

Then Drig was there. He uttered a barked, blood-curdling word which turned Bessie's stomach. It was futile; she knew it instinctively, for in the tumult, few could even *hear* Drig. And how could he hope to match his goblin magics against those of the royal line?

But it was not directed at Rasgha, or Torin. As he spoke, the *bucket* soared upwards in a graceful arc, almost to the ceiling, and then fell towards Bess. Cold metal against her hands, and an encouraging weight to lift; she had it.

She spun about, just in time to see Maggin bring her heavy birchwood broom down upon Torin's neck with a satisfying *thwack*.

Bessie hefted her bucket and swung. Rasgha had only time enough to transfer her attention from Grunewald to Bessie, a look of startled horror in her eyes, before Bess brought her makeshift weapon down upon Rasgha's head.

Grunewald's sister fell like a tree, and lay inert.

Maggin was having a little more trouble with Torin. It was not for lack of enthusiasm, Bessie reflected, for she had already rained two or three blows down upon the Aylir. Her broom lacked the solid weight necessary to fell him with a single blow, or perhaps Maggin herself lacked the necessary height or strength.

Bessie reached Maggin's side in two quick steps and dispatched the dazed Aylir with another quick, efficient swing of the bucket. She watched in satisfaction as Torin measured his length beside Rasgha, and beamed down upon them both. 'Unfortunately for the two o' you, I've always been good wi' a bucket.' She beamed at Drig, whose quick-thinking she had to credit. Magical attacks Rasgha would have expected, but who could have anticipated an assault with cleaning equipment? Drig tipped his hat to her, smirking.

'*Bess!*' roared Grunewald, and his ire rattled the walls once again. 'She was *mine* to dispose of!'

'Mayhap she was, but you was doin' far too much talkin' and not enough dispatchin'.' Bessie put the bucket down neatly against the wall, and fixed Grunewald with a disapproving eye. She was also checking to see if he was unharmed by Torin's magical assault, though she would not have wished for him to know that.

'I was getting to it!'

He looked a little paler than usual, but otherwise whole. Satisfied, Bessie dismissed both Grunewald and his protestations with a wave of her hand, and went to attend to Cassandra. 'That was impressive,' she said, noting with some concern that the lady piper was showing signs of exhaustion.

Lady Thayer smiled wearily at her, tucking her glass pipe into a pocket in her skirt. 'So were you.'

Bessie smiled modestly. 'Aye well, as to that. I ain't blessed wi' magic or music or anythin' so fine, but I do like to keep things nice an' tidy.'

Grunewald continued to spit and snarl somewhere nearby, but Bessie ceased to hear him. She had become abruptly aware of the wound in her arm, ignored in the midst of the conflict but now imposing itself upon her awareness in a disagreeably persistent fashion. 'Oh,' she said vaguely, swaying. It hurt, and her sleeve was soaked in blood.

Maggin was at her side in an instant, together with Drig and Lady Thayer. The two of them guided Bessie to a seat upon one of Maggin's soft, well-stuffed chairs, and from this position Bessie could only smile vaguely at Grunewald as he continued to rage. Her absolute indifference to his indignation combined with her obvious weakness brought him up short, and he closed his mouth with a snap. He eyed her balefully for a moment, then swooped upon her. Bessie found herself swept up in a crushing hug, and even the growl of kingly discontent that came along with it failed to dissipate her growing sensation of peaceful satisfaction. She leaned against Grunewald and permitted herself one soft, contented sigh.

'You'd better deal wi' your sister, I reckon,' she said after a moment.

'Mmf.' Bessie was ruthlessly kissed by way of answer, a response she submitted to without much complaint. Grunewald squeezed Bessie fractionally tighter, then released her as abruptly as he had seized her and sprang to his feet. 'Off we go, then,' he said, scooping up both Rasgha and Torin with remarkable ease considering the probable combined weight of the two of them. The doorway into the Darkways yawned wider in invitation.

Grunewald cast one quick, penetrating look at Cassandra. 'At some point, you and I are going to have a talk about how you came to be so proficient with goblin music.'

He gave her no time to reply. Dragging his prey by their necks, and with a charming disregard for their comfort, Grunewald strode through the door and vanished. The shadows went with him, and the door slammed behind him with a snap.

Bessie was left alone with Cassandra, Drig and Maggin, in a parlour restored to such innocuous peace she could scarcely believe the drama that it had contained but moments before. 'I think,' she said vaguely as her head spun, 'I would like to lie down for a moment.'

Before she could act upon this pleasing resolution, a sparkling grey fog engulfed her vision and she passed into pleasant oblivion.

# CHAPTER FIFTEEN

*Our Bess is right handy wi' a bucket, no? Leave it t' her to cut through the nonsense! Tis fer others to wave about they fancy magics an' what-not! Just gi' Bessie somethin' solid an' room t' swing, an' away goes the problem. I do like a practical lass.*

*Anyhow, that were that fer the time bein'. Grunewald took his wayward sister away someplace. I didn't ask where – oh, not out of any sense o' discretion, or any o' that nonsense. She's dangerous! I've a right to know! But Drig came t' me wi' the details. Seems his Majesty has somethin' by way of a secret prison somewhere in Gadrahst. Sounds excitin', don't it? But it weren't right. Grunewald says as how he's worried she might worm her way out o' that one, bein' as she's royal blood an' all. So he whisks her off to the Hollows – the Hollow Hills, that is. Ye've heard me tell o' them. Tis an in-between place, driftin' somewhere betwixt Aylfenhame and yer own, dear England. Quiet, fer the most part. There's a doorway in not far from here, and them musicians – the ones as runs wi' Lyrriant, the Piper? – they lives somewhere in there. Grunewald's given her over t' Lyrriant's care, an' I've no doubt the Piper will keep her under his eye.*

*As fer Torin an' such of his crew as survived the Goblin Hunt? His Majesty weren't lenient-like wi' them. Not at all. I reckon thas the last we'll ever see o' that lot, an' good riddance.*

*Lady Thayer's gone back to her folk on the edge o' the county. Between you an' me, I heard as it was Lyrriant that taught her how to play them pipes the way she does, and gave 'er the pipe, to boot. Tripped over 'er durin' the summer Rade, an' took her under his wing, like. Mighty sneaky of him. I am a little put out tha' he saw no need t' inform me, I don't mind tellin' you! But thas Lyrriant. Not the most obligin' chap I ever encountered. Anyroad, that heritage o' hers worries me a mite. Mayhap Rasgha ain't the only one t' think she might be o' use in findin' that troublesome Kostigern fellow. I keep a watch on her, secret-like, just in case o' further trouble.*

*Well, but what's next fer the Goblin King? His cover bein' good an' blown in these parts, he don't find it easy to come back. As ye may imagine! There's many as says they always suspected Mr. Green an' his charmin' manners. I find tha' mighty doubtful, but leastwise, he certainly ain't trusted now. Chances are he'll give up Hyde Place, though where he's t' pop up next is anybody's guess.*

*An' Bessie? Ye'll be pleased to know that her arm healed, good as new, an' she weren't much the worse fer wear fer her adventure. Nay, not she! There ain't much as can long dampen that spirit. But what became o' her after? I'm right glad ye asked! I'll tell ye. Just this last note, an' then I'll let ye go on yer way.*

Two days after the events of the Hyde Place ball, Bessie lounged in her comfortable room at the Motley, thinking. It was a pursuit she was heartily tired of, for she had seen scarcely a soul since Grunewald's departure with his sister. Maggin had been attentive enough, restoring her to her favourite room and ensuring that her wounded arm was seen to. But she had seen no one else — not even Lady Thayer, who had been escorted away by Drig two days ago. She had no means of venturing back into England, and no one had come seeking her in Gadrahst.

She was on the point of rising from her recumbent posture and taking herself for a turn about the inn, when there came a tapping at the door. She sat up at once, her spirits lifting, and called, 'Enter!'

The door opened to reveal Drig, a triple-stacked hat perched atop his head and his bubble pipe in his hand. He wore a new jerkin, if she was any judge: a fine, silk confection in a dazzling shade of azure blue. He grinned at her and ducked his head by way of greeting.

'Aye, there you are!' Bessie cried. 'What can you mean by keepin' away so long, horrid creature?'

Drig's grin widened, and he puffed a stream of clear bubbles into her face. 'Apologies, and so on,' he said, shoving the door closed behind him. 'Things to do.'

'Tell me at once, there's a good fellow.' Bessie stood over the diminutive goblin, her hands on her hips, and glared at him.

To her surprise, he wrapped his arms around her legs in a swift embrace and planted a kiss upon her right kneecap. 'You're a good woman, Bessie Bell,' he informed her.

Bessie blinked down at him in amazement. 'Why, thank you,' she faltered.

He beamed at her. The expression was sunny and affectionate, but it occurred to Bess that there was a mischievous and unpromising curl to his lips which suggested something quite different. Her suspicions were instantly aroused. 'Out wi' the mischief,' she ordered. 'What is it yer wantin'?'

He regarded her seriously over the bowl of his pipe, his eyes glinting. 'You do owe me a good turn, now that you mention it.'

Bessie nodded, impatient. 'Yes, yes, I haven't forgotten. Say on.'

Drig opened his mouth, but he was interrupted by a loud knocking upon the door. 'That would be Maggin,' he said.

'Come in then, Mag!' Bessie called.

It was Maggin. She came in beaming, but checked upon beholding Drig. 'Ah! Ye've told her already! What a paltry trick, to be sure.'

Drig shook his head. 'Your timing is impeccable, ma'am. I haven't said a word.'

Bessie surveyed the two of them, frowning. 'Whatever it is, you'd better tell me at once.'

Maggin and Drig exchanged a considering look. 'You first,' said Drig.

Maggin inclined her head, gracious as a queen. 'Well then, Bess. Ye might remember as how I spoke of raisin' His Majesty's sister, when she were a tiny mite?'

'You did say somethin' about that, yes.' Bessie was dying to ask how that could possibly have come about, but she did not want to interrupt whatever it was that Maggin had come to impart.

The goblin landlady appeared to guess her thoughts, for her grey eyes twinkled amusement and she said, 'It's my way. It's what the Motley is for. The name don't refer to the patchworks or the mismatched things, though 'tis fitting enough. It's about the people. I takes in all those as has no place elsewhere, an' poor Rasgha was one o' them, right enough.'

Bessie could well imagine that to be the case. A half-human, half-goblin girl, forsaken by her father and born to a servant girl scarcely able to take care of herself, let alone a child? She would have needed Maggin's help like no other.

'Tis why I brought you here,' added Drig. 'Humans are

uncommon in Gadrahst, and not many bother to cater to 'em.'

Bessie nodded. 'I understand all that. And what?'

'His Majesty has asked me to take care o' her again,' said Maggin. 'He has her tucked up snug in some secret place, but he don't want her to be alone. And there's nobody but me as'd take on the job o' being caretaker and companion to that.' Maggin was brisk and unsentimental, but she was kind-hearted. Bessie was surprised at the note of steel she discerned in the landlady's cool tones. Somewhere under her congenial manner, Maggin was very angry with Rasgha.

'So you'll be leavin' the Motley?' Bessie guessed. 'Is that what you came to tell me?'

'The Motley needs a new landlady,' said Maggin bluntly. 'Someone as understands what it's here for. Someone who'll take good care o' my guests.' She smiled at Bessie, the wrinkles deepening around her eyes. 'Drig says as how ye're looking for sommat to do?'

Bessie blinked, speechless.

'Which brings me to that favour you owe me,' Drig said, stepping smoothly into the silence. 'I have for some time wished to leave His Majesty's service. I would like you to secure my release, and to accept me as co-landlord of the Motley thereafter.'

Bessie had been harbouring a dark knot of tension somewhere within, ever since Grunewald had vanished out of her life and taken Rasgha with him. What she was to do with herself next, stranded as she was in Gadrahst and with no prospects to return to in England even if she could, was a troublesome question – one she had been able to conjure no answer to. But Maggin's proposal was perfect; she sensed at once that she was as ideal for the role of landlady as Magg imagined her to be. And to retain Drig's companionship besides! Her heart soared with gladness, and she accepted both Maggin's and Drig's requests with delight. 'Only!' she cautioned Drig, 'I cannot say as our Gent will let you go. I can but try.'

Drig nodded, serene. 'All I ask,' he said laconically.

'Besides, that also depends on him turnin' up again. I've not seen hide nor hair o' him.'

'He's downstairs,' said Drig, suspiciously nonchalant.

Bessie eyed him. 'Oh, is he? You did not care to mention that before now, I note.'

Drig eyed her in return, his expression a trifle sullen. 'Didn't want him persuading you off somewhere before we'd had chance to talk to you.'

'Tis most unlikely he has any such thoughts in mind,' said Bessie firmly.

Drig merely grunted, and waved a hand towards the door in invitation. 'You can go now.'

Bessie wanted to return some unfavourable retort, if only to punish him for his assumptions. But she could not. The prospect of Grunewald alone somewhere downstairs, waiting for her, set her heart beating a little too quickly, and she could not resist. With parting thanks for Maggin, she swept through the door and hastened down the stairs.

She found Grunewald in the best parlour. He was comfortably ensconced in a large, wing-back chair, smartly dressed in the newest fashions from England. Her right eye saw the red-haired, green-eyed human visage that he liked to wear, but her left still saw him as he was: half-goblin and half-Aylir, with few of the beauties of either.

He was equally beloved in both forms.

She stood in the doorway, studying him for a moment. He had not yet seen her, and he appeared to be so lost in thought that he had not even heard her approach. He looked tired, and a little drawn. His attire might be pristine, but his hair was disordered, as though he had been running his hands through it. There was something new in his air, too; another layer of hard disappointment, or perhaps betrayal. She wondered how deeply lonely he had really been, and for how long.

'Well?' she said tartly. 'Some greetin'! Ignored, and after all we have been through together!'

His gaze focused upon her, and he gave her a slow grin which had a most disagreeable effect upon her heart. 'Ignore my Bess? Never.'

He had been aware of her, she realised. He had merely given her a few moments to collect herself, or to decide how to greet him. And she, uncomfortable and at a loss, had chosen to show none of her real feelings. She returned the smile, if weakly, her brain busily trying to discover how best to recover the situation.

But he spoke, and the opportunity was lost. 'Sit,' he invited, waving a hand at an adjacent chair. 'And tell me something.'

Bessie could see no reason to decline, so she seated herself as invited and directed a look of enquiry at him.

He stared at her, his eyes faintly narrowed. After a moment, Bessie realised he was not staring at her so much as at her eyes – first the left, and then the right.

Oh, dear.

'I am curious,' he said in a hard voice. 'I would be pleased to learn precisely when it was that you stole the fairy ointment from me.'

Bessie hesitated. She had not forgotten – could not forget – how he had kissed her, only two days before. But his manner now was in sharp contrast to his former exuberant display of affection. She read a spark of real anger in his leaf-green eyes, and a tightness about his jaw that suggested he was holding back a tirade.

Well; what matter if he was angry? She had stolen from him, it was true, and she was not proud of herself. But she had done it for good reason. She had been helping him, when he had been too stubborn to accept either that he needed assistance, or that she was capable of providing it! He ought to be grateful to her.

Bessie lifted her chin. 'Not long after Isabel gave it to you.'

Grunewald nodded once. 'I see. And may I be permitted to ask why you presumed to do such a thing?'

'I thought I might need it. And I was right! It was of the utmost usefulness.'

His anger grew, blossoming in an instant from a spark into a burning rage. But his voice, when he spoke, was wintry-cold. 'You had no right, Bessie Bell.'

She lifted a brow. 'Oh? Perhaps you had no right to keep it from me.'

'It was mine, to do with as I chose.'

'Aye. But I have hardly done you or anybody else any harm wi' the share I took, so I dunnot see why you are angry.'

But as she spoke, it dawned upon her. She knew her arguments to be reasonable enough; why had he not chosen to give her a supply of her own, after all? There had been enough for both of them to use; more than enough. It could scarcely have hurt him to do so.

But in his mind, it did hurt. 'You were askin' somethin' else,' Bessie said shrewdly. 'Yer question was not: when did I steal the ointment. 'Twas rather: how long have I been able to see yer real face?'

Grunewald stared at her, the lines deepening around his mouth. He was white with anger, but she read something else behind it: not fear, as she might have expected, but a sense of weary resignation.

'I ain't goin' to tell anybody, if that is what yer worried about.'

His eyes narrowed. 'I am glad to hear it.'

That was not the trouble, it seemed. Then what? Bessie gazed at him, long and thoughtful, and a new idea entered her mind. 'You think I will have naught to do wi' you, now that I know the truth about you?'

He looked away, frowning. 'Something like that.'

Bessie sighed deeply, torn between a desire to embrace him and an equally powerful desire to box his ears. 'Have you learned nowt from yer friend Aubranael's story? Full ruined, his face, but that weighed as naught wi' Sophy.'

Grunewald refused to look at her. 'Sophy is a woman in a million.'

'And I am not?'

He blinked and turned his head, startled. 'That... is not what I meant.'

Bessie threw up her hands. 'A fine pair you make, you an' Rasgha! What nonsense! Wi' yer half-breed worries an' yer vanity. As fine an' finicky as a pair o' English aristocrats, that you are!'

Grunewald growled his annoyance. 'There are some among Gadrahst society who deplored my father's marriage to my mother. Purists, you might say. They wanted a goblin for a queen, not an Aylir, no matter what her connections. Those of my subjects would have despised Rasgha's mother still more. In that, she and I are justified in our doubts.'

Bess shrugged. 'And you care about them lot so much? I find that hard to believe.'

Grunewald muttered something, and at last met her gaze squarely. 'I must care about them to some extent, baggage. There has been discontent for years untold, and I have sometimes but barely retained my throne. It is a matter of some import, especially now.'

'Why especially now?'

His green eyes gazed into hers, dark and intense. 'If I am to raise a human over them as queen, I must expect such discontent to grow. It will not be easy for either of us.'

Bessie's eyes narrowed, ruthlessly ignoring the way her heart fluttered at this declaration. 'That yer plan, is it?'

He inclined his head. 'It is.'

'Seems to me you are forgettin' somethin', my Gent.'

'Oh?'

Bessie stood up, folded her arms, and stared him down. 'You forgot to ask me.'

He blinked his confusion. 'What? But you just said—'

'I said that I dunnot find you repellent! That ain't a proposal o' marriage!'

'Fine,' he snapped. 'If we must go through the charade.' He rose to his feet, took Bessie's hands, gazed into her eyes with a credible approximation of a soulful attitude, and whispered, 'Will you marry me, baggage?'

'No!' said Bessie stoutly, and withdrew her hands. 'Absolutely not.'

He scowled. 'And why am I to be rejected, if I might ask?'

'Because you're still callin' me baggage, for a start.'

'You are quite right. I shan't call you that anymore.' He smiled, as though the question were now resolved, and attempted to kiss her.

Bessie pushed him away. 'I ain't marryin' you! Queen o' the Goblins! Me! 'Tis a laughable thought! Right proper absurd. And that's without takin' into account yer promisin' description o' the reception I am likely to receive.'

'Only from the Purists, Bess! Most of my subjects will love you.' Grunewald captured her hands and insisted upon kissing them. Nor would he be so obliging as to release them, tug though she might.

Bessie lost her temper. 'STOP kissing my hands!' she roared.

Grunewald was so startled as to drop her hands at once. He even took a step backwards, and stood staring at her in wide-eyed astonishment.

'I ain't interested in gettin' wed,' Bessie said, in a more moderated tone. She took a deep breath and let it out slowly. 'I am takin' over as landlady o' the Motley. Did Maggin not tell you?'

He shook his head. 'I had not heard.'

'And for that matter, Drig is leavin' yer service and comin' to help me. You won't object.'

Grunewald detected the warning note in her voice and wisely agreed. 'Very well.'

Bessie glowered at him. 'If we are to be spendin' some time together, you'll need to get over that habit o' dictatin'. It ain't goin' to work wi' me.'

Grunewald blinked.

'For the first time, I have the freedom to make me own choice as to what I do wi' meself! I am to be the boss o' me own life, an' I ain't givin' that up lightly! Not even for you. That clear?'

The Goblin King gazed long at her, his anger visibly dissipating. At last, shockingly, he grinned — swift, sharp and delighted. 'That's my Bess.'

'I ain't yer Bess,' she said shortly. 'Not 'til I say so.'

He bowed, a floridly gallant gesture. 'Very well. Are you my Bess?'

'Maybe,' she said grudgingly. 'Long as you behave yerself.'

'I have never been any good at behaving.' His eyes twinkled merriment, and Bessie found herself smiling in response.

'Eh,' she said. 'We will have to muddle along somehow.'

Grunewald claimed one of her hands again — tentatively this time, giving her plenty of opportunity to object. She did not, and he was permitted to raise it to his lips. 'So I may visit the Landlady?'

Bessie grunted her assent. 'But if you track mud through me best parlour, we'll be havin' words.'

Grunewald laughed and pulled her closer. Bess did not so much accept his embrace as hurl herself at him, and what little remained of her own anger or his dissolved under a rain of kisses.

*An' that's that! Another happy endin', I am pleased to be able to tell ye.*

*Not that everythin's ended, quite yet. I have one or two questions outstandin', meself, and mayhap you do likewise. What o' that Kostigern, fer starters? He is meant t' be long gone, but Rasgha's right certain that he's only sleepin'. Mayhap in the Torpor, like so many others. Can he be woken? And will it be Lady Thayer's blood as does it? I been keepin' a close watch on her ladyship ever since that day, I can tell you. Not tha' she is helpless! Oh, no! What a way she has wi' them pipes!*

*Besides that, Rasgha woke up a deal o' folk wi' the help o' Tatterfoal, an' we ain't managed t' catch all o' them. There's mischief stirrin' there fer the future, if I'm not mistaken. It's vigilance fer me, until everythin' rights itself about.*

*But Bessie's been happy as a lark at the Motley, ye'll be pleased to know! Maggin was right about tha', fer certain: Miss Bell is perfect fer the job. She an' Drig make a fine pair o' landlords-an'-ladies, an' the Motley's more popular than ever.*

*Grunewald spends as much time at the Motley as he does at court, these days. He's becomin' quite the fixture. But the patronage o' the Goblin King ain't doin' the inn any harm! It's my belief he weren't bluffin' when he told Rasgha he'd have handed her the monarchy job. Bored senseless, that he's been fer many a long year, an' weary t' boot. Now there's Bess, and she won't wed him while he's still His Majesty. Tis a puzzle, an' one thas yet t' resolve itself. But they's clever. They will find a way t' manage.*

*But I have rambled on long enough! Ye'll be wantin' to get on yer way. I have detained ye longer'n I meant to, I'll give ye a bit o' help. Just a mite of a Quickly-spell to gi' ye a tiny boost, thas all. Oh, I don't make 'em meself. Mrs. Aylfendeane gave 'em to me! An' a wisp t' guide ye on yer way. There, Mr. Coachman, follow tha' ball o' light an' ye'll be home in no time.*

*Good journey to ye, an' come back soon! I've a feelin' I'll have another yarn t' spin afore long.*

## ACKNOWLEDGEMENTS

As always, a thousand thanks to my artists, Elsa Kroese and the Picsees, for filling this book with beauty and colour.

Books By Charlotte E. English:

Tales of Aylfenhame:
Miss Landon and Aubranael
Miss Ellerby and the Ferryman
Bessie Bell and the Goblin King

The Draykon Series:
Draykon
Lokant
Orlind

The Lokant Libraries:
Seven Dreams

The Drifting Isle Chronicles:
Black Mercury

The Malykant Mysteries:
The Rostikov Legacy
The Ivanov Diamond
Myrrolen's Ghost Circus
Ghostspeaker